The Probable Son

The Probable Son

A NOVEL

CINDY JIBAN

Published by Lake Union Publishing, Seattle
www.apub.com

EU product safety contact:
Amazon Media EU S. à r.l.
38, avenue John F. Kennedy, L-1855 Luxembourg
amazonpublishing-gpsr@amazon.com

ISBN-13: 9781662533808 (paperback)
ISBN-13: 9781662533815 (digital)

Cover design by Olga Grlic
Cover image: © tokar, © Rubanitor / Shutterstock

Printed in the United States of America

The Probable Son

Prologue

2005

Between each labor pain on the ride to the hospital's birth center, Elsa Vargas saw the blur of gold and orange outside the car window. Even the trees of St. Paul were warning against hope: their leaves were dressed and ready for death.

But they were wrong. After sixteen hours of labor and then a cesarean section, her son was born, and he was both perfect and perfectly alive.

Elsa first saw him while she was still in the operating room, her own body shielded from view while they closed her back up. She craned toward a station on the side of the room where her newborn son was cleaned, weighed, checked out, and given a score. He responded with a faint squawk, and they wrapped him up. Finally a nurse brought him close to Elsa's head, and a sob she hadn't felt coming shook out of her. He was real.

"Hi, little muffin," she choked out. "I'm your mommy." The teeny boy's face moved toward her familiar voice, a piece of magic: he was the very creature whose limbs had pushed mysterious bulges across her belly as he listened inside her these last months. His eyelids were pillows, above and below, and they blinked open. Three years before, Elsa had wailed over flat, unmoving brown eyes; instead, these eyes radiated blue, eager and alive.

Two women arranged Ham's hands and arms to receive his son, and a nurse stayed at his elbow as they followed Elsa's hospital bed, wheeled into a recovery room. "Closer," Elsa gushed, happy and impatient as they set the brakes of her bed. Then Elsa's naked son landed on the bare skin of her own chest. He was impossibly compact, tucked as if home again in her womb, pulsing with warmth. She studied each bit of his exquisiteness: his pouty pink lips; his plump cheeks; his strands of dark, still-wet hair.

Finally, mother and son were cleared to move to a more permanent room. As they were rolled through the hallway together on the bed, Ham strode beside them, cupping the baby's tiny damp head securely against her. Elsa dozed off even before arriving. Sometime later, she awoke to a nurse wheeling a cart with its newborn passenger into their room. Had their hours-old little son been in the nursery, away from them? Before Elsa had time to chide Ham for allowing this, the nurse set the baby into Elsa's arms, and she softened into forgiveness.

When she adjusted the thin, light blue beanie he now wore, he opened his eyes. The irises looked darker now. Elsa had done triple readings of *What to Expect*, of course, so she knew infant eye color could change. She didn't remember that it could change this fast.

The boy's chin started to bob, seeking milk, and she looked to his lips. They weren't pouty, but thin. A faint tingle hit the base of her skull. She moved her eyes to the pastel hat, and then she willed her hand to follow. She paused her breathing for a moment, then slid the beanie off his little head. In place of the dark strands that had clung against her son's head was a wispy fluff of lighter brown. *No.* Panic plucked her spinal cord and reverberated through her body.

"This is not my baby." Her voice came out high pitched.

Ham stooped down to her face, his eyes at first confused. Then they turned gentle. "This is our son, Elsa."

"This is not my baby," she said again firmly. "I need *my* baby." She moved her arms forward to give this one back.

Ham scooped the boy from her, looking from the baby to Elsa, twice. Finally he nodded. Then he signaled the nurse to join him in the hallway. Elsa knew what was happening; Ham was explaining about poor Inga, about the shapes and angles of Elsa's own devastation. It pulled Elsa's mind to *then*, and for the briefest moment she considered if *then* was relevant. But no—this was about now, about the living son who had just hours ago been inside her and was now nowhere in sight.

When they came back into the room, Elsa struggled for her regular voice.

"I know this must be rare, but I'm very sure there's been a mix-up. That is someone else's little boy."

The nurse was projecting calm as she explained the maternity ward's security, how a chip in each baby's anklet would trigger an alarm at any exit door. But Elsa heard her own alarm system, shrill and insistent.

"My baby is in the wrong room," she cut in, loud. "He's in the wrong mother's arms." The nurse looked at Ham, so Elsa did too. *"Ham."* Her husband's face registered only pity: betrayal.

Elsa heard the beeps on the machine next to her quickening as the nurse and Ham looked at each other. What was wrong with them? Time was speeding up, and no one was doing a damn thing. Their baby was somewhere else, bonding, starting the wrong life. Her ears rang and a shout tore out of her. "Goddammit, find my baby!"

She tried to sit up, but the force field of her now-worthless post-op abdominals kept her pinned. Flailing, her hands bashed against metal and clawed for grip. She grunted strength into her arms, pulling and twisting hard; she tumbled off the bed, the IV ripping out of her forearm as she hit the floor. Pain leapt above her medication's reach and spiked into her. "Get my baby!" Sounds and words collided into a pileup: Ham and nurses talking loudly over each other, more staff running in, the speaker announcing a code. The faces of her husband and now her sister alternated in front of her as Elsa's limbs fought, fought, fought against restraint and against what she gradually realized was sedation, pulling her into fog and then nothing.

When she climbed back to groggy consciousness, she found Ham's face hovering just above her. She returned his smile. Then she saw the institutional panels of ceiling and she remembered. Her eyes asked him first. She found his wrist and closed her fingers around it, tightening.

Ham nodded. "It's all good," he said, and Elsa loosened her hand. He reached for the baby in its little rolling cart, then hesitated. Instead, he wheeled the clear plastic crib close against the metal railing of Elsa's bed, where she could see. *Wrong.*

Her chest sank into the black hole of her belly. "No! It's that other baby!"

"This is the baby who came out of you, Elsa."

"It's not! It's not who was on my skin!"

He kissed her cheek. "This is our son," he said. Then he put his big hand on the baby's little tummy, caressing the blue dots of the cotton fabric. "He's alive, and . . ."

She squeezed her eyes shut, shook her head. "Why can't you just hear me!" Her loud voice was readying to turn to a shriek. But no—screaming got you shut down. She yanked her head toward the white wall, the room taking a moment to catch up. Then she quieted her voice. "Let's just ask them to check," she said to the blankness.

"Else. I'm his daddy, remember? I checked his ID cuff."

"Then our baby has the wrong cuff," she moaned out thickly, her tongue not fully cooperating. Ham said nothing in response. Then she heard him start to hum. She could sense without turning to look that his hand was on the baby, and she felt tears pricking; he, too, was so ready for a living baby. She tried to place Ham's tune. Was it . . . the Beatles? She hung on, losing track, and again she was swallowed into sleep.

She awoke to her sister, Krista, who was offering the thin-lipped baby to Elsa's chest. Elsa recoiled.

Krista returned him to his crib. "Else, honey. You have to trust us. This is your son, and we all know it." She held Elsa's jaw gently and got close and quiet. "You cannot do this to Ham again. He won't make it through if you go back there."

Elsa begged her sister, pleading: you go find him, go get my son. Krista quietly straightened the covers. Then Elsa clenched her teeth. "Get Mom," she hissed.

Krista shook her head. "It doesn't matter who I get. They might not say it how I'm gonna say it, but here it is: we all need you to snap the fuck out of it, Elsa, and man up."

Elsa turned away, still so very tired. Would they never believe her? Her resistance against her family and her resistance of sleep itself seemed to merge, so that now they were confused into a single opponent. Their arguments lined up against her like a massive army: her marriage, old delusions, the gravity pulling hard on her eyelids. And so, exhausted and fuzzy, Elsa contemplated surrender. For now, she thought. Only for now, while the staples and the stitches and the blasted drugs held her battered body hostage.

Finally she let Ham hold this new baby close to her face. She stared into the too-dark blue eyes while Ham called him their son, his words drenched in love. She wanted this for Ham, wanted to feel what he felt. Eventually, she echoed him.

"Our son," she said, and the chorus of humans outside her filled with relief and rejoicing.

This was the beginning of pretending to believe.

Chapter 1

2019

What Elsa told her principal was technically a lie.

Schusterman had just informed Elsa that the disastrous math lesson she had taught on Friday would be the focus of an Additional Item on the PTO meeting agenda tomorrow night. And unless they were about additional fundraising, Additional Items were not what Schusterman wanted to see the Parent-Teacher Organization initiate.

Elsa raised her own eyebrows to mirror his. "Listen, I had no idea that genes could be so contentious," she fibbed.

Why should she grow qualms about lying now? She had long ago committed herself to a deep practice of deception. Some women did yoga; Elsa Vargas walked a path of deliberate and careful avoidance.

"Of course you didn't," Schusterman agreed, his words dusted in sugar. "But now we know. And I'm sure you can do a bang-up job of putting these rumors and resentments to rest." Then he actually winked at her, as if she were his grandchild instead of his age-mate. "Like I always say: if the parents ain't happy, Schusterman ain't happy."

Elsa found this use of third person reminiscent of Elmo. But she smiled and nodded. As much as she disliked the idea of speaking to the pearl-clutching parents of the PTO about this, she knew she had to clean up the mess she had inadvertently created in class. Such a hassle.

At the time, dominant and recessive genes had seemed like a great way to get the eighth-grade students engaged in the probability lesson.

The "challenge problem" of the week had involved finding the probabilities for genetic traits as they were passed down. Brown eye genes were dominant and blue eye genes were recessive, so having one gene for brown and one for blue would give a person brown eyes.

Suppose, the problem said, that you had two couples, and all four of those people had brown eyes but hid a recessive blue eye gene. If they shared a grandchild, what color eyes would little Timmy have? What was the probability of blue, and what of brown?

On the whiteboard, Elsa had put a capital *B* for brown and a lowercase *b* for blue inside a circle. She explained that this circle person would have brown eyes, and that they could pass down either of their two genes at random—a 50 percent chance of passing down each.

But then the class had gone sideways.

"Brown eyes are dominant? That's so racist," Claire had announced, looking to Darnell for approval.

Thomas snorted. "Claire. Racism is when the blue-eyed people think *they* are dominant." Claire's fair skin turned pink, setting off her professionally highlighted hair and her blue eyes.

Then it got worse.

"Wait, so hold up." Thomas had turned to Elsa. "Ms. Vargas, how did I get brown eyes if both my parents have blue eyes?"

Darnell hooted. "O-ho! Because the mailman has brown eyes, son!"

Thomas broke into laughs, and the two boys slapped hands. Claire only frowned. The room had exploded with an excitement tinged with indignance: think of the secret adoptions and parental infidelities Ms. Vargas's lesson could be outing! Elsa had managed to shut down the whole dramedy for the rest of fourth period, but still it had gone viral after the bell. That it had next infected the parents seemed inevitable, in retrospect.

Elsa left Schusterman's office now and headed back to her empty classroom. She pulled out her phone. If she was to be the Additional

Item tomorrow night, then she would need to stay at the middle school this evening to prepare.

She told her husband Ham about the meeting while he made sympathetic sounds. Then he rambled for a few minutes about his workday, a wash of names that she had heard before populating a blur of sentences. After Elsa made sympathetic noises of her own, Ham turned to thinking aloud about dinner for himself and their two boys tonight, without her. She could guess that in the end he would make what both Bird and Garvey considered a treat: sweaty hot dogs tucked inside ketchup-sogged white buns. These were simply too much for Elsa to bear, let alone eat. They always conjured up painful scenes of tiny death, swaddled in a blanket, a fact she chose not to share with Ham.

At seven o'clock, Elsa finally left school to pick up their older son Bird from his music lesson on her way home. The music store with its basement full of teaching rooms was only a mile from Lowe Hills Middle School, right on Grand Avenue where clusters of people meandered between restaurants and designer eyewear shops and coffeehouses. St. Paul looked so much whiter here. At Lowe Hills, only about half of the students were white, including her own eighth-grade son, Bird.

At the music store, she texted Bird that she was out front.

He seemed to manage being an eighth grader at a school where his mom taught without much problem. It probably helped that Bird's last name was not Vargas, that they had given the boys her husband's last name. Ham was legally Eugene Hamilton, his childhood clowning turning him solidly Ham by first grade. Bird Hamilton, on the other hand, was far more bird than ham.

It was cold, October caving to nighttime's big advance into the dinner hour. Elsa turned up the radio and gave a couple small revs to the engine, confident that a hotter motor would heat the minivan just a bit better. Maybe the revs were also just for kicks; Outkast could give anyone a little extra fire, she thought, slapping two fingers on the wheel to the beat and allowing herself some understated pigeon head thrusting. She looked into the other idling cars lining the street, each with a parent sitting perfectly still, face lit by a phone.

Bird came out and surveyed his options. Elsa imagined he'd rather climb into anything other than her slightly thumping minivan with its equally loud bumper stickers, but he opened its back passenger door. He stowed his French horn case and backpack gently on the back seat, closed the sliding door, and then got into the front.

Elsa pointed at Bird as she sang along, calling him "all right" on loop.

Bird reached over and turned down the volume. He looked at her and gave a couple of slow nods, not to the beat.

"Hey, Mom," he said.

"'Hey Ya!'" she corrected.

Elsa was tempted to reach over and ruffle his curls, but she knew this would double jinx the ride home. Instead, she took a slow breath and tried to let her own RPMs slowly drop. Bird was a low-idle kid; matching that was always a struggle for her. She set the blinker, exhaled, then pulled slowly into the road, waiting at least half a minute before asking how his day had been.

"Good," he nodded. This was followed by silence. Elsa remembered the parenting wisdom: you go first, and then you wait.

She launched into her own substantially longer answer, recapping her day from first period through to the after-school news from Schusterman. "These parents, Bird. I mean, sure, it's Minnesota, but we aren't raising snowflakes here. Before you know it, I'll have to send out permission slips before every damn lesson I teach. It's ridiculous! I mean, what's next, banning math books that call some angles more acute than others?" She elbowed him and waggled her eyebrows. "I just came up with that. Get it? Acute?"

Bird looked at her. After sufficient pause to kill her momentum, he spoke. "Maybe the parents are just trying to protect any adopted kids who don't know, or something. Like, trying to be sensitive." Then he pulled out his phone.

Elsa registered his lack of solidarity as familiar. She tried to keep her voice still light. "Bird, hold off on the video game. Let's take a moment to catch up with each other."

He rolled his eyes and turned to look out his side window. "God, Mom. Do I get any free time to just enjoy myself?"

Elsa clenched her teeth. "I'm sorry that talking to me is a chore. I realize you'd rather be killing your Klingons or whatever they are. But just learn to fake it, Bird. I'm only human."

The light ahead turned yellow, then red. Elsa stared at it hard, willing it to change.

"They're not Klingons," Bird finally said. "They're nixies." Elsa rolled her eyes discreetly. Here it was. "And some are dryads."

She knew Ham would tell her to ask questions. This was what Bird was interested in, so as good parents they should show interest too. But Elsa couldn't make herself do it. She knew that if she asked, Bird would give her three pages' worth of eye-glazing information, during which she would manage to nod her head and say "hmm." Inside, though, her brain would start inventorying the pantry or planning her Halloween costume. Besides, as the lone female in the family, surely Elsa had some responsibility to ensure that she was not raising a mansplainer.

They drove in silence for two minutes before pulling into their alley. Then Elsa said, "I want to hear things about your day because I love you, Bird." He sighed heavily in annoyance, but in the garage he managed a small "yep" before climbing out and retrieving his things.

Elsa let Bird cross to the house and go in the back door before she herself got out. She walked across the backyard in the moonlight, a little bonus made possible by the motion-sensing light having burned out. A life where small shit happened on the regular was a pretty good kind of life, Elsa knew, so long as you set your expectations right.

Chapter 2

The Thursday evening PTO meeting arrived as promised. And so here Elsa was, choosing a seat in the school library at seven o'clock, ready to explain why on earth she had used her whiteboard marker—a marker purchased by these very parents' fundraising efforts, no less—to form the accusatory *B*'s and *b*'s that had injected such familial drama into their otherwise just-manageable lives.

Elsa felt parental eyes on her. But as she scanned the room, no eye contact was returned. She looked for her friend Jennifer, one eighth-grade mom with a healthy sense of humor. Instead, she saw her colleague Aneisha beckoning her from the back wall. With all the cuts to the arts, Aneisha now taught just one period of visual art, one of choir, and two of a grant-funded nothing class called Leadership Exploration.

"My dear Miss Elsa. You seem to have upset the hornet's nest," Aneisha said, her head pulled back and her eyebrows out of symmetry. She pointed at the last line item on the agenda. *Additional Item: Does HOT Stuff belong in math at Lowe Hills Middle School?*

Elsa could see that someone had done their homework—or rather, done their child's homework, plus some googling. The challenge problem had indeed come from a site called HOT Stuff, but the *HOT* stood for "higher-order thinking." She gave Aneisha a long look, face firmly expressionless. Aneisha chuckled.

Soon two people stepped up to the front, where a laptop projected its screen saver, a bouncing Lowe Hills Cougars logo. Their principal joined Natalie Trowbridge, who was both head of the PTO and the mother of Elsa's student Claire. Natalie called out for the room's attention.

"Before we get to any other business, I would just like us to offer our fearless leader a thank-you for an excellent start to this year." Natalie tilted her highlighted head a bit demurely toward Schusterman and gave a nervous laugh. "Let's give a round of applause for our principal." The small crowd responded heartily, three or four of the parents even getting out of their chairs to stand.

Schusterman turned from Natalie to face the room, feigning embarrassment. Then he held up a hand—stop, please!—and began to speak.

"It is the people in this room who make Lowe Hills a community," he announced, looking directly into one face after another. Then he flashed a fleeting boyish smile, and his eyes gave the kind of twinkle that comes with a little "ding!" in the cartoons. He made a few remarks about wonderful children coming from wonderful parents, then returned the floor to Natalie.

"There's our Mr. Schmooze," Aneisha whispered.

Natalie launched into the first order of business, a discussion of who would lead the eighth-grade graduation dinner this year now that the whole herd of Marianne Windell's children had moved on to high school.

As Natalie went on, Elsa noticed a threesome of parents in the same row leaning in for a whispered side conversation. One at a time and very casually, each of the three turned to look around the room, including toward the back wall. Elsa caught the eye of one of them and tried a smile, but the woman whipped her head forward. Then Elsa saw her grab the arm of the dad next to her.

Next came an update on the yearly fundraising events. One mother expressed concern that participation in the events was still very white; she wondered what ideas were being explored to invite more diversity. Natalie looked at her smartwatch and stepped forward.

"Ashley, love your positive engagement. I think you are the right person to get some blue-sky thinking down on paper. Can we put you on the agenda next month for an update, please?" Ashley looked uncertain about how to respond, but Natalie plowed ahead. "I'll connect with you offline about deliverables, since we have such a tight agenda tonight." Then she moved on.

On another night, Elsa might have enjoyed this jujitsu, where parents raising a concern found themselves volun-told to fix it. Tonight, she only noted the speed with which Natalie drove toward the HOT stuff. All that remained on the agenda was a request from Aneisha for funds for a choir competition. Elsa's heart rate rose as this was quickly and unanimously approved.

At this point it would have been good night, Natalie noted. But instead they had one more item to discuss.

"I apologize that we have more than three key points of focus tonight. Unfortunately, we had very little runway, because this only became evident over the weekend." Natalie paused, looking over at Schusterman. "It seems several parents left messages that indicated . . . some concerns with material that was utilized in one or more math classes." Everyone in the room seemed to shift forward in their seats. Natalie turned to look at Elsa, her face conveying just enough motherly concern.

Schusterman interjected, stepping to the front again. "We certainly never want to open up difficult conversations in our community's homes. We know that parenting in this day and age takes everything you've got as it is." Here he shook his head and briefly closed his eyes: empathy. "But a math lesson seems to have led some of our kiddos to start some rumors about adoption and . . . parentage. I have asked Ms. Vargas to talk us through just what seems to have happened and how we can make things right." His eyes connected with those of a couple more parents, and he nodded at each. Then he looked back at Elsa and raised his arm out to her.

She stepped forward. All eyes were on her, and none of them seemed terribly good-humored; none of them were her friend Jennifer's. Elsa started to laugh just a bit, involuntarily. Then she forced her voice to get big and she held out jazz hands. "It was me, folks!" She went to the front and put her thumb drive in the laptop, calling up her slides.

"OK, I'm going to show you the site where I found this terrific math problem about probability," she previewed. "Then I'm going to show you why it's not so terrific. Finally, I'm going to make sure no one has to answer any awkward questions about what Mom was really up to fourteen years ago. Are we ready?" Elsa smiled. "Isn't this fun?" Her gaze found Aneisha, who was nodding: *oh, yes.* Two parents were scowling and shaking their heads. Another parent put a hand up rigidly toward the ceiling. Elsa pretended not to notice, turning toward the screen instead.

She ran through her slides about the problem and how it fit for the lesson on probability. She explained the nature of this unit, noting that no district curriculum had yet been provided, and what the *HOT* on this useful site stood for.

When Elsa turned back toward the parents, she noticed two phone cameras held up in her direction. Also the hand was still up, now somehow a few inches higher.

Elsa nodded at the stretchy parent but held up one finger, asking for patience. "OK, so now let's talk about Not So Terrific. In the setup of the problem I found, eye color is treated as having only two outcomes: blue or brown," Elsa explained. "That's what I was taught. Dominant and recessive, that's it. Who else was taught that?" She asked for a show of hands, the teacher in her mindful of engagement. The rigid hand lowered angrily, but several others rose. Then she revealed that the old eye color genetics theory turned out to be wrong, an arbitrary categorizing of all the many different shades. "Hazel eyes, green, gray eyes—these are all for real." Elsa looked out at the sea of eyes, all staring intently at her. The stiff hand was high in the air again, and she saw two frowning women whispering to each other and shaking their heads.

"It only gets worse, people. More recent science shows that eye color is not determined by just one gene from each parent." Her next slide showed a complex diagram with arrows and circles—a map of how various genes could affect the three factors that determine actual eye color: melanin, pheomelanin, and eumelanin. "If you can make complete sense of this slide, you are doing better than I am. But the basic idea is that there's a continuum of each of these three kinds of stuff. They aren't binary. So all kinds of outcomes open up."

Elsa presented her final slide, a table showing data from a study she had found online the night before. It looked at parent pairs where both had eyes categorized as blue. The old one-gene-per-parent theory would predict all of the kids from these pairs getting blue eyes. "But look at this number here, folks. This study found more than 10 percent of their offspring had a different eye color than blue. And yes, these were confirmed as truly the children of those pairs of blue-eyed parents."

She paused so that the less math-savvy could absorb this. "Bottom line? Kids can have an unexpected eye color, different than their parents have. And that doesn't prove anything fishy went on." Elsa noticed Natalie Trowbridge turning a bit red and stealing a look at the woman next to her.

"I'm sure you are all relieved that any drama that got brewed up is totally unwarranted," Elsa said, looking right at Natalie.

"Yeah, but it's still been brewed up," someone called out from the back row. A murmur rippled through Team Yeahbut.

Elsa imagined herself drinking something brewed up in a taproom, regaling friends with the tale of this meeting. She could taste the brew already. Stuck in the present, she forced her lips into a smile.

"Yes. And I am cleaning up this mess I've unwittingly created. First, I have taken this problematic Problem of the Week out of rotation forevermore. Second, I have already shared this new information about eye color with your children today in class. Your children now understand that, as far as we know, there's no cause for rumors.

Everyone's parents are still their parents." This was where a wink could go. She gave a little smirk with over-widened eyes instead.

A few parents now shared relieved smiles, one dad even chuckling aloud.

Elsa turned saccharine-level sincere as she shut down her presentation and pulled out her thumb drive. "I really want to thank you all for your kindness, your patience, and your forgiveness around this screwup. I have been so honored by those who have reached out with that positive spirit." She nodded, holding her palms together in front of herself for a moment. That was a lie; no one had reached out to her in this way. But what did they expect from a middle school teacher if not a little . . . psychology? "Now, I know that you all have children to get home to, so I'll respect your time. I am more than happy to stay afterward for anyone who has some remaining questions for me, out in the hall." Elsa walked back to her seat next to Aneisha, and that was it. Aneisha looked impressed.

Up front, Schusterman and Natalie both popped up at the same time, then each deferred to the other, synchronized. Finally Schmooze cleared his throat.

"Thank you, Ms. Vargas. And of course, let's thank Natalie Trowbridge for another wonderful gathering," he said. "Those sinfully wonderful treats you enjoyed on your way in were baked by Natalie, and I think there are just a few left. Please be careful that you don't trample each other on your way to get some. Good night, drive safe, and I know we'll see you next month!" He went with the wink.

Elsa stationed herself in the beerless hallway, nodding and smiling. The hand raiser and the chuckling dad turned out to be a couple, both teaching in sciences at the university. The man thanked her for going the extra mile to share the limitations of Mendelian genetics.

"Well, the kids gave me some reason to really get to some answers," Elsa reminded him. The couple finally let her go when the custodian appeared and started taking down the cookie table.

Walking out to her minivan, Elsa massaged the back of her neck where tension had gathered. She stretched her head back. Was the moon waxing or waning? She couldn't recall. All she knew was that she wanted to get home. She fished in her bag for her key fob and saw the lights on her vehicle blip as she unlocked it. She climbed in and threw her bag on the seat next to her, then she dropped the visor and looked into the little mirror. Brown eyes.

Hers had always been this color. She hadn't been one of those babies whose eyes started off blue but kept right on darkening until they were brown. One couldn't really know what color a child's eyes might be just from a first glance at birth.

Elsa flipped the visor back up. Nothing good could come from this line of thought—not for her, and certainly not for Bird.

At home, Elsa took a moment to calibrate before she crossed the backyard. There might be cooking detritus all over the kitchen but no dinner left for her; the homework might still be unfinished; today's battle in the ongoing war against video gaming might never have been waged.

The house, as it turned out, was not in a state of abnormal chaos. Her younger son, Garvey, was in the mostly clean kitchen dancing a spot of light from a laser pointer around the floor, giggling as their retriever-like mutt, Scoopy, pounced and ran in circles. Ham was on the three-season front porch, his feet up and a pint of porter or stout by his side as he yelled jovially into the phone.

"Mom!" Garvey's face lit up. "I have a good one for you, hang on." He dashed into the living room and returned with his book of brain teasers, new from the library. As Elsa parked her coat and work bag, Garvey read the elaborate narrative with dramatic flourish.

"One day, a prisoner has a visitor. Afterward, the prison guard is curious. 'Who was your visitor today?' he asks. The prisoner responds with a riddle. 'Brothers and sisters I have none, but this man's father was my father's son.'" Garvey's neglected laser spot had come to rest, and Scoopy was starting to dig at the wood floor. "So . . ." he wrapped up, grinning with half his mouth. "Who was that unknown visitor?"

Elsa was tired, but good mothers rose to the occasion. She repeated aloud the bits she needed to unwind. "OK. So he doesn't have a brother. Let me think—maybe it's his father . . ."

Ham entered the kitchen. "Hey, Else," he half grinned, holding out his dark beer for her to taste. "I have three words for you." He held up his hand beside his mouth, pretending to block Garvey from seeing. Then he stage-whispered very seriously, complete with intense eye contact: *"Not. His. Father."*

Words like this always clawed at Elsa's attention. But Ham was just laughing here, nothing more.

"I've got it!" she yelled, arms out. "It was his son!"

Garvey and Ham both applauded. She took another swallow of Ham's beer.

Now Elsa felt compelled to see Bird, who was upstairs. On the landing, she collected the crumpled ball that turned out to be sweatpants and a badminton birdie. A dirty towel lay on the hallway floor. She threw these into Garvey's room, where the area rug was barely visible even before the extra donations. As she passed the family bathroom, she noticed Ham had left his gym swim trunks hanging over the shower curtain rod next to her own bra, both now dry. She retrieved these and threw them onto their unmade bed.

Bird's door was closed, and she tapped on it with one knuckle.

"Yep," Bird called out.

She entered and found him in the overstuffed armchair he had placed next to his window. When he didn't look up, she decided against the bear hug.

This was the chair Bird had taken off his Grammy's hands when she had bought a replacement. He kept an emerald-green throw blanket folded neatly over the worn seat and back, which Elsa had to admit improved the look of the chair's awful noncolor. Spider plants—a big one and currently four babies—sat on the dresser next to the window. Amid this tidy green nook sat Bird, his eyes on the pages of the latest in a series of dystopian novels that took place on some kind of moon.

Elsa sat down on the bed, watching him. Then she settled back against the pillow.

"Hi, Bird," she said toward the ceiling.

After a moment he looked up. "Hi, Mom."

"Did you finish your homework?"

"Yep."

Elsa closed her eyes and breathed out. "Good. I'm spent. This day took forever to be over. I think I need to teach in a school with even less parental involvement."

Bird's eyes were back on his book. His blond curls partially hid his face, but she could see him pulling part of his lip into a light bite. The story had him. Elsa watched him until her stomach growled, and then she got up.

"OK, good talk," she said at the door.

Bird looked up, annoyed. "Whatever. I'm trying to read, Mom. You don't have to come in here and interrupt me and then turn all hostile."

Elsa blinked back. "Just trying to crack a joke there, Bird."

"Yeah, you're super funny, Mom."

"But looks aren't everything," Elsa tossed back, and then closed his door firmly behind her.

Maybe adults weren't so bad after all.

Chapter 3

During the middle school's first period, Elsa had no students. When the bell had cleared out the hallway, she retreated to her fraying office chair and looked over her hastily erased whiteboard. The remnants of purple dry-erase marker scolded her. What had she been doing, bringing up genetics? Of all the teachers in the world, it was Elsa who should have known to walk wide around that. It was a sinkhole, and sinkholes were what destroyed whole family homes in unfortunate places like Florida.

Putting the Additional Item behind her, Elsa returned her focus to giving her students the best middle school math education that zero money could buy. This new district requirement of teaching probability had just been shoehorned into her algebra classes this year, and the mandate came with no textbook. It was true that probability wasn't sufficiently addressed in any other math classes, but putting it in algebra was inane. To both teachers and students, it felt like a commercial break on network TV: just when the regular show was starting to get good, here came a total non sequitur, brought to you by our sponsors.

Despite the frustrations of education, though, Elsa felt a pervasive confidence in her own decision to be a teacher. She was made for this. She loved the regular supply of small victories that teaching offered. While a job like Ham's could make you live through a monthlong project arc until the next payoff of success and resolution, teaching returned little dividends of accomplishment many times a day. A student's face would light up with grasping a concept. A good question would be asked. A kid who hardly spoke would finally say goodbye on his way out of the class.

To tee up any of these wins this week, Elsa sensed that her lesson plans needed a little something something. Ordinarily, she might have turned to the HOT Stuff math site, but that safe house was probably burned right now, crawling with parents. She prowled through various other resources, finally landing on a recap of the Birthday Problem. It was a classic of probability, and she decided to make an event of it.

When the fourth-period starting bell rang, Elsa was ready. "Claire!" she called out. "I wonder if you're willing to take my bet. I'll bet you that two people in this class have the exact same birthday. That's without me having looked at your files or anything, pinky promise." Claire looked uninterested. But *uninterested* seemed to be a look Claire was cultivating, so it was hard to tell.

"Shoua, how about you? What do you want to bet that two people in this room have the same birthday?"

Shoua squinted her eyes a bit at Elsa. "What do I win if there aren't?"

"Aha!" Elsa pointed. "Signs of life! If I win, you have to do an extra homework assignment between now and the test. If you win, I'll let you choose one song to play during the Friday work time." Elsa streamed music during half of each Friday's class while the kids caught up or got ahead on homework. The class loved to make fun of her music choices, which tended toward the instrumental in an effort to be less distracting. "If no birthdays match, you win the bet."

Darnell spoke up. "Is this offer just for Shoua? I'll take your bet."

Elsa had seen him counting the thirty-six heads in the class—just inside the union-negotiated limit, Elsa noted—and she knew Darnell had a theory going about his odds.

"Sold," she said. "Darnell is betting me that there are no matching birthdays. Do you want to tell us why this is a good bet?"

He waved both hands in front of himself. "I don't want to convince nobody, Miss. I'm not trying to listen to nobody else's weak music." Darnell was a good math student, so Shoua took Elsa's bet as well.

Thomas had scrawled a few notes on a paper in front of him, and now he raised his hand. "OK, so I think the probability that anybody has a certain birthday is 1 out of 365, and I think if you add that up, you only have 36 chances out of 365. That's pretty low chances that you're right, Ms. Vargas."

Darnell shook his head and reached over to shove Thomas. "Man, you know what some of these girls listen to . . ."

Thomas continued. "So I think people should take your bet."

"So I have Darnell and Shoua and Thomas so far?" Elsa asked.

"No, no, no," Thomas objected. "I said I think *people* should take your bet. I myself am not taking your bet."

Elsa drew her face into a look of confusion. She waited.

Thomas grinned and folded his arms, resting back in his seat. "I don't need any extra homework. Plus, I'm not sure if I'm allowed to gamble, now that I'm Jewish."

Elsa remembered last week: when Thomas realized two Jewish friends had taken the day off school for Yom Kippur, he had immediately announced he was converting.

In the end, she had nine students willing to wager. To get some blood pumping, she made everyone get out of their seats to find any shared birthdays, sending each season to a different corner of the room. Elsa herself moved to the group by the empty hamster cage. The cage held the much-beloved invisible class pet, Furbie; this invisibility had struck just after the hamster had gone home with one of her students for winter break last year. The original Furbie had apparently been shaken to death in the mouth of the student's husky, and Elsa had honored the mother's request that this be kept secret from the other kids.

"So you looked up our birthdays ahead, right?" said a voice close to her ear. She turned to find Thomas, looking conspiratorial.

Elsa gave a half laugh and folded her arms. "I did not cheat in any way, Thomas. I just trust my odds."

"What about your evens?" he tossed out dryly.

"Them too."

Elsa especially liked her eighth graders. Sometimes they gave you these peeks into the fact that when they grew up, they were going to be your kind of people.

A noise erupted from the corner by the windows, where a group had found a matching birthday. Elsa put her hands out, palms up. "Eh?" she asked the students near her. "How you like them apples?"

Darnell groaned. "I think you cheated us so you can keep spinning your elevator music."

Elsa pretended to look guilty for a beat. Moving toward the whiteboard, she turned and put her marker against her chin. "Say, Darnell, what are the odds that someone in the class has *my* birthday?"

Darnell only blinked.

Claire immediately brightened. "It's what Thomas said. It's 36 out of 365." She scrunched up one shoulder as she looked at Thomas, her smiling cheeks blushing just one shade.

Elsa clapped. "You go, girl!" Claire rolled her eyes, but Elsa continued. "Kind of a low probability, if I set a specific date. Imagine I wrote one particular birth date up on the whiteboard, and then bet I could find someone who matches it. That would have been a pretty bad bet."

Elsa stopped a moment, suddenly clear. There was exactly one date she would have written up there.

Darnell's face wrinkled in concentration. "Hold up. Say again how your bet was different?"

Elsa looked at the whiteboard. What had she been doing? Something in her needed retranquilizing.

"Miss . . . ?"

Finally she put her eyes on Darnell. "Sorry," she said. "I'm back with you now, Earthlings." She rewound the tape. "Ah. Darnell, I love a kid who says 'hold up' when they don't get it. That's winning, in math."

He held his arms out high and pointed at his own head while Elsa launched her explanation.

"So instead of matching one date, my bet was about finding any two that match. If we start with whether Claire and I match, then it's like

Thomas said: 1 out of 365. But then along comes Shoua. She can match either my birthday or Claire's. So her chances are 2 out of 365. And then Faviola comes along, and she has three birthdays she could match . . ."

Thomas and Darnell looked at each other. "Oh, snap," Darnell said, his face loosening and his body slumping back in his chair.

Elsa smiled. "Snap, indeed. Adds up to a much smarter bet."

She read out the names of the students who had taken up her wager and lost, assigning them a Birthday Problem video to watch and then summarize. Shoua gave a smack of her tongue and sighed.

"No extra homework for me," Thomas gloated. Then he grinned. "Guess I'll just have some extra time for my Hebrew studies."

Elsa gave him a stern side glance, but underneath it she was entertained. She had high hopes for this generation.

As Elsa relaxed into the sofa that evening, her pocket buzzed. So done with my children. Want either of them? the text said. It was from Jennifer.

The boys had done their homework, and Ham was home. Drink? Elsa replied.

Half an hour later, Elsa and Jennifer brought their beers to a high table in the corner of Mimi's, a newer establishment that their working-mom lifestyles had tried to prevent them from checking out. The new place was located in an old space, as so many of the best ones were. It was a corner building, two walls flaunting exposed brick toward the other two walls of mostly window glass. Various ducts and pipes high overhead were clean and lit like art.

"You know Ted and Ham have been here like five times," Elsa reminded Jennifer. "Fathers of the year."

"Hey, they did their part, with the sperm," Jennifer said.

Elsa and Jennifer had first met in a book club before either had children, bonding during overlapping first pregnancies. But when only Jennifer's pregnancy had resulted in a real live baby, little Sarah, the two women had drifted apart. Jennifer had missed some of Elsa's darker years. They didn't talk about the ancient past, though: theirs was a present-tense friendship, less concerned with the water under the bridge than with what was coming out of the fire hose at them just now.

Maybe eight years back, their husbands, Ham and Ted, had developed a friendship of their own when their sons Bird and Paulie grudgingly tried the same sports. These days, the two families got together often. Jennifer's kids felt like niece and nephew to Elsa.

Jennifer launched into her latest exasperations with Sarah and Paulie. Tonight they had double-teamed their mother, a rare moment of unity as they expressed disgust first at the dinner Jennifer had cooked and then at her asking about new slang she reported reading on Black Twitter.

"Oh my God, Mom," Elsa scoffed dramatically.

But then Jennifer's eyes started filling. "Damn it. So now here go my white woman's tears," she said.

Elsa touched her arm and offered her the chair that faced away from the rest of the bar. Jennifer took off her glasses and blotted, finally admitting her ludicrous overreaction to her children's gripes: she had dumped the pound cake she had just bought into the sink, running soapy water all over it.

Elsa stifled her smile while Jennifer hid her face. "They didn't deserve the damn cake," Elsa chuckled gently, nodding.

This was how Elsa and Jennifer worked. They traded ugly views of their own parenting, and somehow it helped. Elsa was confident that Jennifer was a good mother, so when Jennifer shared something horrible she had done, it served not to change that fact but to add color to it. Elsa now understood that yes, good mothers might drive away from the parking lot without their stubborn son at the end of a soccer game out in the burbs, just for long enough to show that *now* means business. Good mothers might accidentally slut-shame their daughter as she headed out the door dressed like that. There was no point in defending the moment. Shit happened, bumps in the road of good-enough parenting, and confessing helped. Their Catholic friends did it in a dark booth; she and Jennifer held confession over a drink, with the exponential advantage of reciprocity.

They traded their chronic frustrations over screen time. Elsa noted that Garvey wanted a phone; apparently every fifth grader on earth but him had one.

"You know I love Garvey," Jennifer interjected, "but hasn't he lost his school Chromebook like three times this year?"

"I wonder where he gets that," Elsa said. She told Jennifer about how last month Garvey had finished a 3K fun run in the park with only one shoe still on, and Ham had gone to retrieve the other. When he got back, though, Ham found that he himself had lost the shoe all over again, and the whole family had to retrace Ham's steps. They found the shoe in the crook of a tree, where he had paused to lean while chatting with another dad.

"I mean, I lose my keys and my coffee cup on the regular, don't get me wrong. But Ham and Garvey are both next level," Elsa said. "Meanwhile, Bird has never lost a thing in his whole life. Of course." Bird had had his phone for over a year. While he didn't seem to think it was for anything besides nixies, he certainly couldn't fathom misplacing it.

Jennifer was frowning into her IPA again, falling back into the doldrums of her cake fit.

Elsa tried to find a confession of her own to offer. She leaned in. Finally she recapped how the other evening at dinner, she had railed against the drama teacher, who had a passel of girls sewing costumes for the school play. So gender regressive, right? Plus so noninclusive, since only the wealthier families owned a sewing machine?

"Shaking my damn head," Jennifer agreed.

"But Bird is not with me. No, he's sure the drama teacher is being a good person. In fact, his idea is that I should bring in *my* machine for kids who don't have one. And teach my sons to sew." Elsa drank. "So now of course I'm the asshole. Again."

It was a bit of a forced fit to Jennifer's needs, this framing. Sure, it hurt a smidge that Bird found her so irritating these days, but mostly Elsa felt warmed by this latest instance of Bird's charitable view of the rest of the world. It was a humblebrag, really.

"Maybe you can teach Bird to sew a man purse for Ham so he can keep track of his shit," Jennifer offered. "Christmas present? If anyone can pull off a man purse, it's Ham."

It was true that Ham's style had not fully settled into Midwest living—his Seattle roots were often showing. He couldn't understand any man his own age voluntarily wearing a shirt with any form of collar on a weekend.

Elsa could see that Jennifer still felt down about herself. "Hey, so you missed my big genetics fiasco," she started, intending to offer all the details.

Jennifer sat up a bit and her face reanimated itself. "Oh my God," she said, swatting Elsa's hand. "Did I tell you about my neighbor and his DNA testing?" She leaned forward, eyes bright. "This is that guy with the guard mannequin."

Elsa remembered. Last December, Jennifer's neighborhood had developed a package-thief problem, with delivered packages disappearing off front stoops. Instead of a smart doorbell with a camera, this guy had gotten a mannequin and put it right near the front window inside his enclosed, three-season front porch.

Now Jennifer had a new tale about this neighbor. Apparently this neighbor had always known he was an adoptee, and he had decided to send his DNA to that service called MyTree, to learn stuff about himself. But when he received a printout of relatives, he was surprised to recognize most of the names. He had blood relatives from his adoptive mother's side *and* his adoptive father's side. So he wondered: Was he even adopted?

Jennifer beamed, clearly savoring. "So get this. Guess who his mother is?" Elsa was reminded of Garvey's riddle. Since it was probably not the prisoner, she shook her head and let Jennifer continue. "It's his much-older sister. His sister is actually his real mother!"

Apparently this white sister had been discreetly sent away while pregnant with a Black man's child, and when she finally came home, she had a new "little brother." The baby had been reframed as the parents' biracial adoptee.

"Oh my hell," Elsa breathed. She stared at Jennifer, processing the story.

"His parents were actually his grandparents!" Jennifer added.

Elsa absorbed this. This family had kept secrets for a long time. The mannequin man was old enough to have his own kids, and yet only now was he learning the truth. "They never told him?"

Jennifer shook her head, giggling a bit.

Elsa tried to look delighted by this gossip as well, but still her questions poured out. "So . . . so how did he feel about that? Does he still love his family?"

Jennifer shrugged as she swigged the end of her beer.

Elsa continued to press. "Does he hate his sister-mom now, for lying? And is he going to find his biological dad?"

Jennifer wasn't sure, but she wondered if Elsa was up for another beer. Elsa felt frustration rise. How was this even a story if Jennifer didn't know how it turned out?

"You know, I really should get to school early tomorrow," Elsa frowned. She downed the rest of her drink. As she got up, she saw herself in the dark glass of the windows and quickly looked away.

Before finally climbing into bed in her own room, Elsa looked in on Bird. He was a tangle of limbs and caramel-blond curls, mouth hanging open. She watched him for a moment. In spite of the shiny, zit-speckled forehead, his face was still angelic.

Even in middle school, Bird had no real instinct for the kind of social warfare that Elsa witnessed in the halls so regularly. Girls were better at it, sure, but if you looked hard enough, you saw it across the board: students judging, mocking, and excluding each other almost reflexively. Bird, though, seemed to walk around without armor or artillery.

If a bomb went off, Bird would get hurt. It was Elsa's job, then, to avoid detonation. What had she been thinking, opening up these topics recently in math class? It was careless. Sure, good moms sometimes made mistakes. But in Elsa's case, good mothering meant keeping her mouth shut and her feet on the narrow path of deceit.

Chapter 4

The following Thursday afternoon, Elsa was at the dining room table sorting a few late homework assignments when Garvey arrived, shrugging off his backpack in the enclosed front porch and blasting into the house. As he saw Elsa, he sagged his jaw, walked limply into the living room, and dropped to the rug. He flopped out his arms and legs.

"Hi, Fluffle." Elsa waited. She knew Garvey wouldn't last long keeping this display silent.

"Mom, are we secular?"

Elsa pulled out her phone and did a quick search. Secular, nonsecular—which was which, again? "I guess you could say that," she answered. "I mean, *secular* just means 'not religious,' and we aren't religious." She put away her phone and looked at him there on the floor. "You could always tell people you're a *none*, like Jennifer does. Cuz get it? Like if you check off which religion you are, and you choose none?" She remembered when Garvey had told his friends he was an atheist at a birthday party in second grade and how she had cringed for him a bit. Some words were harder for people to hear than others.

Garvey gave a dramatic sigh.

"You can believe whatever you want, you know," Elsa added.

She was fairly confident that the coming conversation was related to one from two days before in the back of her minivan. As she'd driven them home from a game, Garvey's two friends had taken turns telling Garvey about the weekend camping trip their Boys Of America troop had taken.

They called themselves "BOAs," from the acronym, surely hoping to suggest the snake instead of the feathered accessory. Their "BOA" outing, then, had managed to be both a complete disaster and a big, fun memory, one it was tragic that Garvey the non-BOA had missed. After the second of the two boys waved goodbye from under his porch light, Garvey had scooted up to the middle seat and asked Elsa if it was true the Boys Of America said an oath about God. She'd been surprised by the question, but she had told him the truth: "That's what I understand, yes." Now, in her living room, she waited for what seemed likely to be the rest of that conversation.

Garvey continued to lie on the floor. Elsa put red marks on a few homework papers. But when she moved into the kitchen to peel some potatoes, Garvey soon followed. He slouched back into a chair at the little kitchen table, foot propped on the table's stem, and asked why the BOAs cared about the whole God thing anyway.

"Good question," Elsa said. "Seems like they should just focus on sticks and knots. Maybe go-karts and being a good person and stuff. I think that's more what Perry and Oliver do, you know. I don't think they say any prayers or anything in their troop."

"Well, I mean, how could they, right?" Garvey frowned. "It's at school."

Elsa paused. This was like when her sister had said she *might* break up with that lame long-term boyfriend but hadn't yet done so: it was a tricky time for honesty. Maybe Garvey would resolve his dilemma and just join, in the end. She decided to stop short of admitting that she agreed—that something here raised her hackles a bit.

She set her peeler down and sat across from Garvey. "Listen, man. If you want to be the guy in the Boys Of America who kind of ignores this thing, you can do that. I would totally get that. We have lots of friends who do the religion thing, and we just tend to find other things to talk about together." As she said it, she knew this wouldn't sit right with Garvey. "And if you want to become a BOA and then raise a little hell if they tell you to say 'God' in their oath, you can do that too."

Garvey frowned at her, maybe in concentration. Like her, he grew a vertical line between his eyebrows when he was thinking, so "deep in thought" looked more like "slightly pissed off."

"Mom, but I don't believe in God. And if I joined, it would be pretending that's not true, right? I don't think that would be all that good." He shrugged a bit.

Elsa didn't really buy the shrug. "Well, Sugar, I'm really sorry. But I'm totally with you, whatever you do."

Garvey nodded, mostly at the tabletop.

Elsa opened the freezer and grabbed a popsicle for him in sympathy. "Heads up," she said, tossing it his way. "Speaking of sucks. Go eat it outside. And bring Scoopy with you."

Garvey slid off the chair and half-heartedly called out to the dog as he lugged himself toward the coat rack.

Elsa felt a moment of parenting doubt. While she and Ham hadn't told their kids what to believe, they had also never given the boys any real taste of church. Was that so terrible? Neither Ham nor Elsa had been churched themselves, and neither had a high tolerance for the intolerant views they saw some people tie to their religiosity.

Certainly the boys had set foot in their grandmother's Lutheran church once or twice; Elsa's mother, Marcy, remained a half-hearted member. Church hadn't been a whole-family habit during Elsa's childhood, though, because of the resistance offered by Elsa's father, Carlos. His own Catholic, Mexican father had died when Carlos was tiny, leaving him to grow up the brown-skinned cousin among a pack of young Wisconsin Germans in his mother's extended family. He felt robbed of learning Spanish; for the Catholicism, he felt no loss. It had become too much for his young heart to face each week, that enormous figure fixed high up front—that man left to die.

After high school, Elsa had gone to Seattle for college, and she found that the West Coast disinterest in religion suited her. So did a magnetic student called Ham. Love had first sprouted at a street protest, after the Rodney King verdict. The two of them were both up for the shouting, but when things smelled like trouble, Ham had peeled her off their group and walked her to Dick's for a burger.

To Ham, like most Seattleites in their generation, religion was like the color of paint on your closet walls: probably inherited, nothing to get too fired up about. He had plenty of room for someone like Elsa's mother, then, and when Elsa had married him back in St. Paul at age twenty-seven, Ham had been the one to suggest Marcy's church. Elsa's father had been fine with that, walking Elsa down the aisle.

A few years later, her father's cancer began killing him, slowly and cruelly, and people sent their prayers. Elsa felt a kind of anger at that, in her grief. What Would Jesus Do? Nothing, it turned out.

In the weeks after the funeral, Elsa remembered now, she had gone through a box of her father's mementos. There were photos: Carlos's own father when he had enlisted, then young Carlos with his widowed blond mother after his father's death. There was a snapshot of Elsa's mom when she was still Carlos's young fiancée, looking like Audrey Hepburn. Apart from these, the treasure her father left was mostly children's books he'd read to Elsa and Krista.

The strangest of the set was *Struwwelpeter*, a gruesome old German children's book translated into English. Elsa had cracked it open and memories had curled up from it, seeping through her eyeballs and into her head. She remembered wishing as her father read it aloud that she were in his lap like Krista was, instead of sitting beside him. The days of sharing his lap had ticked away; by the time of *Struwwelpeter*, only pudgy little Krista still sat on that warm throne of childhood.

The book was one that Carlos's own German grandmother had read to him and his blond Wisconsin cousins decades before, in English. In the *Struwwelpeter* stories, naughty children met outlandish forms of comeuppance: they burst into flames, they had their fingers cut off with scissors, or they were plucked up by a windstorm and never seen again. Reading these to his daughters set Carlos into great peals of laughter, his body shaking irrepressibly until he had to take off his glasses and wipe his eyes. The girls turned their faces away and held on tighter to their dad, at first. But they requested the book again and again across a dozen bedtimes, until eventually the terror of the pictures on each new page made them giggle too.

When their mother, Marcy, saw him reading these stories to the girls, she objected: too horrifying for children. Carlos usually thought his way through to realizing his wife was right, when they disagreed, but this time he stood his ground. Which was more gruesome, this or the idea of nails driven through hands? The girls had shuddered and squealed in agreement.

Their mother was content to continue her occasional church attendance without them after that. Krista had dabbled in attending one year too, but only so she had a chance to perform in the Nativity play. Apart from this, the girls' version of Sunday school involved following Carlos around while he caulked and sanded and tightened things, sometimes around their own home and sometimes in the home of a grateful relative or neighbor. The girls occasionally tried squeezing the caulk gun themselves, Elsa remembered. He thought they were finally interested in learning skills for female independence; instead, they did it for his laughter and his guiding hand on their own.

When Elsa had flipped through the *Struwwelpeter* after his funeral, she'd found one tale in the book that was unfamiliar. Had their father skipped it? In this story, three fair German children taunted a dark-skinned boy. They teased and mocked his blackness cruelly, and for this they were punished. But their punishment was to be dipped in an inkpot, turned dark as night themselves. Losing their whiteness was clearly meant to bring them shame.

Elsa had felt a new horror. Had his German grandmother read this one to little Carlos, conspicuously dark amid the pale-haired cousins clustered around? It pained Elsa to think of it. This was not a story he could laugh at with his daughters.

That night, Elsa was propped up in bed next to Ham, each of them looking at their phones. Elsa checked the school parents' social media site and found a post recruiting for the Boys Of America informational night at Garvey's school. Did everyone know that girls were welcome now too? Everyone could be a BOA!

"Liars," she said out loud. She thought of young Carlos, othered. She couldn't abide Garvey being made an outsider too.

Before she had time to overthink it, she typed in a reply to the post. It was a question, but of course it wasn't really a question. She already knew the answer.

After clicking post, she held her phone out high and released it with exaggerated cockiness onto the covers: mic drop.

Ham turned from his own scrolling and gave a quick nod of blind solidarity. "Bam!"

Elsa moved her phone to the charger, shut off her lamp, and kissed him good night.

Chapter 5

At 7:55 the next morning, Natalie Trowbridge was pleased to be tactfully early. She had scheduled a touch-base meeting with Principal Schusterman, a time for the PTO and the administration to synchronize their efforts and share information. This kind of meeting felt good: sure, it wasn't yet a corporate position, but she liked the way the insights from her evening graduate courses were improving her contributions to the leadership of Lowe Hills.

Approaching the front counter, Natalie was waved toward the principal's room at the back of the large common office space. As she moved between the countertops and office machines, her hands checked the tuck of her yellow blouse. She noticed Aneisha Reese watching her from her position at the copy machine, hands on hips.

Natalie chirped a bright hello to her. "Claire is so looking forward to the choir competition," she gushed, waggling her fingers at Aneisha as she passed.

At Mr. Schusterman's open office door, Natalie gave a light tappity-tap on the doorframe as she popped her head into the office. Her eyes found the principal. "Good morning, Mr. Schusterman," she smiled.

"Natalie! None of that, it's Rob to you." He stood, gallant, motioning her into a chair across from his desk before returning to his seat.

Natalie launched into a few small logistical questions for the coming History Day event. Then she asked him what updates or concerns he might have for the parent group. She was efficient; this was a man with many responsibilities, and she wanted to convey her respect for that.

"Let's circle back to that eye color issue," he said, leaning toward her on his elbows. "Are we hearing any residual unhappiness, or did Ms. Vargas clear that all the way up?"

Natalie thought about her daughter Claire's theory, which was about Elsa Vargas's own son. Claire said probably he was fathered by someone other than Ms. Vargas's dark-haired husband, and probably the teacher was just playing with fire. It was middle school silliness, of course. But if it were true, then probably the real dad was blond—probably even someone else's husband.

Natalie shook off the thought. Anyway, there was no reason to think Claire's theory would become a rumor, since kids barely knew who this boy Bird even was.

Rob Schusterman stretched his head forward a bit more and lowered his voice. "Some of us have enough common sense that we would have spotted that trouble beforehand, am I correct?" When Natalie laughed and nodded, he pointed his finger at her chest. "I like your judgment, Natalie." She looked at his finger, then his eyes. Somehow they were still on her face.

She leaned in a bit as well, pointing her chin downward a titch so she could look up at him. "Speaking of sensing trouble," she said, glancing at the open door, "are you aware that Elsa Vargas seems to have caused a bit of a reaction over on the Johnson Elementary parent page?" She remembered the way her creation and moderation of that page five years ago had been met with something like cheek pinching at home, how she had laughed along when her husband had teased her about becoming the world's prettiest IT consultant.

Rob looked into his monitor and beckoned her; soon she was next to him on his side of the desk, looking at the social media site. They found Elsa Vargas's reply to the Boys Of America announcement post. Are students required to believe in God to participate in this school-chartered group? she had asked. There was a long reply from the indignant BOA-master pointing out that all faiths could be explored through one of the patches kids could earn, and that no particular denomination or faith was pushed. This reply had seven likes.

Rob looked at Natalie in disbelief, his face starting to grow pink. "The BOAs, now? She's going after the Boys Of America?" He got up and turned Natalie toward a framed certificate perched on one of his shelves: Robert Schusterman, Anaconda BOA. Just like his father before him, he had achieved the highest rank in the BOAs as a teen. After sharing this with Natalie, he shook his head a few moments. "I don't know what kinds of values she was raised with, but I'm wondering why she feels the need to attack people's faith," he said.

Natalie looked back at him. She remembered what little mousey Katharine Humphrey had told her after the Additional Item. Katharine had confessed that she felt sorry for this math teacher; she always had, since Elsa Vargas's first baby had died so unexpectedly right at birth.

"I just don't know," Natalie told Rob. "Of course, I can imagine why she might have lost her own faith, poor thing." Natalie shared Elsa's tragic backstory with him as he listened intently. This was where Natalie shone, she knew: breaking down silos.

"What a soft heart you have," Rob said quietly.

"Oh . . . that's kind to say. I suppose I understand loss," she continued. "I lost my marriage three years ago." That was when she had walked in on her blond then-husband and his personal trainer. It had made a certain kind of sense; the young, supportive trainer was doing a better job than Natalie herself at impersonating the Natalie she had promised to be for him. Now the girl was flailing as a two-weekends-a-month stepmother to Claire and James. "In my case, though," Natalie said to the principal now, hand on her own heart, "it made me focus all the more on what I have to offer my children."

Kids didn't have trophy moms or trade them in for younger ones. Kids didn't prefer that she never assert herself or show her competence, of which she had plenty. These days, Natalie was taking that competence to the bank: her ex was on the hook to pay for her whole MBA program.

It might mean ending up alone, but Natalie was going to show the world that she was more than what they saw now.

Rob nodded, then shook his head. His eyes were warm. His gaze made her smile and tip her head a bit, ready to giggle. After a few seconds of eye contact, they returned their eyes to the computer monitor.

"Wow, another like on that answer to Ms. Vargas's question," Rob observed.

"And someone's typing as we speak," Natalie noted, pointing to the in-process icon. Their eyes met again.

"Word travels fast," Rob said. "Again, some of us have better judgment than Ms. Vargas, I'm afraid."

A loud knock on his open door made the two look up. "Sorry to interrupt," Aneisha sang out boldly. Natalie took a casual side step away from Rob. "Is it too late to add to the morning announcement script? We need a reminder to our scholars about keeping their hoodies off their beautiful heads."

Natalie excused herself. She collected her bag off the floor next to the armchair, feeling Rob Schusterman's eyes on her as she bent at the waist. She suppressed a smile as she continued out the door: thank God for her religious morning discipline on the StairMaster.

Chapter 6

Before there was Bird, there was the baby who died the moment she was born. Baby Inga was how Elsa first learned that love was a forge; it burned what had once been true and bent it into whole new geometries.

When Elsa discovered she was pregnant in 2001, she and Ham had felt both excitement and terror. She was lucky to have succeeded so soon; it had taken Elsa's new friend Jennifer ages to finally get pregnant. But was Elsa ready to stay home for ten months, maybe more? Would the shift from teaching high school precalculus to wiping butts offer enough fulfillment? Then the day had come: contractions. Next came the signs of perinatal distress, the risk of asphyxia. Medical hands and medical hardware up inside her, turning and pulling; pushing and more pushing; more doctors and more nurses barking at each other and wheeling machines around. In the end, their baby Inga was dead. With no air ever drawn into her lungs, she died before ever crying out.

Elsa and Ham returned home with an empty infant car seat in the back of their vehicle. They dragged themselves to their bedroom, realizing only the next day that Elsa's sister had thought to disassemble the infant sleeper they'd attached to the side of their bed. It barely mattered—the presence or absence of objects offered no leverage on their grief. Elsa moved through the hours by changing where she curled up in a ball: on the bathroom floor, in the bed, against the radiator in the kitchen. More tears poured out of Elsa than she could manage to replenish; a constant headache took root in her skull.

For the funeral, Elsa swallowed all the pills that were handed to her. Her recollection of the event was therefore fuzzy. She did remember the Nativity scene outside her mother's church. ("Lucky Mary," Elsa had said to Ham. "Her baby can rise from the dead.") She remembered a frozen breeze blowing through leafless, snowless trees. And she remembered the comfort of touching that old green teddy bear, the one she had hoped to pass on to her little daughter, Inga.

Katharine Humphrey had been remembering that very funeral at the recent PTO meeting. The memory had unsettled her; perhaps this was why she'd told Natalie about Elsa Vargas's tragic stillbirth.

That funeral. Katharine had hoped to attend with another member of Elsa's book club, which Katharine herself had just joined. But that had fallen through, and Katharine had instead brought her sister, Mary Pat.

They'd entered the oddly modern Lutheran chapel to the sound of organ music playing. Up front was the casket, closed and set on a platform surrounded by flowers and an old teddy bear. Off to the left sat a glassy-eyed Elsa and her husband, their hands connected between them as the service began.

At the second hymn, though, Elsa pulled her hand out of his and stood. At first, Katharine thought she only intended to join the congregants in standing to sing. But as the first verse grew, Elsa walked toward the casket. She paused only a moment there, her hand briefly on the top of the casket, then she picked up the stuffed bear and returned with it to her seat.

Throughout the sermon and the readings and the music, Elsa held the bear to her chest. Her husband held his features steady, his hand on her shoulder. At one point, she raised the bear closer against her neck and tipped her cheek against it. Her husband retreated a few inches, removing his glasses and rubbing his eyes. Then after a minute, he put his arm around his wife and her stuffed animal.

As the service ended, the pastor asked that everyone who wished to offer condolences to the parents should please exit the chapel via the center aisle. The couple would receive them all at the main doors to the vestibule, he advised, gesturing for Elsa and her husband to proceed there now. The two of them got up and moved toward the aisle, where a woman who was surely Elsa's mother intervened for a moment. Touching the bear Elsa held, the mother whispered something; Elsa smiled and shook her head, her arms now tighter around it as she moved past the pews to her assigned location.

When Katharine and Mary Pat arrived at the back doors, Elsa stepped toward them and brightened warmly. "Katharine! I've been thinking about your little daughter. I remember how you said she was such a fussy baby. Maybe colic?" At this, Elsa put her free hand on her teddy bear's back. "That must have been so hard."

Katharine felt herself flush at the sympathy. She shook her head a little, unsure of what to say.

Now Elsa leaned in. "We don't have that. Inga just sleeps so peacefully." In her peripheral vision, Katharine saw her sister stepping back, her hand going to her mouth. Elsa continued, her voice now a conspiratorial whisper. "Is it terrible to say that I think she's the most beautiful baby ever? She has these gorgeous brown eyes behind those lids." Elsa gave a little chuckle as she squeezed Katharine's arm, then turned to the next person in line.

Stepping forward to the husband, Katharine looked up, her cheeks still hot. He met her eyes, but she could not think quickly enough what to say. Her eyes were instead pulled back to Elsa, who was rocking her body side to side with a tiny bounce and smiling her next greeting.

Looking again at Elsa's husband, Katharine now felt further embarrassed by her own rubbernecking. He nodded at her, one side of his mouth up in a half grin that looked pained. He put a hand on Katharine's shoulder for the briefest moment. "I'm so sorry," he said quietly.

Only after she had moved past him did Katharine realize: these were just the words she herself should have offered.

After the burial that day, Elsa sat in Inga's bedroom for hours, rocking the frayed green bear in the gliding easy chair. The next day Ham found her swaddling it in one of Inga's blankets, and he removed both the crib and the diaper changing table that very afternoon. He left the chair and Elsa's bear, which either made the days more survivable for her or made them worse—how could he know which?

On the fourth day, Elsa's mother took the bear to her own house. For safekeeping, she said. Elsa's arms pulled Ham's head to her chest each night instead.

Days turned to weeks. They ate and they slept and then they walked the sidewalks, mostly shoveled of snow. They saw that the Clarksons across the street sometimes went out with their baby Emmet, born just three months before Inga. Elsa could not keep her eyes off them. From inside the front porch or from the bedroom's front window, she noted the awkward angle they used to carry in their car seat from the car, sleeping baby inside. She watched when they went out for walks as the weather warmed, taking turns wearing the baby in a carrier on their chest. At first the baby faced inward, but then later he got to face forward with limbs bouncing free. Elsa noticed that when the mother walked down the sidewalk wearing Emmet, she kept her index finger inside little Emmet's fist: holding hands.

As she moved around the house, Elsa began to find that if she focused hard enough, she could inhabit motherhood too. She sometimes put on the baby carrier they had received as a baby shower gift, even loading her sand-filled Velcro ankle weights into the pouch so that she could better imagine the weight and the little grip of Inga. Alone, she sometimes carried the car seat out to the car and snapped it into its base before heading to a nature trail with her weighted pouch. There she could walk and talk in peace, her conjured Inga snuggled up against her body. When Ham discovered the car seat base anchored into her back seat, Elsa retreated into silence, only managing days later to confess and promise that she was done.

But promises were broken. The track of what would have been was so easy to see: it only took a bit of research online or watching the Clarksons with their little Emmet. When Inga would have been ready to try soft foods, Elsa started buying bananas and avocados regularly, cutting them up into a little bowl and using a finger to transport each piece to her own mouth. She ordered larger-sized cloth diapers and duck-printed covers, just right for a one-year-old. These she hid away, only getting them out when no one else was home. Once, Ham found the baby bathtub Elsa had accidentally left inflated inside the regular tub. There were verbal slips too, when Elsa drank too much wine on an empty stomach. She accidentally said "we" instead of "I" about her latest hike through the woods or mentioned an annoying character from a PBS Kids show she had put on while chopping vegetables.

Elsa could see that Emmet Clarkson now rode in a toddler backpack, hip straps tight around the parent. She bought one and loaded it with the increasing weight of Inga. When the Clarksons carried a little toddler training toilet into their house, Elsa knew she needed to see one in the corner of her own bathroom—just once or twice.

Over and over, her moments of make-believe were discovered and her family's hopes were defeated. Her sister or her mother would sit Elsa down, hold her hands, and ask her to please stop. Elsa would cry and nod and agree, and she would not be lying. But within a few days or a week, the hole that ached for more Inga would swallow up her resolve.

Finally, Ham understood that therapy was overdue. Emmet's father had approached Ham on the sidewalk, asking him to please get Elsa some help. He and his wife, he said, were worried about the way Elsa watched their family so intently, the way she showed up at the fence outside the playground down the street when they were there. They had decided to tell their little son to always stay away from Miss Elsa, that she was sick and not safe for children to go near.

Elsa gasped when Ham told her. "Oh my hell, Ham! I would never . . ."

"*I* know that. Your imaginary Inga is all you want," he said. "But I don't know where this leads, Elsa. You have to find a way back to wanting something real."

She knew he was right. And after a few months of counseling, Elsa could see her fantastical world for what it was. It would not save her; it promised only isolation. Somehow, she gradually acknowledged, the empty place of grief was where connection was. There, she could find Ham, reach out for her mother or sister, even chat online with other mothers surviving loss. Together was better; she could see that. Still, it was a painful void.

They could try again, Ham nudged. She tried on the belief he offered: a new baby would help her put Inga to rest. And so before Inga's third birthday, Elsa went off her birth control.

If she were to move forward, she needed to get clean. She needed Ham to see into her dark corners; with him, she could find the chains to pull, illuminate the light bulbs now dusty with neglect. To make time and space for this, Elsa arranged a late winter weekend together two hours north on the shore of Lake Superior.

Setting out early on a Saturday, they drove beyond Duluth and up the shore highway to its collection of state parks: frozen waterfalls, stark cliffs, and rocky beaches. The sun was out and the lake quiet, but they counted two cars in ditches nonetheless. In the first park they visited, the wooden stairways were all closed, with chains draped across their beginnings. The ice near the waterfall was peppered with signage about danger. Up the highway, they found access to a pebbly cove, so they trudged out in their cold-weather gear. At the edge of the trees that lined the beach, something furry caught Elsa's eye: a rabbit, dead. Everywhere was the reminder that winter was out for blood.

One side of the cove had a spit protruding into the lake. Here, the rocks were softball sized, some gray and some black and some iron-ore red, all of them rounded smooth and capped with a thin layer of ice.

The sand below them dropped off dramatically, perhaps carved away by one of Lake Superior's angry waves the night before. One rock had gone missing, fallen out of an icy casing that somehow remained intact around the phantom stone. The ice that lingered was like an upside-down wineglass, posed as if someone were demonstrating not a drop left to give. It was so fragile, this thin glassy keeper of nothing at all.

"It's amazing, isn't it?" Ham said. "We're looking at the past right there. It's like the ice doesn't even know it's the past now."

Elsa turned to look at him. She had to wait a moment, but eventually he looked back at her, snapping into their uncanny synchronicity. His eyes got wet.

"I'm trying to know," Elsa said.

They pulled each other into a side hug and stared at the ice formation together.

"I know. The past is never gonna be gone," Ham said into her hat. "But let's get ourselves a future, Else," he added. She gave a squeeze of agreement.

They headed for their hotel in Duluth. Elsa watched Ham drive, and she felt safe and warm and hopeful. As the North Shore Highway brought Duluth closer, though, Elsa remembered that she hadn't yet told Ham which hotel she had booked. That it was the one with the indoor water park and the splash pad for little ones: it was hard to explain. This was just how she needed to do it. She struggled to find the right tone for her news. Casual seemed . . . dishonest. Instead, she dove in by saying his name, a clear call to serious.

"Ham."

He looked her way briefly, then his eyes went back to the road.

"So listen," she continued. "I booked us at that hotel with the water park."

His mouth tensed. Elsa realized too late that she had over-cued danger in the same way that a soundtrack might, in a thriller movie.

"So this is because of Inga?" Ham asked, voice cold.

Elsa shivered a bit, but she stuck to her conviction. "It is. I know it sounds crazy, Ham, but I just need to . . . go there. I just need to go straight for it." He said nothing. Elsa rubbed his knee, then reclined her seat and closed her eyes. She could give him space.

Once inside the room, Ham loosened. Hotel rooms always sparked a certain excitement for him, and before long his hands found the bare skin of her stomach as they stood at the huge window. Sometimes bodies were better than words, Elsa knew. In minutes, they were on the luscious white softness of the bed's king-size comforter.

Half an hour later, Elsa's teasing about Ham's hotel room fetish had led them to building a list of complaints for the management. Where was the ceiling mirror? Why no vibrating bed? They tossed each other articles of clothing and dressed, content.

Ham suggested they go grab a beer at the pub next to their hotel. Elsa said she wanted to get into a hot tub instead. They agreed to meet in an hour to drive up the hill for their planned late dinner.

She put on her swimsuit and an oversized tank dress and rode the elevator down to the aging indoor water park, refusing to think about Inga pressing the elevator buttons to make them light up. After getting her bearings, Elsa chose a lounge chair near the fountains and dumping buckets of the splash pad, where the younger children played.

Elsa did not close her eyes to fully allow it, but still—from years of practice—she knew just how she could stitch together an Inga from the details the scene in front of her offered. Inga's swimsuit would be both sagging and riding up one butt cheek; her high pigtails would be flattened and dripping; her teeth would be chattering as she stiffly race-walked into the yellow striped towel held by her mother, an alternate-universe Elsa.

Instead, Elsa focused on the real children in front of her. The girl with the butt cheek was realistically more like four years old, maybe even a small five. The hair in the other girl's pigtails was too light and too curly to belong with dark-haired Elsa. And the chattering boy in the yellow towel was not in fact a girl at all.

She watched the girl with the light curly hair for a while. Eventually she noticed the mother sitting on a lounge chair along another edge of the splash pad. Elsa got up and moved to the chair next to the woman.

"Hi," Elsa said cheerfully. "Is that your daughter in the pigtails?"

The woman smiled. "It is, yes."

"She's a cutie. And I have to say, I love that suit." It was pink and had three ruffles across the seat.

The woman mentioned that she bought it in the gift shop. "Which one is yours?" she asked.

"Mine? Um, none of them," Elsa said, perhaps a bit loudly. She was here for this; she was doing this. "I don't have a daughter. I really want one, but . . . we're trying," she added.

After a couple of minutes, the little girl waded out of the pool and ran to her mother, who scolded her for running.

"This is Josie," the woman said.

Elsa introduced herself and reached her hand out. Josie put her wet hand into Elsa's.

Elsa swallowed, then animated her face. "Oh, you're real! You remind me a little bit of a pretend friend I used to have."

Josie lit up and looked at her mother.

"Real is better," Elsa smiled. These words were for herself—for Ham—more than they were for this dripping little stranger.

Half an hour later, Elsa was paying for her purchase in the gift shop when she noticed little Josie, her chubby fingers petting the polished agates in a bin. Elsa scanned the store; Josie's mother was not there. She bent down beside the girl, hands on her lap and a smile on her face.

"Hi, Josie! Is your mom around?"

Josie looked up and shook her head.

"Do you want to come out to the couch out there, where maybe she'll see you quicker? I bet she might be looking for you."

Josie brightened, her mouth forming an O and her eyebrows rising high. She held out her hand to Elsa and went with her into the lobby. Elsa paused to look toward the elevator bank, the hallway, the glass front doors. She saw Ham crossing the parking lot toward her from the pub, but she saw no sign of Josie's mom.

Elsa's eyes kept scanning as she helped Josie onto the couch facing the entry wall of windows. The front desk could help, if a minute or two didn't end in a reunion. She turned to Josie and started to ask her what she liked most in the water park.

"Josie!" A loud voice barked out from behind them, at the entrance to the gift shop. Elsa turned to see a man rushing forward, his face tight. He scooped Josie up abruptly, scolding her and hugging her as he moved away toward the elevators. Elsa's smile was left hanging as the man avoided her eyes.

"Oh, I'm so sorry! I was just . . . you must be Josie's dad?" she called out after him. But all was well. She relaxed back into the couch and turned forward again.

There was Ham, standing in front of her, his brow furrowed.

"New friend . . . ?" he said.

"Isn't she a cutie?" Elsa got up off the couch and grabbed her shopping bag, smiling.

Ham watched her face, trying to relax his own. Then he looked at the sack. "What'd you get me?"

Elsa hesitated. Then she remembered her purpose for this weekend: clean slate, open and honest communication. She opened her bag and pulled out the ruffled pink swimsuit. Ham's face collapsed. He looked toward the elevators, where Josie and her dad were just disappearing into the lift.

"What in the actual . . . ?" he said quietly, slowly.

"I'm giving this suit to Jennifer," Elsa explained. "I want to reconnect, and her daughter, Sarah, is . . ."

But Ham had already started to walk away. She felt panic. "No! Ham. Wait." It snapped together: Josie. The suit. Could he really think

. . . ? "Oh my God, Ham, no. I was just trying to help her find her mother. This suit is for Sarah. It's an actual thing for an actual kid. This is just—this is how I need to do this," she said, catching up to him and reaching for his sleeve. He shook her off.

His eyes were closed, his fingers grabbing his forehead like a claw. "Jesus, Elsa. I thought you were back, but you're not. You need way bigger help. I defended you to the Clarksons, and now I don't even know what you . . . Jesus." He was made of steel now, teeth clenched. "And I'm done. I'm just done."

Elsa frowned, but she took in a deep breath and let it release. It was OK if he couldn't quite understand. She nodded.

Ham was not getting calmer. His nostrils dilated, and he shook his head fast. "Peter from work was in the pub next door, and he's still there." He dug in his pockets and held out his room key and car keys. "And you know what? He'll give me a ride home. He's heading back to the Twin Cities tonight."

Elsa felt fear course through her system. Leaving her here alone for the night? Did that mean *leaving*, leaving? But then she calmed herself. Ham would not give up this easily. Inga belonged to the past, but Ham did not. There was a vast future, and she understood clearly his ultimatum: if she could prove that she was turning toward it, then Ham would be in it. And she *was* turning, even if he couldn't trust it yet.

You couldn't always find shortcuts, she knew. Trust was all about the long game. "OK," she said. *Let him go.*

At home the next day, Ham's plan seemed to be to avoid her. He stayed late at work the next three days; when he finally got home, he left again within an hour. Finally Elsa parked herself at the blanket and pillow he had set up on the living room sofa, and waited him out. She explained again about Josie, about the suit for Jennifer, about why the water park full of real children had been the right place to go. He was distant, but he listened.

A week later, Elsa held a pregnancy test in front of Ham's eyes to share with him the news her painful breasts had already shared with her. Instead of only empty inside her, there was now a little blastocyst. By the fall of that very year, 2005, the two of them could be raising a real live baby.

Ham held her close, and she felt his breath shuddering through him a few times. "Oh, Else," he finally whimpered. "My karma is so fucked up. I mean, this is so great—the world's greatest news ever. It's just . . . I totally don't deserve this."

She pushed her hand against his sandpapery cheek, moved his face so she could look right into it. "You left me all by my lonesome in Duluth," she smiled.

"I fucked up royally, Else. I gave up on you. I'm so incredibly sorry."

"I'm sorry too. And now our sorry asses are going to be parents."

He still looked pained as he nodded. She poked him in the ribs, prodding out a smile.

"You think we're ready?" Ham asked.

She assured him that she was.

And that had been true, hadn't it? Elsa had been ready to bring home a live baby. She just hadn't been prepared for it to be the wrong one.

Chapter 7

On Friday evening after dinner with Ham and her two real live boys, Elsa stepped back from loading the dishwasher. Ham could take it from here. He would face the bowls the wrong way and overcrowd the silverware compartment, but all good things came with a price.

Knowing better than to watch the error of his ways, Elsa picked up her phone and checked her notifications. On the elementary school parents' site, her thumb had to scroll as she took in a tirade of a response.

"Oh my hell, Ham. This guy threw a fit at me about my Boys Of America question," she announced. Ham dried his hands and came to look at her screen. She caught him up on Garvey's mopey dismay about the God stuff the afternoon before.

"Game on," Ham said, retrieving his own phone. He opened the site and hit "Like" on Elsa's comment. "Remember that article I showed you a few months ago about this? That kid who was denied his Anaconda rank after he'd already done all the patches and camps or whatever. He stopped believing in God, and that was a deal-breaker."

The two struck up a duel of search results. As it turned out, the Boys Of America organization was not exactly hiding a requirement of belief; many localities publicized it proudly, sharing the resolution the national group had ratified. Commentary sites described the strategic BOA compromise: just after lifting their ban on gay troop leaders, the Boys Of America had doubled down on a God requirement to appease the more conservative church groups who sponsored so many of their troops. Both leaders and kids were clearly required to state a belief in God to be in the BOAs.

And yet this particular troop, Perry and Oliver's, was chartered by the school's Parent-Teacher Organization.

"In what universe is that not a separation of church and state thing?" Ham snapped.

"I know, right?" They started nodding their matching resolute faces at each other. They were Team Garvey now.

Elsa was pleased to be side by side with Ham in this battle. Sharing crusades was something she remembered most strongly from their earliest years, before they started their family. From the beginning, their political ire had matched, and so had their heavy arsenals of both snark and silly humor. When friends would tire of talking about the idiocy of a latest policy position from the other side, Ham and Elsa would just be getting started. They'd brainstorm ideas for an absurd bumper sticker or, better yet, a crazy piece of guerilla theater. They could riff for days. Sure, their follow-through left something to be desired. But the ubiquitous quote said to never doubt a *group* of committed citizens could change the world. Elsa and Ham weren't a whole group; they were just a pair—the idea people.

Elsa reread the diatribe from the BOA-master. She shook her head. "Classic Minnesota-style tolerance. Call God whatever you like, so long as you call him."

"Right," Ham offered. "You can believe any which way but not." He poured more wine into her glass and grabbed himself a beer from the fridge.

Before Ham, Elsa had figured that pairing up was a matter of finding out who wanted to woo you. But when Ham came along, Elsa realized it was the love flowing out of her that made her feel alive, not the love flowing toward her. So many of Elsa's peers had settled into marriages where they could trust the flow coming at them. Sure, trust in that was important, and Elsa thanked her Lucky Charms that her love for Ham was still requited.

But motherhood had revealed a new twist: some love didn't actually depend on that return flow. Your kids could throw fits at you, resent you, shut their doors in your face; worse, one day they would leave you altogether, and you'd still be thrilled that they bothered to call. They requited sometimes, sure, even in middle school; it's just that they offered these crumbs rarely, at unpredictable intervals. And that worked just like the behaviorists from grad school said it would: a random pattern of positive reinforcement was the most compelling and powerful of all. It was addiction.

Soon a prancing rhythm erupted above the kitchen, followed by Garvey's feet stomping down the stairs into the kitchen. Now that he had left the floor where his brother was actually located, he yelled for him. "Bird, get your butt down here! Movie!" Tonight was movie night for the family in the basement. Garvey started recounting another of the sketchy jokes from his school bus driver this week, but Ham interrupted.

"Yeah, Else—nice response with the attachment," he remarked. "They can't really claim the rules are squishy if the BOA rulebook is that cut and dried about it, can they?"

Garvey shouted once more for Bird. Then he reached to tilt his dad's phone down toward his own eyes, hold it steady, and read. Ham and Elsa exchanged looks, but then Ham went ahead and let Garvey scroll through the thread.

"You should be a lawyer, Mom," Garvey admired.

Bird appeared in the kitchen, having silently descended the stairs in his socks. "Why?"

Garvey launched into a recap, bouncing across the room as he rattled off the evidence: the Boys Of America were for sure officially requiring a belief in God.

Bird nodded. "Yeah, but people don't care if you just kind of ignore that. If you want to do BOAs, you should just do it," he suggested. "Aren't Oliver and Perry in it?"

The family looked at Bird.

"But the BOAs are prejudiced," Garvey ranted, running his fingers into the dark locks above his forehead and making the strands dance.

"You're saying he should try passing, as a believer?" Ham asked Bird. Then he grinned. "I wonder if being a Belieber would do the trick."

Bird shrugged lightly. He pulled out the popcorn popper, plugged it in, and went toward the pantry to find the popcorn kernels. Elsa followed him.

"Do you think it's OK for the school to charter a group that requires a religious belief?" she pressed. "I mean, the PTO sponsors it, and it excludes nonbelievers."

Bird scanned the cupboard. "I don't think they would really tell Garvey he can't do BOAs. They're just regular people."

Elsa leaned against the refrigerator. It was both sweet and infuriating, this benefit of the doubt that Bird tossed around so easily.

Garvey, though, was now in full justice warrior mode. "You can't just say, 'Oh, they'll like you if you just pretend you're one of them.' I mean, racists are probably nice to people on the phone if they sound white."

Bird measured out popcorn kernels and dumped them into the air popper. "You really think Perry is anything like a racist, or Oliver? Cuz I don't. I think they have good values and stuff, and probably going to church is just part of that in their family. Maybe it's you guys who are being prejudiced." He shrugged again. "If you don't want to be a BOA, then maybe just don't be one."

Garvey made a tongue-smacking sound and rolled his eyes. "That's so lame."

Elsa intervened, sending Garvey up to find her favorite blanket. She told Bird to head on down to the TV in the basement while she finished preparing the popcorn.

She took a fraction of the popcorn out, setting it aside before she drizzled the rest with butter. Bird always gagged when he tried to eat buttered popcorn. For his portion, she shot in two quick pumps of olive oil spray and tossed it with salt and pepper. Parenting was this: small instances of love you offered your children almost hourly, most of them simply breathed in without acknowledgment, like so much air.

Elsa headed down with the two popcorns. Garvey trailed her with the blanket, explaining a board game he had heard about and wanted. The basement wasn't technically finished; its drywall was mostly draped with old folk tapestries and strange area rugs collected in her younger years of yard sale scavenging and kidless travel. She'd labeled the basement "boho chic" and called it good.

At the bottom of the stairs, Garvey broke into a run. He and Elsa raced across the room to the highly sought-after corner spot on the L-shaped old couch. He got his butt into the prized location first and threw a fist up in victory, pumping it in tight circles like Arsenio Hall.

Bird was already seated, having chosen his usual end of the L. Elsa sat down next to him. He put his arm across her back and gave her shoulder a small pat. "Sorry I wasn't really agreeing with you, Mom," he said softly. Bird had reserves of sincerity to spring on you when you least expected them—less so now that he was thirteen, but they were still in there. She remembered him as a toddler touching her face while she talked to him, and how it had launched such a wave of emotion and even fear in her.

Elsa leaned over, put her lips on his cheek, and blew a big raspberry. "There's a fart for you, Birdman."

Ham came down with his beer, asking what they'd decided on for tonight's movie. Elsa took her smooth brown hair out of its ponytail and started fidgeting with the stretchy band.

"No stupid fantasy movies!" Garvey proclaimed. Elsa knew Ham, too, was in agreement—nothing was so painful as a movie with magical wizards or elves in it—but she felt Bird's quiet sigh.

Elsa reached over and gathered some of Bird's curly blond hair in her fingers, wrapping it in her ponytail band. "Yeah, stupid anything sucks. Bird, you pick tonight—what's a not-stupid fantasy movie that would be good?" She poked the spout of hair she'd made on top of his head.

Bird turned his head toward her patiently so she could admire her work. "That's OK, nobody else really likes fantasy." He took the ponytail band out and handed it to her. "I might just go read, actually. I mean, we can watch whatever, and I'll stay for a few minutes."

Elsa looked at his face, which bore no resentment or anger—no anything at all that she could read. And yet here it was again, that mysterious force that prevented them from clicking into place, as if he were a magnet turned backward. He seemed almost resigned to not fitting with the three of them.

It made her wonder at times. He couldn't know the truth about himself, could he? Even Elsa didn't know for sure. Not technically. But somehow, perhaps because of how seldom she allowed herself the full thought, it felt like underneath she did know. She would mother Bird always, and she would never let him go. But she knew it was a lie to say she was truly his mother.

Chapter 8

A week had passed since the Birthday Problem, and it was finally Friday. The students who had lost their wager with Elsa passed in their extra homework. Shoua turned around to ask Thomas to pass his forward, and he put his empty hands out wide. "Birthday Problem? I got no birthday problems," he grinned.

"Oh, I forgot, you're Jewish, so you didn't bet," she said.

"Yeah, I changed my mind about that. I might be Hindu instead, because they have a big holiday coming up," Thomas said.

Elsa was at their row. "You're very spiritually inclined, I see," she smirked. "Any chance you're interested in the Boys Of America?"

"Nope," Thomas said. "Why?"

Elsa realized she needed to shut up with this, here at her own school. She shrugged. "Aw, nothing." But Claire lit up a little.

"Oh, apparently the BOAs don't let you join if you say you're anti-religion," Claire offered. Elsa remembered that Claire's mom, Natalie, had a son at the elementary school too. She smiled at Claire and shrugged again.

"But apparently he's Hindu now. No problem."

Claire reached out to touch Thomas's forearm. "You could join the Church of Elvis. You can become a minister, even, online. My cousin told me about it. Then you can, like, marry couples and stuff." Then her smile suddenly dropped, her face blushing pink as she turned abruptly to dig in her backpack.

"Do Hindus do betting?" Shoua asked Thomas.

"Not too sure yet. Actually," he said, face brightening, "I'm thinking about starting a poker game once I get my poker set this weekend. You know how to play poker, Shoua?"

"No," she admitted.

Darnell reached over and poked Thomas's shoulder. "I know poker, man. What do you mean a set, like good chips?"

"Yeah, my grandparents gave me money for my birthday, and I ordered this sweet set—" Thomas looked up as Elsa walked up his aisle. "Hey, Ms. Vargas! My birthday is this weekend, what are the odds of that?"

"Now that you told me, the odds are one hundred percent," Elsa quipped. She wondered if Bird might like a poker set. Probably not; she could picture Garvey and Ham getting excited about it, which made her suspect that maybe Bird wouldn't. "Which day is your birthday? My son's is on Sunday."

"No way!" Thomas burst into a big smile. "For real? Nah, you're messing with me."

Elsa chuckled and kept walking. She could have made the worse birthday bet and still won, in this class.

"OK, folks, turn your attention to the front screen. We're going to hear from Mr. Khan Explains It All, and then I want you to work with your neighbor on any problem you like from the set on page 168." She went to her laptop at her desk and started the short open-source video on combinations versus permutations.

From her desk, Elsa watched her eighth graders. She focused on Claire first, wondering what it would be like to have a daughter navigating these years when "smart" became less prized a trait. Claire was attentive to the video, but whenever Thomas or Darnell behind her spoke, she turned around to listen, pulling her hair around in front of her shoulder. Darnell kept talking to Thomas about poker, and Claire tipped the top of her head toward them a little so that she could look up at them from under her lashes.

Thomas was whispering but animated. He had the kind of expressive face that was easy to read from across the room, and he kept a smile lurking just below the surface even when he frowned or rolled his eyes about something. Elsa knew the effect, this being how Garvey's face worked as well: it made people feel like smiling back at almost everything he said.

After the video, Thomas stared out into space for a moment. Then his face grew intense and he reached out to Claire. "Are you sure the Boys Of America say you have to be religious?" he asked her, loud enough that Elsa could hear.

Claire gave two long blinks and then nodded her tilted head.

Thomas turned toward Elsa and put up his hand for a moment before calling out. "Ms. Vargas, how can the BOAs do that? Isn't that, like, religious discrimination?" He frowned, and Elsa saw the vertical line appear between his eyebrows.

Elsa kept her face blank and shrugged. She moved toward the front of the class. "OK, folks, let's pair up, please, and get to choosing a problem to work on. Page 168."

She strolled the aisles for a few minutes, listening in just enough to encourage the conversations to be mostly about the math. She saw that Claire and Thomas had partnered up, and she walked a route that deliberately avoided their continuing conversation.

By half past, Elsa collected the assignments. Then she turned on the music the students hadn't chosen and declared it now Friday catch-up time. At least half the kids always claimed to be fully caught up, and they just socialized. This was fine with Elsa, who was not without an understanding of adolescent development.

"Aw, Miss," Darnell called out in anguish. "What is this, like Chinese jazz or something? I'm gonna bring you some songs to consider, for serious. I know we lost the bet, but still." He shook his head slowly, watching her to make sure she took it in stride. She shook her head back.

"You can send me a list," she said. "But my standards are high, Darnell."

"Are they, though?" he raised his eyebrows high and looked over at the speaker. Shoua giggled. Elsa got grief every Friday, and she wouldn't have it any other way.

She sat down behind her desk, content to watch her class again. She looked at Thomas over in the far corner, talking to a classmate, chopping his hand up and down in the air a bit and wearing a frown with just a smidge of the underlying grin still in there. Elsa recognized an impassioned rant when she saw one.

She relished his indignance over the BOAs. He, too, saw the real matter of principle at stake. Bird had it wrong: it wasn't just her and Garvey being unduly grumpy. And Ham. At the very least, it was the three of them, plus this kid Thomas.

Thomas clapped his friend on the back and then walked—jaunted, really—back to his seat. He ran his hands up into his hair and shook his dark floppy strands around for a moment. He dropped into his chair, and then he shoved himself low and put a foot up on the bar below Shoua's seat.

Without warning, an extra dose of gravity ran through Elsa's stomach. It was the odd angle of Thomas's head as he slouched, and it was the jaunt. It was hands making hair dance. Everything about Thomas the Birthday Boy suddenly added up, and Elsa felt herself sliding toward a beast awakening from hibernation: the truth.

She put her face on the desk. *Breathe.* Thoughts rushed in; she couldn't think them. She got up and strode to the window, staring blindly through the rest of the song Darnell hated until her mind finally found its meter.

Her world was precarious. It was a mobile, pieces hanging from string on various teetering arms. Touch one piece, and the rest could all spin and bobble. But still—what if . . . ?

The bell rang, and with effort Elsa pulled her teacher-self together. She was practiced; she could act like the world was not what it was. She went to stand by the doorway as the class filed out.

"Happy birthday this weekend, Thomas," she managed as he came near.

"Thanks," he grinned. "To your son too."

"Where were you born, by the way? Was it here in town, and do you know which hospital?"

His eyes looked up at an angle, searching memory. "Yeah, and I think it was . . . actually, I'm not too sure on the hospital. I'll ask my mom." He grinned again.

His mom. Bird's mother. Elsa's core constricted. She shouldn't have done that. She had to undo that.

"Actually, Thomas . . ." She backed up out of the doorway, against the classroom's inside wall. She motioned him toward her. She could see now that his eyes were not just brown, but the same warm brown as Garvey's. Had they always been that color, or had they started out otherwise?

Elsa dropped her voice just a bit. "I shouldn't have asked which hospital, actually. Forget that; it was weird. And . . . maybe don't tell your mom I asked that, OK?" She could feel the red on her face, see Thomas noticing it. "I mean, I was kind of, you know . . . seen as opening cans of worms that should have just stayed canned, with the whole genetics thing . . ." She raised her eyebrows and her shoulders a bit, and waited.

Thomas looked back at her, a frown without the underlying glow. "No, no, I don't think it's weird. But . . . OK. I for sure won't say that you asked." He nodded a couple of times, looking at her with sincerity. A pause stretched out then, but Elsa couldn't fill it. Then Thomas gave a nervous laugh and stepped backward. "Yeah. OK. So, have a nice weekend, Ms. Vargas." His grin came back, then he turned and moved down the hallway with a definite jaunt.

She watched his familiar gait and frowned. What if this boy was really her son? And the boy they had raised as Bird—had he begun life as Thomas Humphrey?

Chapter 9

That evening, Elsa took an electric blanket onto the cold front porch, where she pretended to lesson plan. Her family would not bother her here.

She closed her eyes and contemplated the truth. For so long, the plan had worked: throw it out, bury it, walk wide around it. And then came today.

Everything she felt seemed wrong—too much hope or too much fear; too hot or too cold. Finally the just-right feeling emerged, and it was guilt, sitting heavy on her chest. It forced her face toward the replay of this strange movie that was somehow about her. How had that new mother committed herself to such a lie, all those years before?

Elsa and Ham had named their first boy Baird Carlos Hamilton, and he had most certainly lived. She had held him, looked into his then-blue eyes, and then somehow she had let him go. It was incomprehensible.

The only explanation that made sense now was how quickly a new love had grown. Elsa thought of the Woodstock-era song on classic rock stations: "Love the One You're With." For Elsa, baby to breast and oxytocin flooding her system, it was more an inevitability than a choice. She had fallen in love with the one she was nursing.

It wasn't that it happened all at once. In the days after leaving the hospital, she had tried again to explain that this might not be their baby. Ham continued to bring her water and fluff her pillow and kiss her head, but he ignored her on this topic, hardening under his kindnesses. Elsa stopped bringing it up with him.

She tried Krista again, but her sister stood firm. She reminded Elsa: Ham had stood by his wife's delusion once, but he didn't deserve another struggle to connect his wife with reality. Their mother, home battling a feverish flu, seemed to echo Krista. "Mom says to take care of you, help you know that everything is fine," Krista relayed. "She says it's all understandable, and everything you are feeling is perfectly normal." Perfectly normal had three votes, then, to Elsa's one.

Meanwhile, this baby—his needs could not be denied, and his own mother was not there to meet them. She had no choice but to begin mothering this child who was surely someone else's. *For now,* she thought at first. *Until I can heal up, tote this baby to the hospital, make them check.*

But this baby was not made of sand and Velcro; he was warm, wiggling with life, and drawn to her body like it was part of his own. When unwrapped to the air so she could bathe him or dress him, he flailed and whimpered, the seconds of separation seeming to overwhelm him. In her arms, he melted against her. At first, it was his bobbling little mouth that communicated his need for her, only her. Ham's arms were a solace for only so long before the baby's lips would tell them that it was Elsa he was hungry for. Despite her raw, devastated nipples, the moments when Ham set the tiny cheek against her own bare skin flooded Elsa with something simple and all-encompassing. He was real; so was their love and togetherness.

Meanwhile, the idea of her own son in another mother's arms stayed just that: only an idea.

Across the first weeks with this baby she called Baird, she barely found time to sleep, let alone contemplate just when she might right things. Her brain was crushed small by feelings that had plumped into everything. Eventually her capacity to really think returned, and so did her ability to drive; by then, though, the argument for making things right didn't feel so convincing.

She and this baby here in her arms now pulsed to one rhythm, struggling against their own sleepy eyelids to keep their gazes entwined just one more moment. How could she sever this? Surely giving him back would traumatize him, ruin his capacity to bond. It had become unthinkable—irresponsible. Maybe it was even unhealthy for Elsa herself: she had already mothered just an idea for years, and that had been a problem. Was it healthy to try to trade this baby boy her hands could touch for one only her mind told her existed? Each new day, she reassessed. And each day, what felt most right was to hold tight to the reality in her arms.

The grooves of mothering deepened. This she had expected; parenting meant routine. More surprising was the way this story held her attention, each tiny, new shift a plot twist she couldn't wait to share. Nursing went on just like before, for instance, but now Baird would rest his hand against her breast. Next he began to look around, entranced by the ceiling fan or simply by the place where the walls met; later still, he reached his hand for her mouth while he fed, exploding into a smile when she gummed his fingers.

On the diaper changing table, he began flapping his arms at his mobile, then trying to taste his own foot if she gave it to him when she was all done. When she rocked him to sleep, he held on to her dark hair. When she set throw pillows around his pudgy body for his first attempts at sitting on the couch, he became a low mound, comedy magic to her and Ham. He was Jabba the Hutt; he was a scoop of dough melting toward cookieness, four minutes in. When he finally tipped over onto his face, their alarm was cleared by Baird's own delighted laugh. He was more easygoing than anyone they had ever known.

She and Ham found themselves filling moments away from Baird with recountings of his amazing new developments. Somehow he was stretching out his legs straight beneath himself, in Elsa's lap, trying out the weight as she held him by his armpits. How could it be possible that he would one day stand? But then Ham was holding his little hands above him on the rug while he wobbled like a drunk man, finding his balance.

On the hardwood floor, he seemed to forget his legs, instead pushing and tugging his onesie-covered tummy over to toys and fallen scraps like a hermit crab. Elsa pulled questionable items out of his mouth. Soon she even coaxed in little pieces of banana or avocado, because this baby ate his own soft foods.

Real is better, she remembered telling the water park girl.

When he was just a year old, Elsa's mother brought over the stack of books Elsa and Krista had grown up with, the books their father had saved. The *Struwwelpeter* was all wrong for babies, but there were others: Dr. Seuss books, a book about monkeys drumming on drums. There was also the P. D. Eastman book, one Elsa had not loved as a child but which she chose one day to read to her little Baird.

In the story, a little bird hatched alone while its mother was out looking for a worm. He went to find his mother, tumbling out of the nest and taking a walk past various critters and objects.

"Are you my mother?" the bird asked each one.

"No, not me," he was told time and time again. The cow was not his mother; the dog was not his mother. He walked farther down his path, motherless and searching.

Elsa stopped. She dropped the book and snuggled Baird closer, trying to keep her breath steady. He squirmed, wanting to turn back to the book, but Elsa could not continue. She could not read another "Are you my mother?" out loud.

Ham arrived home later to find her still in the rocker, eyes red and puffy, their son asleep on her shoulder. Her arms were doubled up around him, her elbows all but touching as she whispered to his torso, calling him her little bird.

"What's wrong?" he asked.

Elsa looked at Ham. She had already hidden the book back in the stack. Tears began rolling down her nose again, fresh. She could not explain to Ham that the lie would have to last forever, that she would always answer yes.

"He needs us," she sobbed. "We're who he has, Ham."

Ham melted, nodding his head and looking through foggy eyes at this scene of love and vulnerability. They wept together, cradled him between them, and began that day to call him their little Bird. For Elsa, it was a new commitment to forever. For Ham, she could not clarify what she wanted to ask: Would he promise to father for always a boy who was not their own?

The next day she took *Are You My Mother?* to the big dumpster at the school two blocks away. She looked one last time at its cover, thanked her father for saving it, and then hurled it in.

Years later in a fourth-period math class, though, Elsa had learned that you can't really throw away a question once and for all, just with your hands. Instead, the question lies buried somewhere, waiting: a land mine. So many years later, Thomas had made her hear that ominous click. Elsa had one foot right on top of that buried explosive.

Still, for tonight, paralysis was not an answer. Setting aside the electric blanket and the pretense of lesson planning, Elsa resolved instead to sort through the swirl in her head. She called out to Scoopy and grabbed her coat and his leash.

Outside, her breath came out white, like a cartoon speech bubble. What if she just told the truth? she wondered. She could begin with the adults, Ham and then Thomas's parents. Maybe each of the three knew, somewhere deep down, that the son they were now raising didn't quite fit, not in the way a child did if they shared your blood. Maybe they shared a secret pain, an unexplained inadequacy of connection that all of them would be relieved to finally understand.

A neighbor dog ran barking to his fence, and Elsa tugged Scoopy past it.

But then what? she thought. What if the other couple saw Elsa and Ham's parenting as unworthy, harmful, something to save Bird from as quickly as possible? Maybe they wouldn't understand that sometimes good mothers piss off the PTO or the Boys Of America. What if Thomas's parents got a lawyer?

Elsa shoved this fear aside. That would never happen, because of tit for tat. It was mutually assured destruction: nuclear defense logic, family style.

Scoopy paused at the intersection to wait for Elsa's OK to cross. "That's my good boy," she said, patting him.

So the two families had adoptees, really, Elsa thought. And plenty of people had open adoptions. Just because a child found their biological parent didn't mean they stopped belonging to their adoptive parents.

Neither boy would suddenly move in with a new family, of course. Surely the early days would be full of visits and outings—the big zoo? Saints baseball, or Loons soccer? Maybe the families would go together at first, then separately as each boy felt comfortable. Adoptees who found their parents eventually just had more, didn't they? A new sense of where they came from, of why they were the way they were? They just had more adults in their life, maybe even more siblings.

That thought launched panic. Would Bird find a new sibling who was more like him than Garvey was? Worse, what if Bird felt understood by Thomas's mother in a way that Elsa couldn't offer? Now Elsa's brain filled with adults she knew who barely talked to their parents, who had gradually let that relationship weaken to a shallowness that preserved everyone's mental health. Even if she didn't lose Bird immediately, it felt horrifically possible that she could lose him incrementally. What if he went to *their* place on Thanksgiving breaks in college? Would his future children climb into Thomas's mom's lap instead, calling her Grandma? The truth was full of danger.

Elsa and Scoopy came to the end of a block, and she waited for the dog to let her know whether they should plow ahead or turn back. Scoopy hesitated, waiting for Elsa to lead.

She considered what it would be to do nothing. Right now, she got to see Thomas every school day, and she had Bird all to herself. Maybe the best course of action was not to mess with things at all. That tiny newborn who had first turned his head to her voice, rested his damp head against her breast—he might never be hers to hold close again, not ever. But she could learn more about who he was, see that he was safe and happy. Maybe she would have to call this well enough, and leave well enough mostly alone.

Finally she gave Scoopy a tug. They had gone far enough, she told him, and it was time to return to their pack.

Chapter 10

Sunday morning, Elsa woke up thinking about Thomas. It was his birthday, and he would be opening a poker set with the family who probably wasn't really his. His not-father might teach him how to play Texas Hold'em this afternoon; his not-mother might have baked him an elaborate cake. An unknown child might sit next to Thomas, hoping to be included in the gambling alongside their supposed brother. It would be so easy to look up where Thomas lived, to go sleuth out something about the shape of his life with the wrong family.

But here in Elsa's house, it was Bird's birthday, and no one else's. It was time to start performing the day.

Bird would be sleeping in. He'd had three friends over the night before until midnight, eating pizza and a Whole Foods cake, seeing a movie at the Riverview Theater across town, and then walking around afterward in the dark neighborhood together, like full-on teenagers.

The day was full of readying. Elsa had not yet fully planned Bird's family birthday dinner, and Garvey needed a last-minute trip to Target to find his brother a gift. By afternoon, Elsa was double-checking her to-do list and congratulating herself. Sure, she had forgotten to eat lunch, but she had also kept Thomas mostly out of her head.

At three o'clock, Krista and Marcy arrived to help Garvey decorate the cake Elsa had baked, while Ham took Bird to Twin Cities Running for the zero-drop running shoes he wanted. Elsa retreated to the sun-warmed three-season porch, searching through the photo gallery on her phone. Eventually she came across a picture of Bird from six years before, when his curly hair had been wilder and blonder and his face was still overwhelmed by too-big teeth. What did it matter, biology? He was hers now, this sweet little muffin.

Krista came out to the porch to find her, bringing Elsa some hard cider she had brought down in a growler from a taproom up north.

"Oh fer cute, Else. Look at that guy," Krista cooed at the photo, dropping herself on the wicker love seat next to Elsa. "Do you have any more?"

Elsa got up. "I have the Bird book, hang on." She went into the living room and pulled a photo book off the shelf. She'd made it for Ham for Father's Day the year before, along with one of Garvey. Each book went backward in time, beginning with what had then been the present. For Bird, just now fourteen, the differences from even a year ago were stunning to see.

Krista grabbed the book, putting it in her lap and patting the seat next to her for Elsa to join. Elsa stood for a moment, tentative. Then she scolded herself: today was for celebrating Bird, and looking at memories was simply that. She drank most of her cider, then sat down and leaned in against her sister.

"Look at those round cheeks!" Krista pointed. It was just two years before, but this Bird on the page looked more like a small child than he did like his current tall, hint-of-man self. Krista turned the page, and Bird got smaller. "Oh, I remember Judge Bird," Krista said, looking at the mock trial his class had participated in down at the courthouse.

"He hated that his co-judge talked him into calling the kid guilty," Elsa said. "Then he reduced his sentence. Extenuating circumstances or something."

"He sees the good."

Krista turned the page to reveal Bird throwing a stick into the river. "Oh, no! Dog park!"

The sisters looked at each other, sharing an odd look. It wasn't Bird they were remembering this time; it was their own childhood visit, one day in winter. It was the Iceberg Incident.

When Elsa was seven and Krista five, they were with their mom at the park on the edge of the Mississippi River, letting Schnitzel run around off leash in what was not yet officially a dog park. It was late winter, sunny and clear. The river was still frozen on its edges; a shallow snowpack stuck to both the river's ice and the sand of the bank. You could barely know where you stopped walking on land and started walking on water. Only when a chunk of tundra broke off and began to drift downriver did the answer become clear.

Young Elsa and Krista loved nothing more than helping the ice to break up, on these outings. With rocks and sticks serving as axes and pry bars, they hacked away at fissures in the snow-covered ice nearest the moving water. Other dog owners slowed to watch as the girls chopped, sawed, yelled bossy orders at each other, and chopped some more. Sometimes success would come: pieces of white snowy ice would break free, the size of maybe a bed pillow and the shape of something to be determined. As the piece separated and turned, the girls would yell out labels: "It's a baseball cap!" "No, a mitten!" If it managed to bump away from the shallows and into the deeper water, then they would throw chunks of snow and ice toward it, yelling at Schnitzel to go fetch. Sometimes he would, and when he came back ashore, his wet fur would freeze into tiny icicle sequins, like he was ready for a gala.

The incident that day started off as a victory. While Krista was up on the bank, Elsa broke off a piece of ice so big she could probably lie across it both ways. She hopped on to strike a pose and turned to yell for her family to look. Instead, the person closest was an unfamiliar older dog owner. Aghast, this doughy, bearded man lumbered onto her floating iceberg to save her.

When he landed on the floating island, he slipped onto his ass. This bumped their trajectory just enough: they were no longer inching along the shallows a foot from solid land. Now, they were heading away from the bank and toward the fast open water of the big river.

There was yelling on the shore. On the iceberg, the old man pulled Elsa onto his lap, pushing his white beard against her cheek as he repeated, "We're OK, we're OK." But it wasn't her father's lap; she didn't want to be on this lap. Elsa could see the shoreline moving alongside them, but she couldn't turn to look back. She couldn't see her mother or Krista. She wanted to think that Schnitzel was paddling behind them, that he would climb onto their iceberg and travel with her like Rudolph in the Christmas special. That didn't happen. They floated past the end of the long park, beyond where anything was familiar.

In the end, both Elsa and the old man were rescued. Three big men arrived in a metal boat with an outboard motor, and she was passed aboard. Onshore, Elsa was wrapped up in a blanket from the back of someone's car, then pulled away from the gathering crowd to wait for her family. Meanwhile, the bearded man offered his recounting to those gathered around him, emphasizing how he had kept the girl as safe as if she had been his own granddaughter.

"Creepy old Santa wannabe," Elsa said now, shaking her head as she remembered.

Krista let the photo book lie flat, and she turned to Elsa with a look. "That's what you remember about the Iceberg Incident? That the guy looked like a creepy Santa?"

Elsa stared back. "Yes, Krista, that's what I remember. He held me down on his goddamn lap, and it wasn't a lap I wanted to be in. Plus him jumping on was the reason I went out into the current. I would have been fine if it weren't for him." She emptied her cider, and Krista turned back to the book and flipped the page. Neither of them commented on the photo of little geologist Bird, smashing rocks in the backyard with his snorkeling mask on for eye protection.

Finally Krista muttered, "I guess I forgot about the growing problem of child trafficking by iceberg."

Elsa got up. She went into the kitchen and poured herself a glass of wine. Her mother looked up from guiding Garvey's hand as he piped a frilly frosting edge onto Bird's cake. Marcy had a smudge of white on one of her stunning dark eyebrows, and the other was raised at Elsa just a bit. Garvey wore a furrowed look of concentration with a subtext of delight.

"Shall we put out some food to nibble on if we're starting in on the wine?" her mother asked Elsa sweetly.

"That's so thoughtful, Mom," Elsa said dryly. She watched Garvey for a moment, then complimented him on his decorating before topping off her wine. She reached into the cupboard and pulled down a box of Triscuits, which she plunked down beside the cake. She returned to the porch through the open door and pulled it firmly shut.

Krista was still looking at the Bird book. She looked up at Elsa, then at her wine. She grabbed her own cider, raised it, and said, "To Mom."

Elsa snorted and clinked her glass.

Krista shifted her body toward Elsa. "Because Mom—that's what I remember, Else. Mom, when your iceberg shoved out away from shore. I was running down the beach, and she was . . . I don't know, Else. She wasn't doing anything to fix it."

"It was too late to just fix it."

"Not at first it wasn't," Krista said.

Elsa took a big swig, looking hard at Krista. But then she just shrugged. "Huh." She looked out the porch's windows, thinking about how much she really believed in "too late." Was it too late now, if Thomas were really hers? Finally she sat again next to Krista.

Krista flipped back a couple of pages to give Elsa a quick glimpse at the photos she had missed while in the kitchen, then moved on. On the next page, Bird was peering down at a bundle he held carefully in his three-year-old arms and lap: tiny Garvey, his months-old baby brother. Elsa stared at this picture intently. While the boys wore jammies of matching stripes, that was the end of their matching. Garvey's hair was dark and limp, not unlike her own, and he had his dad's eyes. Bird was blond and curly, and his eyes were blue. It felt impossible to Elsa that no one else had ever wondered aloud about this total mismatch. Did no one even think for a moment that maybe Elsa had been right, in the hospital? Even when she had told Ham and Krista both outright that this was not her Baird, how could that possibility have been so completely erased from their minds?

"Look at how he looks at Garvey," was all Krista said.

It was true, that was touching. But other thoughts were now breaking and entering: Thomas might have been holding Garvey there instead. And because she had missed those years herself, Elsa might always be stuck constructing her own three-year-old Thomas from other kids' parts.

Finally Krista turned to the last spread, a gut punch. Here were Elsa and Ham, arriving home with this baby she had agreed to call Baird. He was the same child as on every other page, of course—but here it was so early. It was before it was too late to get Thomas and Baird correctly sorted. She loved this pictured baby with her whole being; still, this was the very moment of betrayal. The image captured the day when she'd turned away from a child who had now lived precisely fourteen years of life without her.

The ache moved into her throat, and then her eyes were conquered. Elsa tried to stifle her crying, but a quiet sob shook her ribs.

Krista took Elsa's wine from her and set it on the windowsill, then she wrapped her arms around her sister. "Oh, honey," she whispered into Elsa's hair. "I know it doesn't go away. Our sweet, sweet little Inga. I know."

By the time Ham and Bird came back from the running store, Elsa had regained control. While dabbing foundation below her eyes and onto her lids, she had talked to herself about positivity in the mirror.

She grabbed Bird on his way in, reaching up to ensnare him in a big hug. "Happy birthday, Shortie," she said. Bird squeezed her back, then released her and stepped aside, causing Elsa to wobble before regaining her balance. She thought of the Triscuits she hadn't eaten. Ham's gaze fixed on Elsa, and she saw him notice her eyes, still pinker at the rims from the tears. She watched him catch Marcy's eyes next, and she saw the raised eyebrows communicating back at Ham.

"Yeah, don't even start with this," Elsa snapped, looking from one to the other sternly. She had no patience for this kind of husband-mother solidarity.

Krista halted in the middle of her own move toward Bird. Then she shook her head, rolled her eyes, and pulled Bird toward her, immediately launching into overzealous chatter before steering him into the living room.

Her mother stepped closer, putting an arm around Elsa. "Listen, Krista told me you were having a moment earlier. Do you think it would help to talk about some of those things, maybe a bit later? Right now, you've put together such a nice day for Bird." Then Marcy hustled herself into the living room, calling out her demand for her own hug from the birthday boy.

Ham remained. "What's going on?"

Elsa saw the abandoned wine on the windowsill and retrieved it. "Just thinking about babies today, Ham." She stared hard at his face with its false innocence. She raised her glass in a solitary toast. "To our little Baird," she said, and drank.

At dinner, Krista regaled the boys with memories from the months when she had taken care of them each day, when she was on unemployment years and years back. Did Bird remember when she had given him a stack of VHS tapes, thinking he could use them like building blocks, and Bird had systematically taken them apart to investigate what was inside? Next Krista had brought home an old dead printer and defunct keyboard and mouse, and set up a take-apart space in the garage. When they had found a dead squirrel one day shortly thereafter, Bird had asked if they could take that apart too. Bird wore a wide smile as she recounted this, nodding.

"You didn't get that from your dad, that's for sure," Elsa noted. She wondered if the man raising Thomas was into internal mechanics and animal guts.

"You're like your great-grandpa, my father," Marcy smiled at Bird.

"Ugh. Don't say that," Elsa shuddered. "Grandpa was like a giant brick. I think he hated kids, or at least he hated grandkids." She picked up her glass and looked at Krista. "He didn't really think we were all that grand, did he?"

Krista looked at Elsa, then Bird, then back to Elsa. "The man was arthritic and tired, Elsa, but whatever. Apparently he cared about machines and biology, back when he was still a little more . . . vital."

"But Bird doesn't hate anyone," Elsa said. She looked over at Bird. Would this remain true? she wondered. How badly could she fuck things up? "My Bird. Here's to my Bird, a lover, not a hater. He can forgive even his own horrible mother, am I right?" She held up her wine.

Bird gave an uncomfortable smile, looking over at his grandmother.

"We mothers get away with the most," Marcy smiled tightly at Bird. "How about you pass your mother the ice water, and her own mother will go start some coffee?" She popped into the kitchen.

Krista broke her face into a silent laugh emoji and pointed at Elsa. "You're not the favorite today," she sang in a whisper.

Elsa wasn't her own favorite today either. She leaned out for the next while, noting how her mother swooped into the space Elsa was vacating as conductor of this birthday event. It was Marcy who raised her baton and launched them into and through the evening's program: jokes and teasing, clear the table, cake and singing, gifts.

Elsa watched through a slight haze as Bird unwrapped his grandmother's present first. The card played a silly song when opened, the kind of card the boys had loved when they were eight years old. Elsa and Ham exchanged looks. But Bird opened and closed the card again and again, smiling over at Garvey. Garvey got out of his chair and turned around, shaking his booty while Bird scratched like a deejay, making the song repeat its opening bar three times before being released.

"I used to take apart the audio device in this kind of card from Grammy too," Bird smiled.

Now he turned to unwrapping the box itself. Inside was a pair of green striped pajamas: stretchy organic cotton leggings and a long-sleeved top. It was the very same brand that Elsa had seen her boys wearing in the Bird book photo, matching. Elsa suppressed her annoyance. How could her mother have no idea that Bird slept in just his underpants since age nine or ten?

"Sweet!" Bird exclaimed, holding the pajamas up and then touching them to his face. "I love these kinds of jammies; these are the best!" He moved around the table to his grandma and hugged her tightly. "You always give the best presents, Grammy," he said more quietly, turning to look her in the face.

Elsa's eyes filled up with tears all over again. This was Bird, true to form. What did it matter from where or from whom he had gotten this goodness, this ready tuning to the positive in people? He was Bird, and today was for celebrating his arrival in her life.

An hour later, Bird and Garvey headed down to try Bird's new video game as Elsa followed her mother to the front door. She gave Marcy an extra squeeze and whispered a heartfelt thanks into her ear.

"You know I'm always there for you, Elsa," her mother answered, lightly tucking a strand of Elsa's hair behind her ear. Then she headed out to her car.

As Elsa turned back, she found Krista just behind her with a look on her face. "You know she's always there for you, Elsa," Krista echoed, infusing the phrase with more self-righteousness. "Pssshhh, what a load," she added.

"Well, she definitely likes to wear it, but I guess she is," Elsa shrugged.

Krista rolled her eyes. "Elsa. She let you float away on an iceberg with a stranger."

Elsa chuckled. Her sister needed to win every argument, even if the argument happened ages ago. The worst you could do to Krista was to tell her it was too late, that it was no longer an argument.

"That's probably because she had you and Schnitzel to worry about, freaking out onshore."

"You should make her pay for therapy." Krista stood in the open doorway now, both irate and clearly having a good time.

Elsa just nodded, smiling at Krista. "Mom was there downriver when I got rescued. And that's what I remember."

Krista turned and walked out to her car, both her hands up in exasperation.

"I'm always there for you, Elsa," she sing-songed one more time out her window, then drove off.

Chapter 11

At Lowe Hills, Elsa monitored the hallway first thing each morning, a mug of coffee always there in her hand. Monday mornings had their own energy. A few students dragged themselves around, exhausted by the prospect of not just this whole day but four more after that. But most of them buzzed about like pollinators, eager to suck down the tiny particles of drama and anticipation and reassurance that filled their environment. Two days in their separate family-life cages put them all in a state of extreme need come Monday morning.

Sometimes she saw Bird in the hallway. She tried to preemptively look away, knowing that the question of whether to acknowledge his own mother was complicated. But today she saw him stop to help Howie pick up some things that had tumbled out of his locker, and she couldn't not watch. Howie was a difficult kid: small, immature, occasionally blowing up at teachers and tipping over a chair as he stormed out of the room. He met with the school psychologist every week, and most kids either egged him on just to see him go off or they avoided him and rolled their eyes more secretly. That Bird was helping him out almost made her cry right on the spot.

In kindergarten, Bird had been bit on the arm by another kid on the bus: the now-notorious Joey. When she'd reported this to his teacher, Elsa had learned that Joey had an assigned seat, that he was supposed to sit by himself because he couldn't be counted on to treat other kids well. But Joey invited Bird to sit by him, and that was good enough for

Bird. The invitation seemed to be proof that people were wrong about Joey. Even after the bite, when Bird agreed not to sit with him anymore, Bird had stayed secure in his knowledge that Joey was actually nice.

Bird liked what was inside people, and he cut them a lot of slack.

Elsa had worried back then that Bird would end up run over by bullies, but that had not panned out. He now had a few close friends whom Elsa knew and liked—nice fits for Bird. In the hallways, they didn't command much attention from the buzziest kids, and Bird's actions didn't particularly influence anyone to follow his lead. Howie wouldn't get much of a social bump just from Bird's help. But seeing it reminded Elsa that Bird had a generosity that qualified him, in a middle school, as something of an alien.

How right Ham had been that Bird was not the best fit for hockey, she thought. It wasn't that Elsa had really thought he'd love it, or even that she really liked the sport herself. Instead, she'd suggested it the day she watched Bird go into that kindergarten classroom for the first time without her. It killed her, that departure; her melodramatic reeling had lasted all afternoon. Why did their babies have to be boys, she had sobbed to Ham on the phone. Boys were doomed to leave you, to move to wherever their wives' families lived once they started a family. The only men you could count on coming back home to Minnesota were the ones who still loved hockey.

Elsa ducked out of the hallway now—first period was her prep, anyway—and sat behind her desk. She thought about herself as a mother. If Garvey felt there was a fight to be fought with the Boys Of America, she had no qualms suiting up. And what about for Bird? What was the strength of her commitment to him? She would not have this boy wandering through some story asking, "Are you my mother?" It didn't matter what was actually true. It only mattered what she had decided: *Yes, from here on out, I will be your mother.*

Then fourth period arrived, and with it, Thomas.

Leave it, she told herself, as if she were Scoopy and Thomas were a dead fish on the riverbank at the dog park. Only a mess of stink could come from rolling in this.

"Hey, Ms. Vargas," Thomas grinned as he paused in the classroom doorway. "Do I look older?"

The truth was that most of the eighth graders looked older every month. But Elsa stuck out a flat hand and wobbled it at Thomas: *eh.*

Claire squeezed by him just a tad closer than she really needed to. "Thomas, when's the poker night? Shoua and I want in," she said.

Thomas wrenched aside a bit more than he really needed to. He blushed at Elsa as he moved. Elsa knew to always pretend she understood nothing at all about the pollinator dances, so she simply fixed a teacherly level of cheer on Claire. "Happy Monday, Claire. Ready for that probability test tomorrow?"

Claire gave an annoyed sigh and darted away from Elsa. Thomas still stood in the doorway. "Oh, yeah, I forgot the test is tomorrow. We play Nicollet this afternoon—it's a really big game. Do you ever go to soccer games, Ms. Vargas? Our coach said we should really be seeing more teachers show up for at-home after-school games. And he's probably basically your boss, right?" Thomas was pointing at her and cocking his head, trying for humor.

It was Schmooze himself who coached the soccer team. "He is my boss, Thomas. And I'll be sure to let the other teachers know that you're a shill for the administration now."

"What's a shill?" he asked, face briefly more earnest.

Elsa thought of Garvey, who never failed to seek clarification on a new word, even in the middle of a movie scene.

"It means you should be on his payroll." She watched the familiar lopsided smile return to Thomas's face, and it was too much. She forcibly turned herself toward the next student arriving, and Thomas moved past her into the classroom.

Elsa caught the last few steps of his springy gait before he sat. She saw him shove his fingers into his hair and fluff it. *No.* It didn't matter that this could be Garvey's brother—Garvey had a perfectly good brother already.

But by the end of the day, there was nothing left of Elsa's resolve. Stopping herself from attending Thomas's soccer game was as impossible as stopping herself from falling back to earth from midair. She phoned Ham to let him know she'd be late, then she grabbed her rain jacket and wool hat and headed out to the soccer field.

The two teams were already on the field, warming up on opposite ends. Strewn across the small set of wooden bleachers was a Morse code of people: dashes where a few parents clustered together and dots where parents sat alone. Elsa glanced quickly at the parents as she climbed past them to the back row, giving a general nod and smile their way. Natalie Trowbridge caught her eye, perhaps unintentionally, so they exchanged hellos.

"Claire tells me you've just finished up with this probability stuff now. Is that a relief?" Natalie Trowbridge called out.

"Unit test is tomorrow," Elsa agreed. She was confident Natalie's intent was to bring the eye color fiasco back to mind, for anyone aware of it. "Do you have a son playing soccer today?" Elsa asked aloud. This was in lieu of "Why the hell are you here?"

"Claire and some other girls wanted to stay and watch the boys," she shrugged adorably, gesturing across the field.

Elsa noticed the collection of eighth-grade girls draped against the fence at the opposite sideline, trying their best to master this very adorability. A couple of the lone dads in the stands started bantering about how the pack of girls watching might improve their sons' games. Natalie leaned toward them and laughed, pulling her hair in front of one shoulder as she did so. Elsa went up to the corner of the bleachers, sat down, and searched the field for Thomas.

She spotted him in the box: goalie. He kept himself slightly crouched and leaning forward through the warm-up drill, his stance wide and his big-gloved hands low but cocked. He danced his weight from one foot to the next quickly as pairs of his teammates advanced on him, passing and then shooting. Occasionally he leapt and landed his whole body on the ground, which made Elsa cringe for him. She made a mental note to look up the stats on goalies and concussions.

As the exercise ended, the players gathered around Mr. Schusterman on the sideline twenty yards from the bleachers. They each put an arm in before arcing it out on cue, blooming like a synchronized swimming team. Thomas and ten others headed out to the field.

"Let's go, Cougars!" Elsa yelled out amid the hollers of a few parents. "Go kick some grass."

A dad turned and chuckled at her, and Thomas spun himself around and started backward-walking toward the goal, his eyes scanning the bleachers. When he spotted Elsa, he pointed at her and grinned. Elsa remembered the time Garvey confided he felt sorry for his friends because they didn't have her for a mom.

The Cougars were not that great a team, but the Nicollet team was clearly worse. Thomas often stood alone on his end of the field. Occasionally the girls on the opposite side from where the parents sat moved toward him and called things out to him that made them all laugh, Thomas included. Elsa saw Thomas look over at the bleachers whenever this happened, and then pace for a moment or two before landing himself a little farther away from the girls.

Just before halftime, the most talented player for Nicollet got a high pass that he immediately redirected toward the goal. Thomas caught the ball hard to the face before bobbling and finally securing the ball. He looked stunned, and his cheek turned pink almost immediately. He stood a moment, hugging the ball close, while the girls cheered and Schusterman yelled for his teammates to rearrange themselves. Finally he booted the ball toward a teammate midfield, then wiped at his nose with his big yellow glove. There was blood.

Elsa shouted at Schusterman. "Goalie's bleeding, Coach!" Thomas now had a finger from his giant glove pushed up against his nostril, and he twisted it back and forth a bit as he grinned over at the bleachers. It looked like Mickey Mouse trying to pick his nose. Schusterman got the ref to pause the game, and he headed out to Thomas with a first-aid kit. After a full minute, he and Thomas jogged back toward the sideline together, Thomas now holding a wad of gauze saturated with red. Schusterman pointed at another player. "Sub in at keeper," he called out.

Elsa stood, checking her pockets and telling herself to stay put. Several of the other moms dug into their bags. Natalie procured a little travel pack of tissues first, and she ran it down to Schusterman. Another woman—smaller, more drab—headed down after her, and as this woman put her hand on Thomas's chin, Elsa realized it was his mother.

Elsa stared. This was the woman she had let raise her probable son.

When would she just turn her damn face back around, so Elsa could get a better look?

Finally, the woman seemed satisfied that Thomas's bleeding had stopped, and she touched his shoulder before turning back toward the bleachers. There was her face, fairer and more finely featured than Thomas's. Where Thomas had thick scribbles for eyebrows, this woman had the "before" eyebrows in a video showing you how to draw and brush in more color. This being a town people called Saint Small, the woman looked familiar, but only barely. After a moment of haze, Elsa placed her: it was the woman who had joined her book club before Inga's death, maybe eighteen years back. *Katharine.* The two had only overlapped by maybe four or five gatherings before the group's insistently reproductive tendencies had made Elsa stop showing up for good.

Before she had much of a plan, Elsa got up and clopped down the bleachers the kid way, stepping on the butt levels rather than the foot ones. At the bottom, she caught Katharine's eye and stopped in front of her just as Katharine stepped back onto the bleachers. Elsa stood awkwardly for a moment, unsure what to say.

Katharine blushed. "It's Katharine. We met in the book club?"

"Of course, I remember," Elsa said. She realized she was staring. "Thomas is OK?"

Thomas heard her from a few yards away on the bench and called out. "Don't worry, Ms. Vargas. My gloves are screwed, but I think I can still do math."

"I guess we'll find out tomorrow," Elsa called back to him. She smiled at Katharine, who seemed a bit uncertain as Elsa stood in front of her. Elsa looked at her hair—dishwater? greige?—and wondered if Katharine had been as blond as Bird at his age.

Elsa realized she needed to speak words again. "Great kid. He has a real mind for math," she said finally. Katharine agreed solemnly, nodding. Elsa fumbled forward. "Is that true of you too? Are you a math person?"

Katharine raised her insubstantial eyebrows and thought for a moment. "Well, I guess I did all right in school when I had it. I was more of a reading type, I suppose."

Elsa looked at Katharine's mouth and her chin, then back to her eyes: blue. Lighter than Bird's, but . . . maybe.

"Thomas keeps us all laughing, that's for sure," Elsa said. "I bet you're a family with lots of humor, huh?" So much for *leave it*; she was rolling in it now.

Katharine blinked. "Well, he certainly enjoys math class. I hope he's not too much of a clown." She smiled apologetically. Then she leaned slightly to the right to look around Elsa at the cluster of women she was trying to return to.

Elsa jumped aside. "Oh, Jesus, I'm standing right in your way. I'm sorry, I'm just . . . I'm leaving. Gotta get home and start the old second shift." She looked over at Thomas, who was watching the two of them. He looked quickly away. Elsa returned her eyes to Katharine. "Take care of that kiddo," she added. It sounded a bit less casual than she had intended. Katharine's lips made a shape that could pass for a smile, and then she headed back to her seat.

Elsa returned to her classroom. She gathered her laptop and tonight's homework, berating herself for her failure. If she wasn't careful, she could trigger something dangerous. What if Katharine harbored the same deep suspicions that Elsa did? If Elsa put Bird's face and Bird's gestures and Bird's gait into the line of Katharine's attention, what could a flash of recognition lead to?

For now, Elsa only knew that chances to be around Thomas were important. She wasn't sure how to proceed, but she knew she had better do it with caution.

Chapter 12

Katharine tried to concentrate. On the bleachers that afternoon, Elsa Vargas had gotten her attention. Pulling into her garage with Thomas beside her, Katharine realized that she had tuned out from his ongoing chatter for at least the last few minutes.

"Mom? Do you?" Thomas asked, poking her in the shoulder playfully.

"I'm sorry, Thomas. I guess I wasn't listening very well," she said. She turned off the engine and looked at him.

"Do you ever wonder why men have nipples?" he grinned.

Katharine blinked. "I don't know that there is really a reason. They were just made that way, right?"

Thomas opened his door and started to climb out. "So, like, you think God made them that way, then? Do you think it was sort of as a joke or something?"

Katharine got out of the car. She realized that Thomas was just having fun, so she smiled at him as he held the door to the backyard open for her. "That's funny, yes."

"But what's your theory, Mom?" Thomas pressed. "Why the nipples? Like, do you think he was just trying to make men feel hopeful that they could have babies too? You aren't even saying what you think. Why don't you just say what you think?"

Katharine focused on unlocking the back door, saying "OK" to show that she was still engaged. This was just the kind of conversation that she least understood how to participate in. Was there a right answer he wanted her to stand up for, like he had wanted her to go to Washington, DC, for the Women's March?

"I'm thinking maybe it's because one day men will be able to breastfeed," Thomas said. "You know, like evolution is going on and we're stuck in the middle phase."

Katharine set her purse on the counter and nodded at Thomas. She wasn't sure what sort of reaction would be appropriate for whatever it was he was doing—looking for disagreement? Making an extended joke? She felt relieved when her husband, Michael, came in through the front door, announcing his arrival: "What's for dinner?"

She knew his particular greeting was just the kind of thing some of her women friends would rant about. But she felt comfort in it. She and Michael had created a partnership that echoed the world they had grown up in. Katharine did all of the laundry, cleaned the house, and cooked all of their meals; her daughters, Grace and Beth, hovered around to help with these tasks. Michael improved the aging house on the weekends, bringing Thomas on trips to the hardware store and teaching him to use a drill and a stud finder. Michael worked longer hours, because he had a career. Katharine's work life was simply a series of jobs that fit best to the changing family needs as the children grew.

"Can we have spaghetti?" Thomas asked.

Michael put up a hand, like Thomas was already too much. "If you aren't planning to cook the meal, Thomas, then you let your mother decide."

Thomas's face got bug-eyed. "What, so now I'm not supposed to make suggestions?" He turned his voice deep, mimicking his father: "You do not speak unless spoken to, son."

Katharine saw Michael's nostrils react. She interjected calmly. "I need to use the Italian sausage before it goes bad, so that means spaghetti sauce is a good plan. We can eat in half an hour, if that gives everyone enough time to clean up." She put a hand on Michael's shoulder and gave him a kiss on the cheek.

After father and son both left the kitchen, Katharine dug the Italian sausage out of the freezer and thawed it in the microwave. She opened the refrigerator and grabbed the chicken thighs, tossing them into the freezer. There: all fixed. Then she let her thoughts return to Elsa Vargas.

She had first met Elsa in the book club Mary Pat had pulled her into years and years ago. It was a large group—maybe ten women—and Katharine had struggled to speak up, except when someone asked a question that went around the group for everyone's response. While Elsa was quite a conversationalist, Katharine could not recall having ever really talked with her individually, including after her baby's funeral. After that, Elsa had disappeared from the book club, and Katharine had not seen her again until Elsa transferred to Lowe Hills Middle School from the high school two years ago. Since the service, she had never encountered Elsa in person until this year, at the PTO meeting and then the soccer game. She was a force, it seemed to Katharine. She couldn't imagine anyone having to nudge Elsa Vargas in annoyance: "Why don't you just say what you think?"

Katharine snapped out of her memory. "Mom!" A loud yell came from upstairs, and she realized from the tone that it must have been the second or third try. She went up the stairs, answering, "Yes?" as she arrived at the top. She was not a yeller.

"Mom! There's no towels, can you get me one?" Thomas called from behind the bathroom door. Katharine went to the linen closet in the guest bedroom and retrieved a towel. She brought it to the bathroom door, opened it just wide enough, and held it into the room while she remained in the hallway. Thomas grabbed it and started chattering his teeth exaggeratedly. "Th-tha-ank y-y-you," he sang out, shoving the door closed. She remembered him as a little boy jumping right into the towel in her arms. Now, there was always a kind of barrier between them, a door that more often than not seemed to be pulled closed.

Katharine went back to the kitchen and put on water for the spaghetti. Her mind turned to the bleachers, replaying how she might have eluded Elsa Vargas's sudden interest.

After Beth had set the table, the family sat down at their places and reached out to join hands, the way Michael's family had. Thomas hummed "Ring Around the Rosie," and Michael took a deep breath, giving Katharine an irked look.

Katharine nodded, trying to send him some patience. She shared Michael's value for what moments of silence offered. They had first met as college students volunteering on a cleanup and maintenance weekend deep in the Northwoods, at the camp each had gone to as kids. But Thomas seemed to view silence as made for filling.

"Whose turn is it?" Michael asked, taking his time. "Hold on—it's mine. Today I am grateful for . . ." His eyes went to Thomas. ". . . my son's help with the canoe."

Katharine watched as Thomas put a smile on his face for his father. She knew Thomas barely tolerated the slow, meditative steps involved in making their cedar strip canoe, something that had gone on for six months now. Michael didn't see yet what Katharine had quietly come to understand: the annual family Boundary Waters trip was not a tradition that their son would carry forward. She imagined him passing other traditions down to his own children instead, perhaps something from a future wife's lively upbringing.

Seconds after delivering his perfunctory smile, Thomas half stood, heaping pasta on his plate and recounting the tale of his goal-saving nose. Beth accused him of bragging, turning to her father as if she expected him to throw a flag at this foul.

"Your brother has worked hard at his goalkeeping, Bethie," Michael ruled. "I'm proud of his dedication and effort. Maybe he could tell us more while staying in his seat at dinner, though." He reached over and clapped Thomas on the back a couple of times, and Thomas grinned. Then he pulled his chin and body into what Katharine supposed was a caricature of an upper-crust Englishman sitting primly in his chair.

Katharine recalled Elsa's comment: "I bet you're a family with lots of humor." She looked around the table. Surely they were. But it was truer that it was mostly Thomas who brought levity to their family. Katharine frowned. Perhaps she herself had simply struck Elsa as terribly humorless all those years before, so Elsa was just surprised to find that Thomas was such a clown.

Katharine wound her spaghetti around her fork for an extra few rotations. She looked over at Thomas, who was now trying to engage his older sister Grace in a debate about whether the school should ban pork like they had banned peanuts. Was it any fairer for the Muslim students to have to see pork than it was for the allergic ones to have to see peanut butter? Grace was shrugging, listening to his assertions, glancing at her father. Thomas was now waving his hands around about multiculturalism and EpiPens. And while Katharine was again unsure of whether this was humor or just stirring up a good fight, she knew that either way it was what made Thomas different.

That and the brown eyes.

After dinner, Katharine cleaned up the kitchen as her daughters loaded the dishwasher. Her husband settled in the living room to read his weekly news magazine in the overstuffed chair. Thomas, though, was hovering around him, telling Michael first about a few more of his saves in the game and then about how you could figure out all the combinations of triple-scoop ice cream cones using math.

"Oh, yeah," Thomas said, interrupting himself with a new tone to his voice. "I forgot to ask you. Could you tell me about when I was born, like the story of that?" After a pause, he added, "It's just something I want to add to my personal memoir for English, actually."

Katharine felt the possibility of panic sprouting.

After she finished scrubbing around each of the stove burners, Katharine retreated down to the basement laundry room. She pulled out the wrinkled clothes from the dryer. It was last night's laundry, because she was always behind. She gave each T-shirt a good shake by the shoulders, trying to make the wrinkles magically fall off. Then she spread the shirt on the table, smoothed it with her palms a few times, and folded it up into a tidy rectangle. It was a truth to live by: if you were diligent, you didn't have to let a wrinkle get the best of you.

She stood back and looked at her folded stacks. It was hard to tell herself that things looked great. But maybe she could go ahead and ride this out. She put the stacks into the clean laundry basket and resolved to do just that.

Besides—if riding things out didn't work the way it usually did, then maybe Michael would bring up his ailing mother again. Then Katharine could plant another seed about relocating the family to Iowa, Thomas included.

Chapter 13

When the weekend finally came, Elsa felt her body loosen. She needed the break from Thomas to clear her brain.

Tonight, Jennifer and Ted were hosting for drinks and take-out pizza—bring the kids. Elsa's family arrived by six, and as soon as they had their coats off, Ted pushed a tulip glass at Ham. "Double IPA from Michigan. This is the one, Ham."

"You're in love?" Ham asked, holding it up to look at the beer in front of the light.

"Yes," said Jerrod and Craig in unison. They were a married couple from two blocks down, fathers to Garvey's friend George. They both held mostly empty glasses of the same stuff. Jennifer, on the other hand, was wrinkling her nose.

"Elsa, let me interest you in a gin and tonic."

"Real men drink big hops," Elsa said, happily following Jennifer to the kitchen.

"Are you womenfolk going off to eat quiche?" Jerrod called after them.

Bird and Garvey headed straight up to the attic to join Paulie and George in the rec room where, in spite of Jennifer's investment in both a Ping-Pong table and an electronic dart board, the video games remained king. Jennifer's daughter, Sarah, was in the kitchen, so Elsa insisted that she demonstrate the top two TikTok dances of the moment. Sarah laughed until Elsa got her phone out, ready to film. "No! I'm not good,"

Sarah screeched. Then she asked her mom if she could head up to her room now, and Elsa pretended to be stabbed in the heart by this request. It wasn't so far from the truth; being around Sarah always brought a slight ache to Elsa, since she was the age that Inga would have been.

The adults gathered in the living room. It was only maybe the third time that Jennifer and Ted had had Craig and Jerrod over, always with Elsa and Ham so far since they were the initial connection. The six of them were just settling into a groove that no longer smacked of a first date.

The rest of them watched tennis-match style as Jerrod and Ham debated whether youth ukulele choirs were a net good or just cultural appropriation. Then Craig started in with some new gossip about the state legislators. Craig was a lawyer at the capitol, and this month people were laughing about a guy named Johanson, senate district 7, who had convened his staff for a briefing on the growing tiny-home movement.

"So apparently, up in Two Harbors, a guy is converting shipping containers into super tiny homes, and the staff is telling Johanson about the pros and cons of this," he said. "I mean, shipping containers, right? Then somewhere in there, the senator brings up 'Smells Like Teen Spirit,' looking all proud of himself, and the staff are confused. So the senator starts singing." Now Craig bent his face into what must have been an imitation of Johanson and sang out loudly, complete with air guitar: "Here we are now—in containers!"

Jerrod turned to Elsa with a huge smile. "The guy thought that was really what Nirvana wrote," he explained. "In containers!" Elsa adored the way Jerrod supported Craig's stories.

Predictably, they all chuckled their way into inventorying the song lyrics they themselves had misunderstood. Elsa went with the Go-Go's hit she had told her fifth-grade crush was her favorite song. "I thought it was called 'Honest I See You,'" she admitted.

Craig and Jennifer blurted out the punch line in unison: "'Our Lips Are Sealed!'" This made Jennifer say "Jinx!" and count to ten fast, which got them all sharing next just how exactly they'd called jinx in their own families and neighborhoods and whether it had involved a Coke. Soon Ham and Jerrod, both immigrants to the Twin Cities from out west, were trading which words and phrases had been the most baffling when they'd first arrived. They agreed that while it was strange that Minnesotans got "Duck, Duck, Goose" all wrong, it was more confusing by far that *outstate* turned out to mean a bunch of places *inside* the state.

At this point a metal crash came from the kitchen, and then Garvey and George poked their heads around the corner. "Sorry, Jennifer," Garvey smiled sheepishly. "Paul told us to get chips, and it kinda got loud. Nothing broke. Can we have chips, by the way?" Elsa loved it that Garvey and Jennifer liked each other so much.

Jerrod motioned George into the room not so discreetly. George kept glancing at his dad while he stepped a little closer to Jennifer shyly. "It's my fault. I thought we should serve them in a bowl, so I tried to grab one. It turned out to be two." He looked up at Jennifer with a nervous smile. "I'm definitely going to wash the one that fell on the ground."

Jennifer laughed out loud. "I love that you felt the chips should be presented in a bowl instead of just in their bag, George. You're a natural-born host." She reached out and touched his elbow. "And you can just throw that other bowl back in the cupboard. I'm sure the insides are pretty clean." George looked relieved, and they dashed off to the kitchen. The adults heard the sink running for a moment, and then a cupboard closing.

"And he washes it anyway," Jennifer whispered, smiling in delight at Craig and Jerrod.

"Like father, like son," Craig said, pointing to Jerrod.

Jennifer nodded in appreciation at Jerrod. "Is George—I mean, this is weird to ask since I know you're both his dad, but are you the, I guess, biological . . . ?"

"I'm the sperm daddy," Jerrod confirmed. "We actually had to get a paternity test to make sure the mom wasn't fucking with us."

Elsa looked into her drink. It was nice that they could just know, once and for all. They had the truth.

"Well, she definitely wasn't *fucking with us*, fucking with us," Craig clarified. "She was just a little cagey about things at one point. So yes, we've confirmed the paternity."

"I can tell, Jerrod," Ham said. "He has your green eyes."

Elsa felt something else rise in her. *Really?* So now Ham was someone who drew conclusions from eye color?

Jennifer got up to look at Jerrod more closely. "Yep, those are lovely green eyes," she confirmed. "I'll have to inspect George later." She sat, and then suddenly she brightened. "Did you all hear about Elsa's trouble? With the PTO at the middle school?" Jennifer glanced at Elsa, who was rolling her eyes. "Apparently she taught her students just enough about eye color genetics that it made some kids go home and accuse their parents of cheating," Jennifer announced.

Elsa groaned and recounted the Great Apology, admitting that she actually still felt a bit terrified up in front of adults like that. To lighten the vibe again, she told them how disappointed Natalie Trowbridge had looked when the old approach to genetics didn't work well enough to fuel some really great drama.

"Oh, yeah, I'm with Natalie," Craig said. "What a killjoy you are, Elsa! That could have been juicy."

"I'm somehow wired to piss people off at PTO meetings, apparently," Elsa sighed. "Stay tuned. Up next, it's probably the Boys Of America . . ."

Jerrod perked up at these words. "Yeah, now there's a juicy history. You know, I am just blown away that that organization finally got its shit together. I mean, there have always been gay boys in the BOA troops, you know? Both Craig and I did it, although let's point out that I am the only Anaconda between us."

"Well," Craig smirked. "That's true in this context only, I have to say."

Jerrod continued. "But who would have thought we'd have both yes to gays and yes to girls, both in one short period of time? It's unheard-of! It's the great takeover of the Boys Of America. We just yanked it out of the clutches of the homophobes," he gushed.

Craig nodded. "If only George were at all interested. Jerrod would make the perfect troop leader."

Ted and Ham looked at each other, and then at Elsa. She paused, unsure of how to proceed. Apparently neither Craig nor Jerrod spent time on the elementary school's social media site.

"Hey!" Ted jumped in, practically waving his arms with distraction. "Speaking of perfect. I thought of you, Craig, for something else. Paul's school has History Day coming up, and you would be a great judge."

Topic safely changed, Elsa slipped off to the kitchen to find some more tonic. She didn't need more gin, not while her brain was filled with Thomas, with Katharine, and with a growing recognition that the "do nothing" solution might not hold, long term. Could she let sleeping dogs lie? Maybe. But if a dog lay sleeping forever, was it really living its best dog life?

Chapter 14

The unit on probability behind her, Elsa was now safely back in the land of algebra. The curriculum was provided, including options for her challenge Problem of the Week. The only thing that felt insufficient was one area where her students chronically struggled, year after year: the vocabulary of math. When she said *linear equation* or *binomial expression*, it was like she had become a hypnotist. Their eyes would all dilate and lock into daydreaming position. Vocabulary, then, was where Elsa supplemented the curriculum with the occasional game day or group peer-teaching project.

Claire, Shoua, and Thomas were in the same group this week. Their task was to help the class make lasting sense of *slope-intercept form*, based on their mini-lesson of ten minutes or less.

"So if we have to teach instead of you, can we get a cut of your salary for that ten minutes?" Thomas asked.

"Only if you've gotten licensed as a sub," Elsa said. "If you have, then I'll give you ten minutes' worth of what a sub makes per day in this district, after taxes."

Shoua perked up. "How much is that?"

"You tell me," Elsa said as Claire rolled her eyes.

"We need to unionize!" Thomas announced, looking over to another group. Elsa suppressed a smile and went to her desk.

"You have the rest of class today and twenty minutes tomorrow," she announced. "Then it's showtime!" She leaned over to her ancient relic of an iPod and put on some music. Darnell groaned.

She opened her tablet to the chapter they were starting next week, planning to select homework problems. But her eyes were drawn back to Thomas. The three in his group were all leaning in, looking at something that Thomas was drawing on paper. Shoua giggled and covered her mouth, and Claire grabbed the pencil from Thomas.

"No, that's confusing," Claire objected, tapping Thomas on the nose with the eraser playfully.

Thomas howled, "No, not the nose! It's a bleeder!" He turned toward Elsa, hand on his nose, and caught her watching them. Elsa moved her eyes to another group reflexively, and then wished she hadn't. She felt embarrassed for herself, continuing to watch Thomas. She tipped her tablet a bit higher, positioning it between her face and most of the class, and tried to focus on the task of selecting math problems.

After maybe two minutes, though, she turned on the tablet's camera. At first, it showed her face, looking slightly horrified at herself for doing this, but then she found where to switch it to its back camera. The legs of her students' desks appeared, and she corrected the angle. She looked beyond the tablet for a few seconds, checking to see if any students were onto her. After adjusting her chair and the three-ring binder on her desk, she found the posture that best conveyed carefree casualness, one where she could see Thomas on her screen and yet not telegraph that to her students.

Sure, this spying would seem a little creeper-van-at-the-playground. But there was a wall behind her, and really, this was critical information gathering. Was that Ham's nose? Was this forehead crease or that gesture her own? It was a stakeout, a tool TV had taught her was key for all detectives. Elsa already knew whodunnit, how it would turn out. But did she have enough evidence?

She toggled to the search bar and typed in MyTree DNA. When the site came up, her foot started bouncing her leg a bit.

The site offered a lot of information, much of it about health. You could pay more to find out what kind of risk you had for various bad things, apparently. She scanned further to find the part about family trees.

The upshot seemed to be this: you sent in saliva, and if you checked yes for finding any relatives also on MyTree, then you could find out who was related to you. And, Elsa thought, who wasn't. What's more, you could have your child's results sent directly to you, the paying adult.

The bell rang, and Elsa jumped. The tablet fell onto her notebook, face up, and she scrambled to turn off the screen. Thomas was watching her, and he laughed.

"Ms. Vargas, we won't tell if you're watching Netflix over there," he said, and Shoua covered up her mouth, giggling. Elsa closed out of MyTree and the camera.

"Just had to check how many likes I got," Elsa said, adopting an overeager look, "since I've just learned from you youngsters how to post and all."

Claire's eyes narrowed, and then she reached out for Thomas. She leaned in to whisper something in his ear. Thomas listened for a moment, then pulled away. He loaded his backpack and glanced back at Ms. Vargas. After he saw Claire walk out of the room, he turned back to Elsa. "So I hear you're posting what you think about the Boys Of America, actually." He grinned.

Elsa paused, then shrugged a little. "It's a topic at the elementary school where my son goes. I have some concerns about who they might be leaving out."

Thomas nodded vigorously. "Yeah. No, that's cool." He put his backpack on one shoulder. "I mean, I totally agree with you, actually. Sometimes it seems like people expect everyone to just, like, go along saying nothing about things. But yeah, I think that's bad." He looked at her earnestly and nodded again. Elsa felt a pang: she wanted to have seen this boy at seven years old, and four. She wanted to see the fits he threw at the grocery store, the howls of protest at bath time. Would she ever get to see pictures, even?

Thomas grinned and ducked toward the door. "OK, well, see ya, Ms. Vargas."

Elsa raised her hand in response, and he was gone. She heard Darnell shouting to Thomas as he entered the hallway.

During her prep period and on the way home, all Elsa could think about was MyTree. What if she got real proof? It seemed important to have proof. She could send in Bird's saliva with her own, and then she would have facts. But obviously she'd have to do this clandestinely; she didn't want Bird knowing what she was up to. And if Ham knew—well, that would be bad. Maybe Ham was why she wanted the evidence. Really, the only way she could tell him would be with proof positive.

She considered how she could get a sample from Bird secretly, then. His toothbrush would be easy enough to get, but MyTree required collected saliva, sent in a little tube. Then it came to her: the French horn.

The most disgusting thing about Bird's French horn was when he had to clean out the spit valve, pouring saliva into the kitchen or bathroom sink and then failing to run the faucet afterward. Maybe she could nab the horn when it was good and juicy, and pour its nectar into a funnel. A whiff of doubt plagued her, though: sample contamination.

At home, she searched the internet for information on French horn saliva and DNA. Soon she found a discussion among French horn players where one of them ridiculed the others for thinking the spit valve was actually full of spit. Apparently it was mostly condensation from their breath, instead. No good.

Elsa thought. Surely people wanted to send in samples from tiny kids who hadn't learned to spit yet. A memory flashed of adorable little Bird, his curly blond hair all cattywampus, trying to teach his little brother to whistle.

After a grueling workout on the search bar, she found an ingenious solution: sponge on a stick, a tool used with babies by genetics researchers. Apparently they could set the little absorbent end inside the cheek of a baby until it filled up, then squeeze the saliva out with a sterilized squeezer. What was so different about a sleeping middle schooler and a baby? Elsa perused the not-so-user-friendly site that carried the tools, eventually finding where one could order with a simple credit card. She entered her information and finalized the order.

But as with most of her online shopping, her next step after purchasing was to really think it through. Unlike his unwakeable father, Bird was a light sleeper. She'd have to insert the tool maybe three or four times. Maybe she could slip him a massive dose of melatonin?

She cringed. Now she was taking her cues from Bill Cosby, apparently. Sponge on a stick was a no go.

That evening Elsa sat down at the kitchen counter, exhausted by the day. She drummed her nails against the surface a time or two and let her face rest in the other hand. Then Garvey came sliding sideways into the kitchen in his socks.

"Mom, did you see that?" he asked. "That's a new record—I made it past the end of the oven!" Then he climbed up on the stool next to hers and put his face in his hand too. "What do you want to do?" he asked her.

"Homework?"

"Done."

"Yeah, me too." Elsa sighed. Then she remembered that she did have an idea, one she had been toying with all evening. "Hey, do you want to help me with something?" she asked Garvey. "This new science teacher is doing something in class tomorrow with pH strips—you know what those are?"

"Do you have pH strips?" Garvey brightened.

"No," Elsa admitted. "But I told her I could try to get some spit. She needs a couple of samples she can use that aren't hers, and she doesn't live with anyone else."

Garvey grinned. "So she needs our spit?"

Elsa nodded. Then she got two bowls from the cupboard.

Elsa spit into her bowl. Garvey tried to as well, but his came out partly on his chin. Elsa leaned over and looked into his bowl. "Garvey, what have you been eating?"

Garvey moved the bowl away quick, but he laughed loudly. "Dang it! Busted!" He squished up one side of his nose and mouth a bit, his take on sheepish. "I might have found out there's a bag of chocolate chips open." Elsa reached around and swatted him on the backside. An open bag usually lasted almost a month, when she got to make her way through those by herself.

"Should I brush my teeth first, for the spit?" he asked.

Elsa nodded. "Yeah, actually you need to give it half an hour after you do that, or your spit will be wrong for what she needs. Maybe see if Bird will give us some spit too, when you go up to brush?" She had to hand it to herself with this.

But when Garvey came back down, he informed Elsa that Bird would not join them, not now and not later. Bird thought this whole spit collection thing was gross.

Elsa sighed. Bird was a more formidable opponent. Worse, now she'd probably tipped her hand. But there had to be a way.

Chapter 15

While the question of DNA samples churned in the back of Elsa's mind, the rest of life rudely proceeded. For one, the Boys Of America issue had come to a head. One of the dads who lurked on the social media site was a zealous member of the local atheist advocacy group, and he had emailed Elsa and Ham to invite them to join this organization. Perhaps they would like to come to the atheists' game night, this man named Brian offered. Did they know that there was an atheists' night at the local minor league baseball stadium? They had politely declined his invitations. It seemed to Elsa and Ham that huddling up with a like-minded team was not so different from doing church.

Brian had nonetheless continued to loop them in as he pursued the BOAs-in-schools issue. He had drafted one email to an atheists' organization he was in and another to a contact at the local American Civil Liberties Union. Thanks to his efforts, the St. Paul school board had now received some number of emails as well. People were asking the board to clarify whether the district allowed its schools to directly sponsor BOA troops, groups that these emails asserted were "explicitly discriminatory on the basis of religious belief." The school board had called for public input on the topic this Tuesday night.

A lawyer named Joanna from the ACLU had asked Elsa and Ham if they'd be willing to attend the meeting. She wanted to refer to their family's angle in the questions she hoped to raise.

"Everybody knows we think it's discriminating, Mom," Garvey told her, sounding proud rather than embarrassed. "We kind of started it. We have to go so we don't look like we changed our minds." Here they were, then, leaving Bole Ethiopian where they had eaten dinner and pointing the car toward the district administration building instead of toward home.

"Wait, so what's happening there?" Bird asked. Elsa gave Ham a look; he gave the same look back. They realized neither of them had brought Bird up to speed.

"We're helping to get the school board to discuss the Boys Of America thing," Elsa said. She watched his look of exasperation in the rearview mirror and felt her arms push harder against the wheel. "Bird, your brother found a way to fight for what's right. I just don't think it's too much to ask that we stand with him as a family."

Bird turned his face to the window. He sat without comment for a few moments. Finally he asked, "Do you have to make a speech or something? I mean, could you not?"

Elsa willed looseness into her shoulders. She turned to look directly at him at the next red light. "You sign up to speak at the microphone, and we did not sign up. But we will get mentioned as having concerns, if I understand this ACLU woman right."

Bird met her eye, looking pained.

Elsa tried again. "How cool is that, right? Your brother and the ACLU?" She saw Garvey look at Bird's face; Bird shifted to look out at the street again. The light changed to green and she turned back to driving. None of them spoke until they pulled into a lot full of cars outside the board meeting.

"Wow," Ham said. There were families climbing out of vehicles and clusters of people greeting each other near the door. Several children and a couple of adults were sporting a bandana tie over a navy or tan button-down: BOA garb.

They got out of the car and crossed the parking lot, walking a bit closer to one another than they might have on another evening. At the entrance, Ham reached ahead and opened the door for Elsa. She felt enormous gratitude that rather than letting her walk through first, he slipped his arm around her shoulders and walked in next to her. They were advancing their tiny line of resistance together.

A wispy, disheveled man in a black button-down and black jeans appeared at Ham's side: Brian, the atheist. He struck up a conversation full of nervous chuckles, introducing himself to Ham and thanking Ham for the family's attendance. Would Ham like to meet the lawyer from the ACLU, Brian wondered, or a friend from the atheist group? Elsa fixed her smile on Brian steadily, waiting for him to acknowledge her, but it took Ham's intervention for this to occur.

"Oh, oh right, of course. I believe Joanna talked with you. Elsa, is it?" Brian extended his hand while looking away awkwardly. They followed as he led them to Joanna, a younger Black woman with freckles. She wore a smart blazer over her jeans and tall clogs. Elsa immediately warmed to the attorney as she described the likely shape of tonight's proceedings.

"We're going to focus on troop sponsoring. We'll ask for a position statement against the district's schools taking that direct a role," Joanna said. She explained that if the troop were chartered by another group, outside of the school, neither the members nor the activities would need to change; it just wouldn't be an official school activity. Garvey listened intently, and Elsa and Ham nodded. "You probably already know that there will be some very passionate people speaking on the other side. People love their BOAs," Joanna said. She looked at each of them. "But just remember that most of them wish this 'oath to God' requirement wasn't there. People in St. Paul like inclusivity, even if they're not always achieving it."

They moved into the meeting room, Elsa steering Garvey gently. Finding a row near the middle with four seats open, she held Garvey back to let Ham duck in front of him. A parent on either side felt like the strongest support. Elsa realized as she sat that Bird wasn't directly behind her; she craned her neck and saw him trailing a few people behind. He took the seat on the aisle, next to her, and kept his eyes on his knees.

Though there was space for at least sixty people, the room was reaching capacity. Someone announced that there was overflow seating in a larger room with a video link to the meeting, and Bird looked over at Elsa. He bounced his knee against hers twice and raised his eyebrows.

She sighed. "It's your brother, Bird." But his eyes still sought permission, and finally she shrugged. "OK."

Bird leaned over Elsa toward Garvey. "Um, good luck?" he said. "I'm gonna go watch from the other room." Then he got up and walked out, head ducked and eyes stuck to his phone as he went back down the center aisle.

Elsa tightened her mouth and shook her head a bit. Then she reached over to ruffle Garvey's hair, noticing that Ham had his hand on Garvey's knee. Her eyes met Ham's for just a split second, enough to confirm their shared thinking. They were a small team, and it didn't feel great that they were only getting smaller. But Bird had a right to be Bird.

When it was time for the Boys Of America topic, people who had signed up to speak lined up behind the podium.

Joanna was first. She thanked the board members, then read excerpts from several Boys Of America documents stating that a belief in God was central to being a good citizen, and was therefore a requirement for all BOAs. Then she paused and smiled out toward Elsa. "In St. Paul, the present issue surfaced at Johnson Elementary when a family raised questions about whether, as advertised, everyone was actually welcome in the BOAs." Many eyes found the remaining trio of Elsa's family. Garvey straightened his posture and held very still.

Joanna continued, explaining that were the troops sponsored by a private organization or church instead, she would have no beef with a faith requirement. But direct sponsorship by the district's schools, she said, was another matter. She asked the board to prohibit this, and then she thanked them and left the podium.

Garvey leaned over to whisper. "She did good, right?"

Elsa nodded.

Next to speak was a mom in a Johnson Elementary sweatshirt. She looked familiar to Elsa from last spring's Family Math Night.

"OK, so you know what this really is?" the woman began, fist on her hip. "This is just a hurtful attack on kids. And it's coming from people with no intention of actually being BOAs. We are being slandered. In fact, your own district employee is calling BOAs prejudiced." Heads turned to follow the woman's eyes, which now pointed at Elsa. "If you think we're prejudiced, then you don't know us. You don't know that every child in our troops is *insulted* by this, because they have friends with beliefs of *every* kind. And they are not prejudiced against *any* of them."

A group off to the right of the room started clapping loudly. Elsa kept her face neutral as she took Garvey's hand and squeezed it. She felt her phone buzz with a new message, but she refused to drop her eyes from meeting the hard stare of the woman at the podium.

Finally the mom turned toward the school board. "Please let our kids know that they haven't done anything wrong. Let the BOAs continue at Johnson Elementary."

Applause spread more widely across the room, with a couple of troop leaders in uniform standing and clapping vigorously.

"Amen," someone called out. Some people turned their heads to see who said that, then whispered to each other through uncomfortable expressions.

A few more speakers explained their support of the Boys Of America, including a particularly moving speech from a gay troop leader. This time more people got to their feet and clapped, but no one shouted any amens.

Last to speak was Brian Routledge, the atheist in black. Clearing his throat, he read from his trembling note card about the historic rationale for a separation of church and state. People began checking their phones. Elsa watched Garvey as he tried to absorb quotes from John Locke and James Madison.

Then Brian took a deep breath, setting aside his notes. "So I'm a dad of a really great kid who loves the outdoors. I'm raising him to be honest, helpful, and brave. He doesn't believe in a god, no. But it's hard to explain to him why that means he can't do something at his own school." Now Brian frowned toward the top of the podium. "I guess some people's advice is to just ignore it, just kind of keep quiet and go along. But I don't know. I guess to me that sounds like I should teach my son to lie."

Silence blanketed the room. He left the microphone and moved toward the aisle. Elsa put out her arm and motioned to the seat with no Bird in it, and Brian took his place.

Garvey and Ham both leaned forward to smile past Elsa at Brian. "Thank you," Ham said with sincerity.

"Good job," Garvey added.

Elsa's phone vibrated again, and she pulled it from her back pocket. She took in the accumulated texts from Bird. Can we leave yet?

"That was very effective, Brian," she said, shoving her phone back in her jeans.

Finally the chair thanked the last speaker and brought the topic to a close. "The board has heard a lot tonight, and it is our typical practice to take time to process before making a determination. The chair will entertain a motion to vote on this issue in two weeks . . ."

Brian craned forward and whispered into their row. "Joanna said a delay would be a good sign."

Elsa turned to exchange an optimistic look with him, but he looked over her head at Ham. "I'll make sure to relay that to Ham," Elsa said, perhaps too pointedly. Brian just gave her a thumbs-up.

As the topic was closed, the board called for a five-minute break. Elsa's was not the only family to gather up their jackets to leave now, filing out to the wide hallway and receptionist's lobby.

Perry's mother hurried over to Elsa and Garvey. "There you are!" She put her hand on Elsa's arm, and then she looked intently at Garvey. "How are you doing, Garvey? We just want you to know, me and Perry both, that we totally understand and respect your decision to not do BOAs. We really wish it were, you know, a better fit." They all smiled at her, not sure what to say. "I just didn't want things to feel weird or anything."

Elsa's phone buzzed again: Bird. I'm by Ted. Near bathrooms.

Elsa thanked Perry's mom and mentioned getting the boys together that weekend. After a quick cheerful nod, the woman hustled toward another BOA family, holding out her arms. Still, Elsa appreciated her care; none of the other parents they knew were even looking their way. One angry dad in uniform glared at her, but Elsa met his gaze and tried a small smile. He slid his daggers off of her and onto Ham.

Eventually she spotted Bird, who was leaning against a wall and scrolling on his phone. When he headed outside with the rest of them, Elsa fell into step beside him.

"What did you think?" she asked.

Bird was intently focused on his phone. After a few seconds, he said, "You know."

"Not really, no," Elsa said. "What did you think?"

"I didn't like it." Bird acted like something intriguing had suddenly happened on the other side of the lot, looking abruptly in that direction and then keeping his head turned away from her.

Elsa's eyes went back to really seeing him. Bird, the boy in a whole 'nother room, watching them and probably wishing they were something different. She'd been disappointed that he hadn't stood with them, but now she could see: surely he had been disappointed to be alone. "I'm sorry, Birdie. Sometimes the rest of us just kind of . . . roll full steam ahead on something. I know you aren't always too into that."

Bird looked back at her for just a flash. Then he nodded. "I'm not like you guys," he said as they arrived at the car.

He was right. He wasn't like the rest of them. On the drive home, Elsa couldn't help but think about why, which she knew and he didn't.

Maybe it would actually be a relief for him, if he learned the truth. For Bird, it could mean finding the people who *were* like him. Maybe by keeping quiet, she was denying him a certain kind of belonging, one that he needed but she couldn't give.

It was a terrifying thought. He had been inching away these past years already, and the truth ran the risk of turning those inches into yards. But she would still be there for him; she would always and forever be there for him. The question was what was best for Bird, not for herself. Wasn't this exactly what made parenting so painful? The more your child knew you were always there, the more bravely they hopped on a current that pulled them away from you.

Elsa turned the car into their alley, thoughts still churning. Funny how people focused on the mom jeans; clearly what mattered was the big-girl panties underneath.

After the boys had read in their beds for a few minutes, Elsa went in to say good night to Bird. She pulled the covers up to his neck and kissed his cheek, and he didn't object. She stretched out next to him on top of the covers.

"I'm sorry that you got pulled into that tonight," she said.

Bird sighed and shrugged. He turned his face to her and shrugged again. "That's OK."

"You were saying before how you aren't like the rest of us, and I . . ." Elsa paused to form the right words. "I think you are like us, Bird, in the ways that matter. But you're not really itchin' for a fight, in life. If I could be more like you on that, that would probably make me a happier person."

Bird looked up at the ceiling. "But Mom, you're happy that way. I think you're really really into stuff, a lot of times."

Elsa waited.

"I'm just more medium feeling about a lot of things." He turned toward her. "I still like you." Then he patted her head a few times like she was a puppy, making them both smile.

Elsa pulled one of his corkscrew curls out to straight, making a "sproing!" sound as she let it go. Then she stood up, told him she loved him, and left him to go to sleep.

She climbed onto the bed, where Ham was reading something on a tablet. She stared forward into space until Ham noticed and set aside his device. He rearranged himself into a conversing angle.

"That was fun, right?" he opened.

Elsa gave a little laugh through her nose, but she frowned and looked intently at the cuticle she was scraping at. Finally she said, "Bird really thought so, huh?"

Ham reminded Elsa of Bird's age and said they were probably lucky he even got out of the car with them.

"Exactly," Elsa said. "We stand by Garvey so much more easily." She felt herself starting to tear up, and she cursed her hormones and apologized.

Ham pulled her to his shoulder. He didn't say anything for a few minutes.

"Maybe Bird needs us to do something different than Garvey does," Ham said. "He doesn't want us to join his battles, because he doesn't do battle."

Elsa nodded. She told Ham about Bird's description: medium feeling about most things. They both smiled at that. Ham liked the idea of it appearing under Bird's graduation picture in the yearbook at the end of high school, a summary. They tossed back and forth other candidates.

Baird Carlos Hamilton: Likers gonna like.

Baird Carlos Hamilton: Keep calm and nixie on.

Elsa felt the little muscles of emotional tension loosening in her torso. Ham, her ally. The more she could confide in him, the better things felt. Unless she went too far.

She gave his hand two quick squeezes.

"Basically, Bird is chill," Ham said. He turned to look down at her, and she met his eyes. "And we're not actually all that chill, Else."

Elsa had to agree. Try as she might, she really sucked at *chill.*

Chapter 16

Saturday morning was sunny, perfect for an overdue sister walk. Besides, Elsa had a lot on her mind, and a good stroll always seemed to help.

Krista was all about the fast walking, now that she was deep in her forties. She pumped her arms and everything. "Oh, get over it," she told Elsa. "If I could run without injuring something every year, I would do that. But I've got to do something." Elsa had to put a few strides of jogging in every now and then to keep up, making her feel like the little sister instead of the big.

They were halfway around Lake Phalen, a three-miler on the east side of town. The windstorm midweek had stripped the trees of all but the hardiest of the orange and gold; those leaves that had succumbed clustered in drifts against trunks and boulders, crispy as potato chips waiting to be crunched. Krista left no silence: she was relaying how their mother had subtly reorganized Krista's kitchen over the last year, gradually turning it into a mirror image of her own setup. Their mom lived in the other half of a 1920s side-by-side duplex Krista had bought two years before, when Marcy had started to think about how to age in place. Krista loved to throw shade at their mother, but the duplex showed that was mostly cover for the fears seizing Krista since the day Carlos died.

"She does this kitchen thing right in front of me," Krista emphasized. "And it's never a bad idea, right? She'll just be putting away the whisk for me, and she'll mention how she's opened the wrong drawer again, silly her, since it's right by the stove . . . and before you know it, I'm realizing that yes, the whisk drawer and the scissors and tape drawer should definitely be swapped." Elsa nodded as Krista continued. "Or she'll be saying 'I'm parched, would you like some water too?' and then she'll reach up to where the glasses are not located. 'Oh, Krista, honey, I'm losing my mind. I always look for the glasses near the sink!'" While Krista was giving these so-sweet impersonations, she seemed to speed up even more.

Elsa ran a few steps. "She does have a point there."

Krista's balled-up fists flailed about violently for a moment, like an exasperated Kermit the Frog. "Elsa! This is what I'm telling you! She's always right, and I always end up resisting for like two days before I finally cave in and move things to their better spots. So now I have Mom's kitchen, but blue."

Elsa took on her mother's voice for a moment: "Krista's kitchen really does express her personality, doesn't it? I would never have the courage to use such color." Krista had installed Mexican Talavera tiles on the backsplash to go with the bright blue cupboards.

"Express my personality!" Krista rolled her eyes. "She just prefers to forget that we have any Mexican ancestry."

Elsa made no comment. She couldn't imagine their mother wanting to forget anything at all about Carlos. But the mention of ancestry got Elsa thinking again about MyTree. She for sure needed to find a way to submit samples, even if she wasn't yet clear what would come after the results.

"Speaking of ancestry, get this," Elsa said. She retold Jennifer's wild tale about the mannequin neighbor who turned out to be his sister's child.

"Wow. His sister's kid?" Krista said.

Elsa thought about Thomas, how Krista might never know he was her nephew.

"I used to dream about being adopted," Krista reminded Elsa. "But I can't say I ever dreamed about finding out I was yours."

Elsa shoved her off the slightly elevated path in jest. Krista yelped, barking out something resentful about old injuries. Elsa rolled her eyes: *please.*

Krista was drama and always had been. The world was her stage, as a child. Their mother had stumbled through, accidentally recycling bits of cardboard that turned out to be cherished thrones and swords and microphones. When Krista's already-big emotions got even more expressive in her teen years, Marcy made the mistake of remaining calm and offering perspective. Their father did better: he knew how to commiserate or marinate with her in righteous indignation. But even Carlos sometimes chuckled that he wasn't sure where Krista came from. "Not from this stupid family," she would yell, slamming doors.

"If you were adopted, then we could've returned you," Elsa jabbed now. Then she heard herself. She remembered her thought of telling Bird he had a different mother, as if that would be a kindness. Maybe it would only be cruel.

Krista leaned into a good limp for a few strides, then seemed to tire of it. "Did you know Aunt Lois is on MyTree?" she asked. This was their mother's sister. "She's trying to find the Swedish relatives. Personally, I thought mail-in anything was just stupid after that Theranos fraud. But apparently MyTree is good—blessed by His Eminence David as the best one." Marcy and Lois adored that their brother, David, was an actual medical expert. Elsa didn't mind that fact at the moment either.

Krista continued. "So far no actual Sweden Swedes for Aunt Lois. I guess she found some third cousins in Kansas or somewhere. She tells Mom every time someone new pops up on her tree. Mom thinks it's just delightful, of course."

Elsa watched a brown leaf flutter, indecisive. "Pops up? How does that work?"

Krista shrugged. They'd finished the loop around the lake, and she went to a curb to stretch out her problematic calves. "New people join MyTree all the time, and if they're relatives, they pop up on Aunt Lois's chart somehow. I guess there's sometimes extra mystery at the beginning, because they might use just a number ID or something until you reach out to ask their name."

"So they all show up, even if they don't want to . . . ?"

Krista joined her on the bench she had occupied. "I don't know. Maybe you can turn that option off. You mean like if they don't want to find relatives?"

Elsa nodded, and looked out through bare oak limbs at the glistening lake. Could she do something to make sure she wouldn't pop up on other people's charts? She didn't want her mom and Krista knowing about her doing DNA testing. Most of all, she didn't want that fact getting back to Bird before she figured out what was right. It was hard enough to keep Bird in the dark with whatever spit-nabbing trickery she would eventually come up with.

"Yeah, I think you can just focus on finding out if you have some risk for blah-blah-blah syndrome, that kind of thing," Krista said.

Elsa pulled in part of her lip, thinking. "Syndromes Only" wouldn't work for her. She needed the proof that Bird had fallen off an altogether different tree.

"Hey, it's after eleven," Elsa said. "I should get home." Bird and Garvey were supposed to do chores before they went to the basement for video games, but they usually borrowed a section of her brain for remembering that, instead of using their own. Ham would be rounding up groceries from two stores, because as a couple they were both picky and pennywise.

Her sister pulled her in and put her cheek against Elsa's: "Mwah!" Then she headed toward the other parking lot.

Elsa got in her car and watched Krista disappear across the walking bridge. Then she pulled out her phone and opened the MyTree site. How could she get the relevant facts, but not pop up for Aunt Lois?

Chapter 17

With the Boys Of America decision due in a matter of days, the elementary school community was atwitter with anticipation. Elsa's attention, though, was elsewhere. A mother could only surreptitiously watch her newfound son for so long before she needed to hold the proof in her hand.

After learning about Aunt Lois, Elsa had systematically run through her MyTree options, logically interrogating each possible route until she was clear. Getting spit from Bird was not the right path. It failed on three key questions.

First, was it right? While Bird had little need for Elsa to fight next to him in battle, he did need her to stand by him in life. And Elsa was clear: testing Bird's DNA to prove he was not hers was difficult to construe as standing by him.

Second, would the logistics work out right? If she wanted a report on Bird's relationship to her, she would have to opt for the relatives-seeking part of MyTree, for both of them. That meant that Elsa would certainly pop up for Aunt Lois, and it would all get back to both Marcy and Krista almost immediately.

If Elsa were the only one to pop up, she could explain away why she had submitted her DNA: random gift from Jennifer or something. But here was the thing: What if, somehow, Bird popped up too? Elsa knew this couldn't happen, but she didn't *really* know it. She didn't have the facts. Her gut objected: *obviously* Thomas was her son, not Bird.

But yeah, gut feelings were a little squishy; there was a reason she was a math teacher instead of a psychic. She had to admit that the likelihood that Bird was her actual son was not actually zero. He *could* pop up, the Lois-Marcy grapevine could activate, and Elsa could be stuck having to explain to everyone why in the hell she had submitted Bird's sample. Bird would get hurt; Ham would wonder why he had trusted Elsa to live in reality.

Damn those pop-ups. Aunt Lois was an inconvenient blood relative, it was turning out.

The third and final question was strictly pragmatic: Could she pull it off, surreptitiously? Bird was too light a sleeper for the sponge on a stick and too savvy for giving saliva without questioning why. This one didn't look good either.

So, no—getting spit from Bird was not the answer. Instead, Elsa had to consider getting it from Thomas, a path that passed all three questions just fine.

First, it was right. With Thomas, she was looking for evidence *for* a connection rather than *against* a connection. It was way more morally defensible, trying to confirm a long-lost son.

Second, the logistics would work out right. Elsa would still pop up on Aunt Lois's chart: still annoying. But the Thomas part sorted itself well. If he somehow didn't show—wasn't related—then no one would ever know. More realistically, though, Thomas would show up on Aunt Lois's chart alongside Elsa. The blood relatives would need an explanation . . . but how long would she want to keep this secret from them anyway, really?

That was the part that helped Elsa get new clarity. Wasn't the truth what she was pursuing, when it came right down to it? Didn't she want to share this good news, talk to Ham about what they should do next? If she had proof that Thomas was her son, that cat was getting out of the bag eventually anyway; it was a lion, after all. It would mean that she had found them their son. If she could get the proof, Elsa would finally tell Ham the truth.

And then there was that last question: Could she get saliva from Thomas without him knowing what was going on? That one required some thinking. She could ask the whole math class to start spitting in tubes, but then she might as well change her legal name to Additional Item.

Elsa had been sitting with her developing DNA strategy for a couple of days when there was a break in the weather, of sorts. One evening Garvey called out to her from the living room, where he lay on the floor looking at a celebrity gossip magazine. "Mom, what does *gleek* mean?"

"Hmm. It might be a guy from this crappy old show called *Saved by the Bell*," Elsa called back. "Where's your dad?"

Garvey got up and shouted into the basement. Ham was watching the news, and he had the answer: "He's the monkey that hung out with the Wonder Twins." Garvey walked into the kitchen with the magazine, frowning and rereading.

"Time to set the table," Elsa said. She called out to Bird as well, who answered in a resentful tone that he was coming, Mom, jeez. Eventually they all sat down to dinner, everyone but Bird pouring out random strange bits from their day and interrupting each other, fishing for good punch lines.

As the boys cleared the table, Garvey showed the magazine to his dad, pointing at the word he didn't get. Ham googled and scrolled, then grinned and turned his phone toward Garvey. A video played of a talk show guest showing how to gleek. "We called that 'snake spit' in Seattle."

Spit? Elsa went to look. *Gleeking* meant spraying a little saliva out of your mouth from under your tongue, something that happened to some people when they yawned. The guy was demonstrating how to gleek on demand. It was too good to be true.

Garvey and Ham spent the next few minutes finding more video tutorials on gleeking. They pushed their tongues upward and their jaws forward, trying their best to get a wet spray to come out. Elsa started making attempts as well.

"Is it actually saliva that comes out, or something else?" she asked, all casual-like, thinking of the French horn. "Find out what it is that sprays out!" Ham and Garvey ignored this and stayed focused on the how-to videos.

Bird continued to put dishes into the dishwasher. Then he went to get his own phone. After a minute, he spoke: "It's from a saliva gland called the sublingual gland, and compressing it can make saliva spray out." He nodded as he continued to take in information. "Saliva actually has enzymes that can kill germs, so it's kind of similar to venom in a weird way." Bird had Elsa's attention, but Garvey and Ham were busy contorting their tongues in their wide-open mouths. While Bird wanted the science, Garvey and Ham just wanted the party trick. Elsa still wanted the saliva.

Bird wandered off upstairs by himself.

Elsa joined Garvey and Ham, the three of them jutting their chins out and squeezing various mouth muscles, looking completely foolish. This was definitely something Thomas would try too—she could picture it easily. She could see Thomas asking Ham, "Did anything come out?" She imagined Garvey looking up at Thomas, the two laughing together.

Then Elsa squeezed her eyes shut. *No.* Pretend friends were not healthy.

A surge of anxiety went through her; it started at Inga, but then it landed on Bird. What had she done with Bird, in that imagining? She had disappeared him, that's what. She had replaced him with Thomas, right here in Bird's own home.

She left the kitchen and went to the living room, thinking about self-flagellation, hair shirts, and walking on her knees until they were bloody.

The next day before dinner, Elsa sat in the basement staring toward the TV news when Bird came down to find her.

"Mom, watch this," he said. Then Bird gleeked. Elsa stared. He gleeked again, then beamed at her. "It's just a gland, but you can control it."

"How much comes out?" Elsa asked, her brain three steps ahead. They considered this together for a moment and decided it was surely too little to measure. But maybe if you collected eight or ten gleeks . . .

Bird nodded, his face more serious. "What would we measure it in?"

Elsa looked at him, uncertain. Then she told him to try the little plastic cup that sat on the lid of the children's cough medicine, its sides marked in milliliters. Bird headed up the stairs immediately, intent.

It was tempting to see this for more than it was. She had to talk herself down. His natural skill with gleeking was a coincidence, not a sign; this wasn't manifesting or some other woo-woo nonsense. It was just her human tendency to imbue meaning in randomness. She had to stick with collecting Thomas's saliva, as planned.

Well, maybe "planned" was a little generous. But she would get there.

On Wednesday, Elsa and her coffee stood watching the hallway fill and empty. She noticed a cluster of girls down by Mr. Anderson's room, all of them in hoodies with the hood up.

She knew where this came from. Schusterman had reiterated several aspects of the dress code at the last assembly, including that the hoods of their hoodies were to remain down at school. Tiana Mosley had made a big stink about that, and then she had been escorted out. Her argument deserved an answer: If the Muslim girls in hijab were allowed to cover their heads, then why not the rest of them? But because she was Tiana, deemed too loud and unruly, the logic of her objection went unaddressed. Things had gone quiet for a couple of days, but then

Halima Farah wore a hoodie hood up over her hijab. Now Elsa counted seven girls with hoods up on this morning alone.

Middle school students were not big fans of "because I said so."

Back in her empty room, Elsa let the hoodie thoughts stew while she tidied. She watered Phillipe the Philodendron, the plant she and the boys had named at home before she brought it to her new classroom two years ago. Then she sat down at her desk, popped open her laptop, and found a site where you could design your own stickers and signs. She could do this.

Ten minutes later, she had a sticker designed. It was a modified emoji, its tongue up, a spray of dotted blue line arcing out from under the tongue. Over that face was the red *Ghostbusters* slash, and below it Elsa had typed in NO GLEEKING.

Bird was no influencer, but that didn't matter. For less than ten bucks, Elsa was confident she could get this strange skill to catch on with Lowe Hills students.

There was a tap on her door, and then it opened. Aneisha had the same prep period, and now she leaned herself against the inside of Elsa's doorframe.

"Darlin', what's all this I hear about you and the school board?" At tonight's meeting, the board had promised a verdict on the Boys Of America. "Do you just seek out trouble?"

Elsa closed her laptop. She sighed and wilted her head into her hand. "Apparently."

Aneisha pretended to scold. "My brother was a BOA. Hell, even my father was a BOA." Now she pointed at Elsa. "And both of them would tell you that, girl, you need Jesus, Mary, *and* Joseph." Elsa smiled while Aneisha laughed and laughed and then finally recovered. "You going to that meeting tonight, or you gonna stay home and keep your hoops in your ears?"

Elsa said that she was going, yes, but Aneisha's attention was drawn to the hallway; she straightened up and smiled at someone. Then Thomas poked his head around the doorway.

"Hi, Ms. Vargas," he said. Then he blushed and looked back at Aneisha. "And hi, Ms. Reese, sorry," he added. Then he looked back at Elsa, whose heart was leaping at this bonus appearance.

"What's up, Thomas?" she asked casually.

He took this as permission to enter. He moved past a couple of student desks before turning back to Aneisha, his hands shoved in his pockets. "Sorry, I didn't mean to interrupt . . ."

Aneisha raised a hand at Elsa, wished her good luck, and left.

Thomas leaned against a desk and took his hands out of his pockets. Then he put them back in. "Yeah, so I heard from some friends how there's a meeting tonight on the Boys Of America thing. And I know you're trying to change things there . . ." He paused, and Elsa watched the forehead crease emerge. "So anyway, I just wanted to tell you I think that's cool. I think what you're pointing out is right."

Elsa nodded. "It seems like that might not be such a popular opinion."

"But it's a public school. I mean, they'll have to agree with you, right?" He could have been Garvey. Elsa couldn't help but smile at him.

"I'll tell you tomorrow how it turned out," she said. She wanted to keep him here, ask him about his family, ask him about his latest religious conversion, ask him anything that would feed her need for more. Instead, she told him he'd better get back to class.

Chapter 18

That evening, Elsa darted all around the main floor like a Roomba, desperate to find her car keys. The board meeting could fill up, she knew, and she wanted to be in the room where it happens. No overflow seating for her—in fact, no overflow seating for anyone this time, since Bird was firm in his decision not to attend. Ham was coming from a racquetball date and planned to meet them there. He might be even later than they were.

"Don't you have that tracker thing on your keys?" Garvey asked, increasingly worried. "You should just buzz them."

Elsa paused, finally looking at Garvey and taking in what he was saying. "That's right! I can buzz them." She squeezed Garvey around the shoulders. Then she felt her back pocket, which was empty. "Now where's my phone, so I can buzz the keys?"

Garvey moved quickly, scanning the kitchen and then dashing into the dining room. "I found your phone!" he announced.

Elsa dug into her leather bag one last time. "And I just found my keys. Let's go, man!" They raced out the back door and across the yard to the garage.

When they pulled into the parking lot at the administrative building, they saw Ham walking in from his parking spot. Elsa gave a tiny honk and then immediately regretted it. Three clusters of humans now looked over at her and Garvey in the minivan, and she could see them turn to one another right afterward: *It's them.*

As she turned off the engine, she looked over at Garvey.

"I hope we win," Garvey said.

Elsa reached to touch his leg. She realized that this might be his first taste of adult-level disillusionment. "Just remember, Bug, that what they say doesn't tell us if we're right or wrong. It's just what a group of regular people think, see what I'm saying?"

Garvey nodded.

They found Ham and went in to find seats, pausing at the back of the center aisle. They could see single seats only near Joanna or Brian, and two seats but not three in a few other places. Elsa saw Jerrod and Craig seated together between Natalie Trowbridge and Mr. Schusterman. She looked away quickly, feeling her pulse pick up. Jerrod, the Anaconda.

Someone leaned in behind Elsa and Ham and muttered in a low grumble, "There's those atheist assholes."

It was Ted. He chuckled and held up a hand to Garvey, who gave him the high five. The four of them moved together to the back wall, where they decided to just stand and lean.

"Jennifer got home late, so she needs to eat some dinner," Ted said. Elsa wished for Garvey's sake that she'd make it.

The board members filed in, and Elsa reached over to her left to put her hand on Garvey's head. She turned to look at him, and instead her eyes were yanked to a boy just entering.

Thomas.

He saw her, grinned in relief, and came to lean against the wall on the other side of Garvey. "Think we'll win?" he whispered, leaning out across Garvey. Garvey turned to look at Thomas, curious.

Elsa felt incapable of breathing. Garvey and Thomas. They stood right next to each other. This was too much: surely they would see it, or someone else would. She tried not to look at them, tried not to draw attention, but her eyes kept darting over. They wore the same nervous expression, held the same stance as they leaned against the wall. Sooner or later one or both would do that same goofy thing with their hair, and anyone looking would know.

She felt eyes on her, and looked out at the crowd. Two women on the far left looked away fast. On the other side, Craig. He raised an exaggerated eyebrow at her, but he didn't smile. His gaze took in Garvey and Thomas and Ham. He shook his head slightly, and then turned forward again.

Obviously Craig had seen the resemblance.

Things were said up front, but Elsa's ears were not listening. They were busy turning hot, and probably red. It felt impossible that no one was standing up and pointing, calling out that these two boys were clearly brothers. What about Ham, on her right? She couldn't look at him to find out what he was or wasn't realizing.

Elsa pointed her face toward her feet, shaking her hair forward to cover her ears. She concentrated on her boots. They were made from shiny, not-for-everyone fake seal fur. They had been a prized thrift store find back in Seattle, perfect despite the cracking seams that rendered them worthless in rain and snow alike. What was Ted muttering to Garvey? Was he asking about this new brother? She focused on the fur's sheen, on the boots' metal eyelets, and on the little hill her big toe could make as she raised it. *Breathe. Let time roll forward.* She concentrated on bringing her face and her ears back to their regular hue.

"It's all down to Willis," Ham said, and Elsa looked up front. In her peripheral vision she saw Thomas with one fist at his mouth and Garvey with two. A couple of women off to the right were watching Elsa's group on the back wall, surely noting these matching gestures.

The chairwoman of the board was taking a roll call vote, and it was three votes to three. Only Director Willis was left to respond. Elsa tried to imagine horse blinders, her eyes adamantly forward. Tim Willis cleared his throat, and she heard the stretched silence of the room.

"I understand that people have deep feelings on both sides of this issue," Willis began. "The Boys Of America have made some great strides that are really important to the LGBTQ community, and they no longer exclude girls. I can understand why open and accepting families might support the organization." He looked up briefly, licking his lips.

Elsa could see Ham's head shaking no, just slightly.

Director Willis continued. "However, it is clear that officially, belief in God is required. That policy is not compatible with public school sponsorship." Elsa felt Garvey's hand grab her arm. "Madam Chairperson, my vote is in favor of the resolution, calling for our schools to no longer sponsor troops."

The room buzzed to life, opposite emotions erupting simultaneously. A man in a BOA uniform stood up abruptly and stormed out; Garvey went onto his toes and yanked on Elsa. Then he turned to look at Thomas, who pulled a victorious fist toward his own gut. Garvey copied him. Elsa was horrified.

She grabbed Garvey in a quick hug and pulled him hastily through the doorway behind them. She maneuvered him into the lobby and through it, ahead of the crowd who might have seen. She pulled Garvey out into the crisp air just beyond the entrance.

"We won," Garvey said, his eyes already crinkled up with delight. Then he busted out a huge smile.

Elsa couldn't make her mouth return the smile yet, so she just hugged him again. She had succeeded in separating the secret brothers, and that was foremost. No one had yelled out a realization; maybe only Craig had seen something uncanny.

"Good job, brave guy," she said, holding him at arm's length now. "We'll have to celebrate."

Ham and Ted found them a minute later, and they all went back into the lobby to find Joanna.

Craig and Jerrod were headed directly for them. Ham reached out to Jerrod for a handshake, and Jerrod blinked for a few seconds before grabbing the extended hand and pulling Ham in for a hug. Craig took half a step back, and he turned his gaze toward Elsa. She felt her head getting warm, but she managed not to run.

"Hi?" she said.

Craig was about to speak when Garvey spoke up. "Is George here?"

Craig relaxed his posture a bit and said hello to Garvey, telling him that George was at home with only the cat for company. Garvey frowned, looking around at the crowd of adults, then mumbled something about going to find the restroom.

Craig turned back to Elsa. He pressed a finger across his mouth for a long pause, then spoke. "So I had no idea until tonight, Elsa, that you guys were involved in this issue." He looked a bit hurt. "After we just went on and on about Jerrod and the Boys Of America that night at Ted and Jennifer's. Did you feel like you couldn't tell us? I feel like we were probably fairly insensitive. Was Garvey just flat-out rejected by the BOAs?" He reached out to touch her arm. "That is so bad."

Elsa was taken aback. His odd raised-eyebrow look had not been about Thomas, then. "Oh, good God, Craig, we were the insensitive ones. I know getting rid of the gay ban was so important . . ." She explained the circumstances leading up to tonight, including her social media tiff. As she spoke, Elsa saw Joanna moving toward her across the lobby. "Turns out there are some pretty strong voices on both sides," she told Craig, reaching out to welcome Joanna and give her a hug.

Joanna squeezed her back and asked where Garvey was.

"He's here somewhere," Elsa said, turning to survey the lobby. "So hey, we're getting ice cream to celebrate, and I think he'll really want you to come with us. Can we buy you an Izzy's ice cream?"

Joanna agreed, and she and Elsa spread the plan to Ham and Ted and Brian. Then Elsa turned in place to look again for Garvey, and there was Thomas.

"Hey, Ms. Vargas," Thomas smiled. "Congratulations. You guys did it. I guess I should have told people: do not bet against Ms. Vargas."

Elsa laughed.

"So yeah, anyway. That's pretty hardcore," Thomas added.

Elsa tapped Joanna's shoulder as she smiled at Thomas. "Here's one of the people who did it, actually. Joanna Taylor, meet my student Thomas, who is . . . a fan of religious liberty, I believe? Thomas, Joanna is a lawyer with the ACLU." Elsa tilted her head once toward Joanna. "Hardcore."

Thomas looked like he had breathed in big air but forgotten how to push it back out. His eyes were wide and happy. "Oh, cool, nice to meet you!"

Joanna struck a humble tone, mentioning the role of Brian's organization. "Maybe you'd like to meet them as well. Are you coming to Izzy's Ice Cream?" Joanna asked, then turned to someone else trying to get her attention.

Elsa saw Thomas look at her, his hand going to his hair for a moment. *For real, could no one else see it?* It seemed impossible, but maybe they were safe. Finally she smiled.

Thomas pulled out his phone to text something. "So, Ms. Vargas, this is probably really bad manners to ask, but if my dad is OK with it, could I maybe get a ride with you guys to the ice cream place? I mean, I'd be pumped to go. He would pick me up there . . . ?"

Elsa was used to shuttling extra kids around, what with Bird and Garvey both having teams and activities. "Let me see his text saying it's OK, and then I can do it," she said. Then she turned her attention again to scanning for Garvey.

The group in the lobby had mostly dispersed, and those pleased with the outcome were beginning to head to Izzy's. Ham stood next to Elsa. "Garvey's been in the minivan, to avoid all the stares," he said. "I'll meet you guys at Izzy's." Elsa let him know that Thomas was riding along, and the three of them walked out together toward their two vehicles. She asked Ham to remind her which block the ice cream shop was on, since she was perpetually getting lost in her own city.

Ham hopped in his Civic, chuckling. He called out to Thomas before he shut the car door. "You may want to turn on your navigation there, son."

Elsa dropped her keys and felt a jolt run through her. *Son.*

Thomas picked up Elsa's keys and held them out to her. "Is . . . are you OK, Ms. Vargas?"

Elsa took the keys and looked at his face. Could Thomas see it, maybe just a little bit? "He called you *son*." She watched for his reaction.

Thomas just grinned. "Aw, that's just like saying 'homie' or something, Ms. Vargas." He tried to stop smiling, but he was obviously kind of entertained.

Elsa quickly adjusted her face into a snarky expression and gave a heavy sigh. "I know. But my husband is an old white guy, so that's super dorky. Sorry you had to hear that, Thomas." She pointed the keys at the minivan and unlocked it. It was parked at the far end of the lot, but this would give Garvey a heads-up. Her worry shifted to him. Had one of the BOA fans said something to him?

Elsa opened the sliding door. "Hey, Mom," Garvey said, happily working some kind of puzzle with a pencil. When she told him her student Thomas was coming along to the ice cream shop, Garvey scooted over quickly to make room. "Cool, so are you an atheist too?"

Elsa interjected. "Actually, Thomas has a project you might appreciate, Garvey. He's basically speed dating through different religions that have major holidays on school days."

Garvey shoved the brainteaser book back into the seatback pocket in front of him and turned his full grinning attention to Thomas.

Elsa pulled out of her spot and aimed for the back exit. Only a couple of cars remained in the lot, but her headlights skimmed across a sports car with a woman leaning into the driver's window. The woman had quite a bit of herself inside that window, Elsa noted. As they rolled past, Elsa turned to look. Like any of the moms would have, Elsa immediately recognized that gym-toned ass in those suburban-white jeans.

She smirked. Natalie Trowbridge could have the men in fast cars. Elsa and her ass were going to eat victory ice cream.

Chapter 19

As he climbed out of the minivan, Thomas turned to Elsa. "Thanks for giving me a ride, Ms. Vargas." Then he jogged ahead and opened the glass door to the ice cream shop. He stood aside, holding it open.

"Oh, well, thank *you*, sir." It had been a while since Garvey had given up racing to do this.

Inside, Elsa saw most of their group standing in line to order at the counter. One of them was Jennifer. She rushed toward Elsa, fists raised and then arms collapsing to give Elsa a hug. "Nice job, Supermama. Keeping the world safe for science, am I right?" Then Jennifer reached her hand out for a handshake with Garvey, only to slip it away from him at the last moment. "Psych," she taunted, then swallowed Garvey in a hug as well. "I had to miss the vote, but I'm in for the celebrating. Way to show them your double stuff, big man."

Then she turned to Thomas. "Hi, I'm Jennifer." She held out her hand, then laughed. "I promise I won't hug you."

Thomas shook her hand and introduced himself, glancing nervously at Elsa as he did so. Then he looked past Jennifer to the ice cream line. "Hey, it's Paul Myers," he grinned, then moved to talk to Paulie. Garvey followed him, and the three stood in line together, awkward only for a minute before laughing about something. Thomas glanced back at Elsa, smiled, and shrugged.

"He's your student?" Jennifer asked, turning her back on him a bit. Elsa explained his interest in the Boys Of America resolution. "I don't know, Else, are you sure he isn't just interested in you?" She raised her eyebrows twice.

Elsa struck a pose, hand on hip and chest a little higher. "Ms. Vargas, boys. Wait until you see what she can do with your . . . linear equation."

Garvey broke away from the other boys and came back to Elsa. "Mom. Money, please."

Jennifer reached out and pushed his head. "Garvey, I got your ice cream since you're my hero. Just point at me from the counter like Paulie does, and then I'll pay. And I guess Thomas is Paulie's friend, so I can get his too."

"They used to get chased by the same girl at recess in second grade. She used to lick people."

"Ew." Jennifer and Garvey laughed.

Elsa hadn't even laughed before it hit her brain: saliva. She stood in thought for a moment, then took out her phone.

She brought it over to Thomas and Paulie. "OK, guys, here's the skill you needed back in second grade, with Licking Girl." She played them a video of a YouTuber. "Gleeking, a.k.a. snake spitting. People can teach themselves to do it on command."

"O-ho, check it out," Thomas said enthusiastically. He reached for her phone and pressed for it to replay. He and Paulie leaned in. Elsa stepped away as the video ended again, and both boys pulled out their own phones and started searching and comparing finds.

Elsa played herself a little "ta-da!" horn sound in her head. The hook was set. She would bring in the "No Gleeking" stickers when they arrived, and then once Thomas could gleek, all Elsa would need next was . . . well, the rest of the plan. But it was coming together.

Once they all had their ice creams, Joanna turned from her own little table toward the boys, who were seated at the neighboring table. Thomas brightened at being invited into conversation, and he started asking Joanna about her job. Paulie soon returned to looking at his phone. Thomas, though, seemed especially interested in the legalities of religion.

Soon he moved over to an empty chair at Joanna's table, asking her what Elsa considered to be some pretty good questions: "So do they really not pay any taxes?" and "How are they allowed to say you can't be married, for some of their jobs?" Elsa casually moved forward a bit, intrigued.

Garvey draped himself across the back of his chair to listen intently and nod at the conversation at this other table. Half the time he just gazed at Thomas like a victim of Cupid's arrow. Elsa glanced around the room, still trying to convince herself it wasn't obvious that these were two peas from the same pod. She saw Ham watching them as well.

When their eyes caught, he grinned and moved toward Elsa. He took up a spot against the wall next to her, and both of them turned to listen in. Joanna was laughing and explaining, and Thomas was always quick with a follow-up question.

"How can there be priests or whatever in the army, like in movies? Isn't the army public too?"

Joanna explained the establishment clause and recapped settled case law around chaplains.

"So does the military have to have a chaplain for every religion? Like a whole battalion of them? I mean, I know they probably don't, because how would you even fit that many on one submarine or whatever. And what about atheists, don't their beliefs mean there should be no chaplains?"

Ham shook his head and chuckled quietly. "This kid," he said. "And Garvey is quite the fanboy, right?"

Elsa looked at her husband, his eyes stuck to these two boys. She turned to watch them again too, letting herself fall toward a rare moment of shutting out future, past, or anything other than this little bubble of immediate present. Here they were, these two parents watching these two boys.

Ham draped his arm across her shoulder, and Elsa leaned into him. She wanted to fall in all the way.

But bliss was not her strong suit. She tried, but tendrils of thought started creeping outward. Could she really have all this, now? When he was a baby, she had let go of this. She had caved to Ham's insistence, given her husband what he understood as sanity. And then she had let this son drift away.

She thought of Krista's beef with her mom, during the Iceberg Incident. "It wasn't too late at first, Elsa." Good mothers didn't just let their child go, and that was exactly what Elsa had done.

Somehow, here she and Thomas both were, though, way downriver. When she had been pulled ashore off that chunk of ice and reunited with her mother, young Elsa had felt no resentment of Marcy. At least she didn't remember any. She had felt only relief, hadn't she? Maybe it wasn't so impossible to hope that Thomas might feel the same.

Brian and a gangly friend of his came through the door and found their group.

"Hello, fellow victors," Brian announced awkwardly, pulling out both of the empty seats at Joanna's table.

She smiled up at them. "Thomas, this is Brian and Karl, members of an atheist organization." She told Thomas their role in reaching out to the ACLU. "And Karl, I don't know if you've met Garvey." She held her hands like a spokesmodel to present him.

Brian offered further clarification. "These two are Ham's boys."

Elsa's blood pumped to her face.

But Garvey was quick with a cheerful objection. "No, that's Thomas." Then he dropped his smile. "My brother, Bird, didn't even come." Ham and Paulie both immediately defended Bird: there was the history project, the Spanish test, the other homework.

Elsa moved toward a corner and pretended to look in her purse for a moment. *Bird.* Again she had dropped him from her consciousness for a while and shamelessly swapped Thomas into his place.

Jennifer appeared at her side and spoke toward Elsa's bag. "So Bird said, 'Forget you,' huh? Remember, Else—they're teenagers. If they weren't rejecting us right now, we'd be doing something wrong."

Elsa was definitely doing something wrong. Confession would help, but that was impossible. This was no cake in a sink.

The three of them walked into the house at about ten o'clock to find Bird in the living room. He'd heard about the victory by text from Paulie. His first question was about how upset the BOA families had been.

"They're fine, Bird," Ham said, his eyes going to Garvey. Ham reminded Bird that BOA life would go on, that no boys had been de-trooped in the making of this episode. Bird shrugged and went up to his room. But after ten minutes, he emerged again, covered in his striped pajamas. He went to lean on the doorway to Garvey's room, just across the hall from where Elsa was reading.

"So I guess congratulations," he said into the room. Elsa heard silence. After a bit Bird added, "I know you were probably nervous about it all. So yeah. Good job standing up for yourself, I guess." Bird turned to head to his own room, catching Elsa's eye as he passed her door. He shrugged at her, and she gave him a thumbs-up. Then she heard him close his bedroom door behind him.

"Thank you," Garvey eventually called out.

The next morning, Elsa made a point to drive to school late enough to give Bird a ride. When he pulled out his phone to fight the pixies or whatever they were, she took a deep breath.

"Only one round, OK?" she said lightly.

Bird grunted a syllable that Elsa knew how to translate: it meant she was annoying and clueless, and he understood she would take his phone if he didn't respect her limit.

After a minute, Elsa put enthusiasm on her face. "Hey, so Mr. Anderson seems pretty interested in your History Day project. He was telling me that Civil War soldier reenactment happens at Fort Snelling. You know those old barracks, up from where we used to walk around Pike Island?" She remembered the panic she and Ham had felt one time on Pike Island when they lost six-year-old Bird in the woods for upward of half an hour. They had run around in widening circles yelling his name, Ham carrying little Garvey. Elsa had been sobbing, numb, imagining Bird gone forever.

Here in the minivan, his face got more irked. "Jeez, Mom. So when you said one round, you were lying?"

When they had found little Bird, he'd been on his stomach among yellow fallen leaves, carefully brushing away dirt from a shrub's roots as if they were ancient Egyptian artifacts. He was surprised to hear he had scared them, and when he saw that Elsa had been crying, he wrapped himself around her and patted her back like he was burping a baby doll. Then he tugged her by the hand to show her what he'd found: a puffball mushroom, a colony of harmless ants, the confused shrub that had two different kinds of leaves. Bird knew how to see. He had beamed about each, talking into her face that she kept drawing so close to his, and he had petted her hair to make her all better.

Elsa put her eyes on the car ahead of her. "No, Bird, I was not lying. But you can still hear me talking while you play, right?" He skipped the grunt this time. "I just wanted to tell you how we could look into that reenactor stuff, see when it happens. Maybe the soldiers would have their shotguns or whatever."

Finally Bird put his phone into his backpack. After a good ten seconds of nothing, he gave a small shrug as a response. Elsa ran through a few radio stations, settling on a Janelle Monáe song with lots of tongue clicking. Bird cupped his hand a few inches in front of his mouth and gleeked.

"So the little plastic millimeter cups don't quite cut it, right?" she tried again.

"It's not really a large enough surface target," Bird agreed. "You need something wider for catching it. But then you could still transfer it into those cups for measuring." Elsa noted the whole sentences, the lack of heavy sighs. So this was the magic to connecting with Bird—trying to prove they weren't related?

Elsa brought him into the teacher's lounge when they got to school. She pulled a cone-shaped paper cup off the dispenser next to the water cooler and held it up. Bird brightened.

"I could make it go in this for sure," he said. He looked happy. Elsa gave him the pointy cup, and he held it in front of his mouth to test it out. He nodded and smiled, then headed off to his locker. Once he was gone, Elsa shoved aside her guilt and grabbed ten more cups to stow in her bag.

Within two days, Bird had managed to take two measurements of his total collected gleek and divide each by the number of gleeks that had contributed to it. His per-gleek average was different enough across the two collections that he felt he needed to accomplish a third. Watching Bird pour his second batch of saliva into the little measuring cup, Elsa had felt the tiniest wobble of temptation to somehow grab it. But no; she would hold out for Thomas's, waiting for the perfect moment.

Chapter 20

The following Tuesday, Elsa tried once again to talk herself out of going to a soccer game. But the rain decided things for her. Experience with her own sons' sports told her that kids often had no one watching them when it rained, and the idea of abandoning Thomas—well, that was just what had gotten her here.

She walked out to the field in her Seattle-worthy rain jacket plus a large umbrella. Sure enough, only a handful of parents huddled in the stands, and none of them were Katharine.

Thomas was in as goalkeeper, and he saw her coming. He gave her a goofy, happy wave followed by a series of sporadic glances, always with a grin or a funny face. Unfortunately, this meant that he took his eye off the ball at an inopportune moment, and the visiting team turned the ball quicker than Thomas's feet would turn on the mud. He made a nice leap that landed him on his side, but the ball had already passed him for a goal. Thomas got up slowly, hanging his head toward his muddy body and no longer looking Elsa's way.

Coach Schusterman soon subbed another player in at goalie, telling Thomas his focus was off and he was done for the day. Eventually, Thomas wandered over to where Elsa sat, on the far end of the front bleacher. She adjusted her umbrella to include coverage of the space next to her, patting the seat.

"It's not raining under here. Plenty of room."

After looking nervously at his coach a few times, he sat next to her, making sure not to lean in too close. "Sorry if I'm kind of a mud duck," he quipped. Then he looked at her for clarification. "Wait, is that expression . . . ?"

"Dirty?" Elsa interrupted. She laughed, and he smiled. "No, but I think it means 'ugly.'"

"A stick in the mud?"

"That means 'boring.'"

"Mud in your eye?"

Elsa thought. "I think that means you're an old duffer drinking with your friends."

"Huh. It sounds more like something from the Bible."

Conversation was easy with Thomas. Maybe it was the shoulder-orientation thing that she'd learned in college psychology: males were supposed to talk more comfortably when side by side rather than face to face. Previously she had tested this supposed magic with Bird, to no avail. She had ridden a chairlift up the summer sliding hill at Lutsen Mountain with Bird at least five times this year, and still she had failed to get more words out of him than she had fingers.

But here was Thomas, rambling on about how he and Paulie had been looking into joining that organization Brian and his friend belonged to. Thomas wasn't sure if he was exactly an atheist like Paulie was, though; that got in the way of Thomas's religious creativity.

"I might start my own religion, actually," he announced.

Elsa smiled. "Let me guess. Will it have quite a few holidays?"

"Founder's Day, for sure. I'll never go to school or work on my birthday again." He held up his hand; Elsa laughed and gave him the high five.

"We'll have all the usual religious stuff," he explained. "Foods that are banned, and then other ones that you eat in a ceremony. But we won't ban things that taste good, just ones that are gross, like anchovies or cilantro. What is the deal with cilantro, anyway? Ew."

Elsa liked cilantro, but the rest of the family hated it, so she just nodded.

Thomas continued. "And I think the stuff you pass out during rituals could have a little more zip. In my church, we're giving people Pop Rocks each week, when they come up front."

"Way more inspiring," Elsa agreed.

"Also, probably only women are allowed to lead a church service or read aloud from the Bible. Well, actually, I don't know if it will be called a Bible; that part I don't have figured out yet. It might be something shorter than a whole book."

"More people might read it if it's short," Elsa pointed out.

"It could be a graphic novel; that could help a lot too," he grinned. Then he continued. "So you know how women in some religions are supposed to be all covered up or not wear pants or whatever? In my religion, women and girls can do whatever they want, but there will be rules about men's outfits. Like maybe men are banned from showing their bare feet. I mean, that rule is just a favor to the whole world because men's feet are usually gnarly anyway. Nobody wants to see that."

"Much appreciated," Elsa said. She noticed a mother in a rain poncho arriving to climb the bleachers, and she nudged Thomas, giving him a wordless look and tipping her head toward the mom subtly. On the topic of religion, it was easy to offend. She wasn't sure Thomas understood her meaning, but he did keep quiet for a moment. His face flushed just a bit. The mom climbed up to the top bleacher and sat, well out of earshot given the rain.

Thomas glanced back at the woman, and then he looked again at Elsa, leaning toward her with a conspiratorial grin. Elsa smiled as he launched into the rest of his ideas.

This new faith would ban weekend homework, of course. And instead of baptizing a baby with water, Thomas's ritual was a bit different.

"You don't have something done to you with water; you do a thing yourself." His eyes smiled, waiting for Elsa to ask.

"Give it to me," she said.

Thomas opened his mouth a bit and pointed his jaw toward the field. After a moment, he managed to gleek out a small spray. Then he beamed at Elsa.

"Did you just . . . ?" Elsa's eyes and mouth both went wide.

"Yep! That's how you baptize yourself. The priest woman says some special words, and your parents put their hands on your shoulder and all that. Then you gleek, and you become a member of the church." Thomas tried to nod casually. But he glanced at Elsa and broke back into a grin.

Elsa chuckled and looked out at the field. So Thomas could gleek. She smiled at the universe: you didn't have to believe in magic to feel gratitude for the improbable. Knocking Thomas's knee with hers, she smiled. "I love it."

The steps forward were so easy now. She could see them in simple pictures, like a set of IKEA directions. 1: Gleek goes into cup. 2: Cup pours into vial. 3: Vial gets shipped to scientists in white lab coats.

And then it would be step 4: Truth and reconciliation.

That night and the next morning, Elsa solidified her sample collection plan, one that would cast no shadows on Elsa herself while managing to keep Thomas in the dark.

The "No Gleeking" stickers had arrived, so she went full stealth, secretly venturing into both the boys' and the girls' bathrooms to put one at eyeball height on each exit door. Then she sat back and put her faith in middle school oppositionality, allowing a few days for her students to master this new skill.

By the end of the week, she started spotting kids standing around face to face, at least one of them with their mouth wide open and jaw held forward. A couple of kids had joined Thomas among those who could actually gleek.

"This has got to stop," Aneisha complained, repulsed.

"I'll shut this down," Elsa promised.

When her fourth-period students filed in on the Tuesday before Thanksgiving, Elsa greeted them at the door with her stack of pointy cups. "Gleek cup?" she offered as students arrived. She held out a marker and asked that each person put their name on their cup, if they accepted one. "Today we find out who's our best gleeker, and then we put this disgusting practice behind us once and for all. Enjoy it while it lasts, my young friends, because anyone doing this after today gets sent to Principal Schusterman. Am I clear?"

Before starting the math, she announced that no one would gleek anywhere but in their cup. Moreover, everyone would turn in their cup on their way back out to the hall, for her to judge the day's winner. "We are not sharing saliva. Not during class and not after class. Not on purpose and not by mistake," she decreed.

"Not in a box, and not with a fox," Thomas added. Then he held his cup to the lower half of his face and gleeked in it. Claire tried to follow suit, in her own cup.

Darnell tapped her shoulder and insisted on a peek into her cup. "Pssshhh, this girl can't gleek," he announced.

"Yeah, well, this girl can," a voice called out from the back row. It was Lyda, her menacing stare firing out like lasers above the loon on her Minnesota United soccer sweatshirt.

Claire gritted her teeth briefly before regaining her composure. She turned back around, pulled her hair onto her shoulder, and gave Thomas a look. "What a shocker, Lyda's flexing on you," she said, telegraphing boredom.

Elsa hid her excitement. She remained calm as she went over the previous night's homework, explaining again about a negative sign before a parenthesis. Next, she introduced how to multiply both sides of an equation by negative one, a move that sometimes turned a mess of a problem into sleek simplicity. Then she assigned a set of problems for them to try themselves.

The gleek competition had clearly begun while Elsa wrote on the whiteboard. Hopeful, Elsa made a point of rolling her eyes a little and shaking her head as she moved past gleekers and into her seat at her desk. She propped up her tablet, again pointing the camera discreetly toward where Thomas sat, and she set up a pile of homework assignments to correct on the desk in front of her.

Her red pen poised, she glanced back and forth at her screen. She could see Thomas raising his cup about every minute, which had Darnell in a tizzy. He prodded at Thomas to keep up with Lyda. But

Thomas seemed to be pacing himself, his head nodding a bit as if he were counting. Elsa was pleased: as an athlete, Thomas probably understood strategy for long-distance endurance. She scanned two more homework assignments, marking them as complete at the top.

As she glanced back at her screen, she saw Thomas still nodding, but now with his lips moving. Elsa stretched his face a bit larger. He closed his eyes occasionally too, nodding and mouthing words until Darnell would poke him again to gleek. Elsa now understood: Thomas was listening to music—not her own wordless background music, but his own, an earbud stuck in the ear she couldn't see. It was entrancing to watch.

"Ms. Vargas?"

Elsa jumped. It was Shoua, somehow at her elbow. When Elsa turned, she saw Shoua's eyes on the screen filled with Thomas. Shoua frowned a bit and looked at Elsa.

"Shoua! Oh, how embarrassing." Elsa breathed in. She held herself still for a moment, taking control of her pinkening cheeks. Confidence was the "con" in con man, after all. She leaned toward Shoua, dropping her voice lower. "I'm trying to figure out how it works, how you guys gleek. I know I'm supposed to be disgusted, but I actually really want to show off some gleeking skills to my husband. He'll be delighted." Elsa smiled at Shoua, whose eyebrows were up high. "I think Lyda and Thomas might be the ones to watch."

Shoua nodded; she seemed to accept Elsa's explanation. She set her math textbook in front of Elsa and pointed to a problem she was stuck on.

Twenty minutes later, Elsa noted the time and pulled open her lower drawer. Then she cleared her throat dramatically, stood up, and pulled on the latex gloves, letting each one make a squeaky snap as she stretched it onto her hand. Next, she reached into her leather tote and pulled out a white plastic kitchen garbage bag, pulling it apart a bit and then filling it with air in one dramatic swoop. She walked over to stand in the doorway, opening the door in anticipation of the bell.

"OK, everyone who took a gleek cup, that cup is your exit ticket today," she announced, one hand holding the garbage bag and one hand perched and ready to receive the first wet pointy cup. She saw several students moving to huddle around Thomas and Lyda as they held their cups together for comparison. Thomas and Darnell both exploded in a ruckus of groaning: Lyda must have been the clear winner.

Elsa took two cups with seemingly nothing in them as the first students left, tossing each into her white bag. Lyda passed her next, and she handed Elsa a cup with a bit of visible liquid collected in its tip.

"Lyda, you're a girl of many talents," Elsa offered.

Lyda marched wordlessly into the hallway before throwing her hands up into rock-on devil horns. Elsa saved Lyda's gleek cup upright under one finger of her garbage bag hand, freeing the other to grab Thomas's as he approached.

"I'll take that, please, for official judging," she said. "The baptismal gleek, right?"

Thomas tilted his paper cup forward so she could admire what he had accrued. Elsa's heart dropped: it was hardly more than nothing at all.

Elsa took his cup, unable to listen as Thomas gave her an excited update about online ordination. Was this gleek even enough to pour? She rocked the cup back and forth, watching it intently like a wine connoisseur. It was no good. She'd have to do this ten times or more to get what MyTree needed.

She let Lyda's cup fall into the bag, and then she dropped in Thomas's as well, fighting off tears. The gleeking angle had seemed so serendipitous, a gift. But then it turned out to be the opposite: not only had it not worked, but now it would be harder than ever to meet her saliva objectives without suspicion.

Elsa looked out her doorway after the students, scanning for Thomas. Across the hallway she saw Shoua and Claire, huddled. Shoua felt Elsa's eyes on her and looked up; their eyes caught. Then Shoua turned away quickly, grabbing Claire by the arm and yanking her down the hall.

"Bye, girls," Elsa called after them in cheery defiance. It had to be the screen filled with Thomas. She thought she had sold the con pretty solidly, but apparently Shoua was no easy mark.

Chapter 21

The next morning during her prep period, Elsa slumped into her desk. She stared at the three pointy paper cups that had gone unclaimed, finally picking one up and setting it on her own head: *dunce.* Of course you couldn't get enough saliva from an obscure skill that hardly anyone could learn, let alone master. She thumped her finger on her desk rhythmically, focusing on a distant point beyond the wall. Now what? There was the sponge on a stick, sure; that was clearly a fine solution if you had someone drooling and asleep right next to you. But . . . Thomas?

Elsa let the little cup hat fall off her head as she went to her doorway. No Thomas was coming; no one was in the hall at all. This was fine, she realized, because she didn't believe in stupid little serendipities anyway. She had grown an appetite for forward progress, for executing a plan and moving toward resolution. She could no longer tolerate waiting.

It was time to make spit happen.

She called the front office and asked them to get a message to Thomas in class, telling him to report to her room.

Moments later, the PA system addressed the whole school. "Thomas Humphrey, please see Ms. Vargas in room 210."

Elsa frowned at the incompetence. Why not interrupt just Thomas's class instead of all of them? She moved to her stack of extra textbooks and opened the front cover of one. In almost illegible handwriting, she signed Thomas's name on the first open line on the "This Book Belongs To" sticker.

Moments later Thomas appeared, looking uncertain. She smiled and held up the book. "There's not an emergency. I just found your book on the hamster cage and thought you'd be missing it. The office may have overreacted just a hair."

He relaxed into a smile. Then he looked puzzled and put his hand up in his hair. "Huh. Cuz I think I have my book," he said. He took the book from her and opened the cover. "Oh, that's not mine. I have way better cursive than that, Ms. Vargas."

Elsa apologized. Then she made like she was sending him on his way again, until—oh!—she interrupted herself, even snapping and pointing at him, for effect. "Hey, wait. That's right. Now that you're here, there is one other thing." He looked happy for the delay. Elsa parked herself on the edge of her desk, then twisted her hands together a bit as she continued. "So. I have to be straight with you about something, Thomas. It's probably going to sound a little . . . strange."

Thomas nodded, then frowned. Then he laughed nervously. "Yeah, OK," he managed.

"So with the gleeking yesterday," Elsa continued. "I was actually planning to keep some of the collected gleek. It's saliva, and I know that's a super strange way to collect saliva . . ."

He blushed. "What for?"

Elsa leaned forward now. "This is kind of on the down-low, OK?"

Thomas raised his eyebrows and shoved his hands deep into his pockets.

"I used to teach at the high school, and a friend of mine is a science teacher there. She's trying to get a wider sample of saliva for her class to compare their data to. So I was hoping to give her at least one more sample from outside my family. I'm not sure Principal Schusterman really wants me doing anything besides teaching math right now . . ."

Thomas's face clicked into understanding. "Right, you had the eye color thing and then the BOAs. I get it."

"So anyway, I failed at my secret mission to nab a large enough saliva sample. I just wanted you to know the truth." She waited a beat, feeling slightly slimy. But it worked.

"Hey, I could totally give you a bunch more gleek or even spit, if that would work," Thomas offered with a big grin.

Elsa smiled back. "I guess I was hoping you might be up for that. It would be great. And yes, regular spitting is what works best." She went to her big leather bag and fished around in it, finally pulling out the vial.

"Maybe think about foods that make your mouth water," she said.

He was clearly delighted, and he started scrunching up his mouth to get the juices flowing. Elsa could hardly believe it.

A tap came on her doorframe just then: Aneisha. "Hello, friends," she said, her eyes moving from Elsa to Thomas. "What brings you to our part of the hallway today, Thomas?"

He stopped working his mouth and closed the saliva tube inside his hand, moving his hand discreetly to his side and then finally into his pocket. He smiled at Aneisha and only glanced fleetingly at Elsa. "Hi, Ms. Reese," he managed. Then he looked around the room, eyes landing on the textbook that wasn't his. "Oh, I'm here to get my book," he said, moving quickly to retrieve it. He stood with it for a moment, adjusting how he held it. Then he offered another grin.

"I see," Aneisha said. "And you're still here missing class because . . . ?" Her eyebrows were up, and her arms were now folded.

Elsa spoke up. "I was complaining at him about the office, actually. They treated it like a natural disaster, using the whole school PA channel. It's like he might need a defibrillator if he went without his textbook for another three minutes." She rolled her eyes at Aneisha. "But yeah, you can head back now, Thomas. Thanks for coming down, always nice to see you." She nodded at him and smiled reassuringly.

He went to the door and then turned to look at Elsa. "So, um, sorry about that one homework thing." He shrugged and then turned to

Aneisha. “Bye, Ms. Reese. Sorry for missing class, but it’s just español, and yo hablo español muy bien.”

“No problema,” Aneisha nodded. Then, as he left, she focused her gaze on Elsa. “So. How are we doing, after that school board meeting? Staying out of further trouble, I hope?” She moved to Elsa’s whiteboard and picked up a marker, holding it up for borrowing approval, and then moved to the door. There, she turned back, face growing more serious as she put her hand on her hip and leaned against the doorjamb. “Listen,” she finally said. “I think you see this some, but I’m gonna tell you anyway. Once they put you in a box, hon, you gotta be on your best. That’s just how this world turns out to work.” She held Elsa’s eyes for a long moment. Finally Aneisha gave her face a quick shake, a reset that cleared the intensity. Then she turned. “Lie low, girl. Keep your head down and teach ’em some math.”

Lie low. That, Elsa thought, was exactly what she had been doing for fourteen years. She’d been alone in her knowledge that Bird was essentially their adoptee. It was ridiculous. What was the shame in being adopted? Nothing. It didn’t mean you were loved any less. In fact, it meant someone had chosen you. At least usually . . . at least eventually, in her case. And maybe even in Katharine’s. Might Katharine have realized she was raising an adoptee? Maybe they would all ultimately welcome a day with no more deceit, a day when the biological truths were out on the table for all to see.

Just thinking it made it clear to Elsa that was what she wanted. It didn’t feel good, scheming and deceiving. But the only way beyond it was through it. She had to get the proof, or else telling Ham would be a disaster.

At this point, she was so over being creative or squeamish or indirect about getting the evidence. Aunt Lois’s chart, the blood relatives? Forget all that. Instead, her mind pulled her back to Ham, the one living in a dream that things were fine.

It must be nice, Elsa thought. Here she was, telling lies and creeping around, and ultimately she was doing it all for him. He was the one who needed convincing, but she was the one who had to do it. Ham would just get to sleep through it all, blissfully unaware of all her covert maneuvers in the dark. One day, he would be shaken awake to their real son. He would learn about her skeeviness with the DNA. Still, even then, Ham would get to be the magnanimous one, granting forgiveness.

No matter. The time for lying low was over. If she had to stoop lower before she could stand straight up, then she would do it.

For the rest of the day, her resolve only grew. She would get his damn saliva, whatever it took.

At the final bell, she watched her last-period students empty into the hallway. Energy was high as students flitted about, madly cramming in enough contact to survive the long Thanksgiving weekend apart. Before long, Thomas appeared next to her, and she moved aside so he could enter her classroom. He went over to Elsa's desk, set something there, and then jaunted across the room again toward the hall. As he passed her, he dropped his voice low and leaned toward her. "Hope your science friend likes the spit." Then he moved into the hallway and called back at her. "Happy Thanksgiving, Ms. Vargas. See you Monday!"

Chapter 22

Ordinarily Thanksgiving Day was the apex of a climbing slope of stress for Elsa—maybe for most of the women in America, along with her. But this year, Thanksgiving itself was the first day of tremendous relief, and not just because her mother was hosting. It was because finally she'd sent off two perfect saliva samples in the mail.

Elsa felt thankful for that. As she moisturized, she realized that she liked her face a bit better today, in the mirror. She was a woman who took steps toward the truth instead of staying in perpetual limbo and denial. The stress of knowing but not *quite* knowing had accumulated since the day Thomas had told her his birthday, and now she was just a few weeks away from resolution.

She went to her tiny, old-house closet and contemplated her clothes.

Maybe it was cheating to be grateful for something she didn't quite have yet. Gratitude was about being present, seeing what you had right now. What she had now in the way of blouses wasn't doing it for her—none of these sparked joy—so she moved instead to her shelf of indoor-day sweaters.

The present day offered plenty to be thankful for, she thought. She and Ham and Bird and Garvey were all safe. They all knew they were loved. Life at work and at school was mostly good, all around, and they all had strong friends surrounding them.

She grabbed an olive-green sweater and held it up, checking her reflection. Their world would be rocked, not long from now: a new son, and new brother. And a new Elsa, one who it turned out had never been completely truthful with them. Surely they would understand why, though—wouldn't they see that her choices had held them together all this time? Besides, she had tried telling the truth in that maternity ward, and her own family had let her be drugged into silence.

She put the sweater back; that color did nothing for her. Today she would go with red.

Elsa and her family arrived at the duplex at two o'clock to help out or hang out, either on Marcy's side or on Krista's. Two more guests would join them at four o'clock for the actual feast. One was Marcy's brother, David, and the other was his date. Uncle David hadn't dated anyone in a long time; it had been since Marcy was widowed. After Carlos died, David had insisted on taking his sister out for a weekly lunch and bringing her as his guest to evening events at the medical school where he taught. He'd only started backing off this last Christmas, when Krista had gifted their mother a subscription to the dating app Krista used herself.

"Every man I meet wants someone less direct," Krista had reasoned aloud.

Marcy hadn't yet tried to find a match online. Still, she was thrilled for David that he'd found someone besides his own sister to spend time with, and she was going all out to make the feast a warm welcome.

"Who will help me finish building the pies? The apple gets a lattice, and the pumpkin gets some cutouts," Marcy announced.

Garvey shouted out to make sure he was first, and followed her into the kitchen.

"I have wine and strange sodas," Krista said, beckoning them to her side of the duplex. When they got there, she handed Bird an apron and a knife, pointing him to a cutting board with a bulb of garlic on it. "Could you do two cloves, minced? And before you do that, could you fix the music situation for me? Please please please find me something besides

NPR and their damned turkey cooking show." Bird cheerfully followed her directions, and Elsa gave Ham a look. This happy cooperation was not what they had experienced before leaving their own house, where Bird had insisted that his horrible screen-printed black T-shirt was fine, Mom, because nobody else judges people by what they wear.

Ham put a few things in the fridge and peeked in the oven at the turkey. Marcy was the turkey chief, but she used Krista's oven so that she could rotate various pies and casseroles through the oven in her own kitchen.

"Sure enough, he's dead," Ham said. "I've got a green bean thang that could get warmed up later, either stove or oven. In the meantime, got any more assignments?" He went back to the fridge and grabbed a beer they had brought. "Or can I interest you in some coffee stout, Krissy?"

Krista accepted a small glass of the beer, then parked herself next to Bird, waving off other help. Elsa suggested that she and Ham call his parents in Seattle for the holiday hello.

The two of them sat close on the couch as Ham dialed his dad, holding the phone so that their faces were both in view. His father answered from outdoors, wearing a jacket and hat. A windstorm early that morning had knocked their power out, so he was lighting the charcoal barbecue as a backup plan for the turkey, just in case power wasn't restored soon.

"We had to barbecue the turkey one year when you were little, Ham, you remember that?" Ham did not. "When you found out there were no mashed potatoes, you locked yourself in your room and started destroying it. You couldn't have been more than four." They laughed with him. Ham's dad called his wife outside to join the conversation, and as she joined him, he seemed to forget the phone's camera. His dad recapped what he had said to this point while Ham and Elsa watched the deck railing. Ham's mom laughed and then adjusted the phone so she could see them.

"Oh, hi, you two. Such a sight for sore eyes." She turned emotional. "Listen, I think you should come out again this summer and let us look after the kids while you get some time. Remember when you let us have Bird to ourselves a few days that one summer?"

For their tenth anniversary, Elsa and Ham had gone back to Seattle, the place where they had fallen in love. Bird was a two-year-old, and Ham's parents eagerly took care of him all day, letting Elsa and Ham return only to sleep each night.

It had been a pretty lovely setup. For most of the day and all of the evening, the two of them had hit the Elsa-and-Ham greatest hits—minus the breweries, since Elsa was pregnant with Garvey. It had brought them closer, revealing more to Elsa about a husband she thought she already fully understood.

He had his own geography hardwired into his bones, for one. In the Twin Cities, Elsa had grown up taking nice thirty- or forty-minute walks around a lake. But for Ham, these sorts of walks were like scratching near an itch, but not quite on it. Elsa remembered finally understanding this on that trip. They'd gone down to Seward Park at Ham's insistence, a peninsular park below the breakfast place. It was a half-hour walk along a lake, and yet it was a complete inversion. The insides and outsides were reversed. You didn't walk around the water here; instead, you had the water around you while you walked.

They had rented kayaks on Lake Union, paddling along and between little houseboats moored to wooden piers strewn in connected paths across a field of water. They visited two city beaches: one was sandy, sporting beach volleyball, while the other hid little intertidal crabbies below its barnacled rocks. Behind you on a Seattle beach was always a hillside or cliff, all up in your face. But in front of you were huge swaths of wide blue expanse, tiny boats dotting the distance.

In Minnesota, water was drops of paint on a canvas of land. Out there, water was the canvas itself.

Ham's mom was selling the visit. "You could take the ferry out to have dinner on Bainbridge again for your anniversary."

Elsa felt Ham's arm pull her against him. They'd had a moment on the ferry, on that trip years before. At the back of the boat, they'd looked out from the deck railing as the Seattle waterfront receded. Eventually Ham pulled some linty lump from inside his jacket and threw it into the wake, and then after a few moments, he started to cry.

"It's still tough sometimes, Else," he said. "Just knowing that Bird's big sister . . . our daughter." They watched the churn of water below them through their own saltwatery eyes. But their grief had matched less than Ham thought it did. Elsa had felt, even two years in, a tug of mourning for both of the babies she had birthed. Inga was dead, but her true baby Baird was adrift somewhere, with them powering full speed away from him.

Now, fourteen years later, maybe he was found. With the saliva samples sent off to MyTree last night, it would be a mere three weeks—four weeks, tops—before she'd know. Ham had no idea what was coming.

He was telling his parents to enjoy the day now, and signing off. Elsa puckered her lips at them and sang out, "We love you." Then Ham hung up.

Elsa put her chin on his shoulder. "I was thinking about Inga for a second there." They sat together in silence. Then Elsa put her hand on his knee. "It's Thanksgiving, so let me just say that I'm grateful you stuck around through all of that."

He sighed and pulled her against him. "Back atcha, Else. I'm just thankful you made it out the other side."

Elsa curled her toes under tightly, then plowed ahead. "Remember how I told you Bird wasn't my baby, that he had been swapped?" She kept her voice low. She waited a moment while Ham just sighed again and shook his head. "What do you remember about that time? I mean, do you think you would have left me if I hadn't given that idea up?"

Ham was still, so Elsa tilted her head back to look at him. He was frowning. When he turned toward her, she saw that his eyes were glistening.

"Jesus Christ, Elsa. What do you mean, leave you? What would I have done, left both of you, with you raising a son you were rejecting? Or maybe the alternative, where I just take my son away from his mother?" She recoiled, hearing him tick off the options so clearly. "It was scary, that's what it was, Else. But no, I wasn't going to leave you." Ham looked at her, and eventually seemed to breathe out the tightness. "Just don't ever do that shit again, OK?"

Elsa's face heated, and she opened her mouth. She wasn't sure what to say. She couldn't really promise not to do that shit, since she was currently doing it. Finally she said, "I'm sorry. I'm never trying to mess with you, Ham."

He squeezed her, hearing what he hoped to hear. She let it ride. There was no point in saying more until she had the evidence.

They sat there for a moment before Krista and Bird came in and flipped on the TV. Krista trolled through channels. "Fútbol, ¿sí o no?" she asked in a Mexican accent when the screen showed a soccer game.

Bird said, "Fuck soccer. It's so lame."

The three adults all turned to look at him, then Krista and Ham looked at each other and started laughing. Elsa did not; Bird's hate-drenched side-eye was landing squarely on her.

"Wait, I thought you were Bird," Krista said. "Who are you, and what have you done with my nice nephew?"

Bird looked a bit embarrassed, but his jaw remained clenched. Krista flipped the channel, and she and Ham both announced "fútbol americano" at the same time, good-naturedly.

Elsa watched Bird a minute more. *Soccer?* But she decided to let that ride too.

"I'm going back over to Mom's to help out," she announced, and left.

Chapter 23

Natalie Trowbridge felt thankful the evening after Thanksgiving. Earlier that day, she had successfully nabbed the best doorbuster sales, and now she was having sex.

She didn't mind much that her man had headed off to the bathroom, clueless, without her having actually orgasmed. It was part of the deal, sleeping with someone new: you couldn't count on what a man might have learned from his previous partners, and it didn't help anyone to embarrass him. Besides, Natalie was perfectly capable of getting herself across the finish line in a pinch, if she had the good fortune of the man leaving the room or falling asleep. She got to it, keeping herself quiet enough, then slipped off to his other bathroom down the hallway, naked. She grabbed her handbag on the way, mostly for the sake of the phone.

I need the mess in the kitchen gone, Pumpkin, she texted Claire a minute later. I'll be home in an hour max. She remembered the way her daughter had screamed at her full-length mirror last night, angry at her thirteen-year-old image. When Natalie tried to offer comfort, Claire slammed the door in her face. It wasn't easy being beautiful so young; the attention made you think it was your ticket in life.

ILY, Natalie added.

After a quick check in the mirror, Natalie strutted down the hallway back to the bedroom, her pert top-handle green leather bag on her elbow.

"Holy shit, Natalie," Rob Schusterman said from the bed. Natalie stopped in the doorway and turned a shoulder toward him coyly.

He patted the bed next to him.

"I have to get back home soon," Natalie announced, knowing that round two was always a bad idea at their age. Then she reached for her clothes draped on the chair in the corner and started to dress while she spoke.

"So I missed the game last week, and you guys lost. You've never lost when I was there, Rob . . ." She scrunched up her nose a bit as she smiled cutely at him.

He winked at her. "That's right. But it was raining cats and frogs, babe, and you would have been miserable. Bet you'll never guess who was there, though," he added, head shaking and eyes toward the ceiling.

Natalie hooked her thumbs in her jeans pockets and leaned one hip forward. "I don't know, tell me," she said. She liked to cover her breasts up last.

"The Boys Of America castration queen," he spit out. "Elsa Vargas."

Natalie had already heard his full rant on the BOA topic twice. The last time had been just after she leaned into his car in the parking lot, after the school board had voted against them. She'd been ducking Elsa herself, in fact. Even the faceful of Natalie's breasts between Rob and the steering wheel had failed to distract him then as he'd railed against the anti-BOA injustice. Here in his bedroom now, Natalie sighed and rolled her eyes in solidarity, pushing herself into her bra.

"That woman keeps showing up, and she doesn't even have a kid on the team. Should I be worried she's too big a fan of our coach?" Natalie teased, giving a little pout.

"Seems like Thomas Humphrey is a pretty big fan of *her*," Rob said, annoyed. "After I pulled him out of the game, he sat under her umbrella for the next hour. It's a good thing Coach managed to focus on the rest of the game, I'll tell you what."

Natalie tried not to notice the way he called himself Coach. At least it hadn't happened during sex yet.

She plunked herself on the bed next to Rob. “Interesting. And she gave him a ride after that school board meeting, remember?” He looked at her blankly. “She and Thomas got into her minivan together. I saw them.” In the moment, she now realized, she’d been so preoccupied with whether Elsa Vargas had seen her. But mentioning this ride now made Natalie think.

Rob looked at her, his eyes narrowing. “That’s not a good look, come to think of it.”

“Exactly,” Natalie said. Bad optics, certainly—but was that all it was? “And this morning I heard from someone else who’s started thinking something along these lines too.” She leaned forward. “An independent source.” She recounted the conversation outside the spin class with Craig, one of George Smith-Ryan’s two fathers. They often caught up on school district happenings, and so of course they had been talking about the Boys Of America decision.

“I asked if he’d noticed how she recruited a student to her side of the issue,” Natalie said. “But then Craig said how Thomas looked so pained by this big crush on Elsa Vargas. He went on and on, really. He said he knew that look—he’d grown up with that look, since his every crush was all guilty and painful and secret. You know, because he was gay.”

Natalie had mostly been annoyed at Craig’s whole crush assertion this morning, honestly. That boy Thomas was lucky to have her beautiful daughter’s interest. But she certainly remembered the way boys in her own junior high had stared at grown women’s chests instead of her own.

Rob rubbed his chin. “He has a crush on her. She gave him a ride, and then she sat with him in the rain with this umbrella. I’m just trying to figure out how killing off the Boys Of America fits in,” he said.

Natalie stood up and pulled on her blouse. If she were the boss, she would call the woman in and talk to her about boundaries. But she wasn’t the boss; she was his love interest, and bossiness was not how to keep that interest alive. “Your job is so hard,” she purred. “I wonder if a talk with her . . . ?”

“Teacher’s union,” Rob muttered. He stayed put on the bed, still pondering, as she found her coat in the hallway and called out to him from the door. “Night, babe,” he managed.

Natalie drove home hopeful. She liked the way Rob talked with her like she could understand and contribute, even when she wasn’t fully clothed. Sure, one day a young athletic trainer type might come along, one with firmer breasts and less well-developed leadership skills. But for now, she was going to enjoy it.

Chapter 24

On the Tuesday after Thanksgiving, Jennifer felt it was still unreasonable to cook for real. Instead, she unboxed the Trader Joe's appetizers in her kitchen and poured Elsa a glass of wine. Tonight was the History Day showcase, and she'd invited Elsa to come over beforehand and make a date night of it. This was, after all, the St. Paul mom version of a gala premiere. No red carpet, sure—but there were those red lines painted on the gym floor. In place of champagne, bad coffee. And who needed celebrities when they had kids in braces, grudgingly standing next to their trifold poster boards?

Her son, Paulie, was still at school with Bird, the social studies teachers having fed pizza to students who helped set up. Her husband, Ted, was at their daughter's volleyball match, so it was just the women and the begging dog.

"He's a ridiculously good boy," Elsa said, bending down to ruffle up his ears and slap his back end. The black lab had his chin in her lap.

"Apart from being racist, he's perfect," Jennifer agreed. He was a rescue; embarrassingly, the dog always barked energetically at Asian men, on walks. When she'd mentioned another instance of this last week, her son said it was probably Jennifer herself making it happen.

"Paulie's kind of a dick now," she said.

"Well, he's not a dick to anyone at school, as far as I can tell," Elsa offered.

"I know. He reserves it for me."

Elsa said she knew the feeling. On top of the animosities from Bird, she dreaded having to spend any more time feigning continued interest in his History Day topic: the pluses and minuses of the various weapons used in the Civil War.

"We're both doomed on that front," Jennifer agreed. Still, as much as their sons would treat them like piles of stinking compost tonight, she knew that attending kids' events was—like composting—the right thing to do in the long run.

They ate the samosas and the artichoke dip, mulling over the parental catch-22: damned if they see you there, damned if they don't. Then Jennifer had a brilliant idea, if she did say so herself. Why not swap? Neither boy was mean to the other's mother, and neither mother was already driven to poke her own eyes out by the other son's topic. Elsa could focus her attention and encouragement on Paulie tonight, and Jennifer could do the same for Bird.

"Maybe we can even get video of them to trade later, talking to the judges and stuff," Jennifer gushed. They clinked wineglasses to congratulate themselves on their advanced and highly adaptive parenting.

At the school, they surveyed the gym and the wide hallway, both crowded with presentations perched atop tables. After a quick lap, they each found their respective destinations and wished each other luck. Jennifer headed toward Bird at the back corner of the gym.

A woman with a clipboard had just arrived at Bird's table. Bird noticed Jennifer and gave a little wave before turning his full attention to the judge. Jennifer held up her phone and started adjusting, moving her own position and setting the zoom level just right.

"Ah, how interesting. Now what can you tell me about your source material?" the judge asked. Jennifer hit record as Bird nervously explained how, after reading a book and an article, he had found a university site with letters from the battlefield that you could search by keyword.

"Wow," Jennifer said out loud. Then she held her hand over her mouth by way of apology. Bird turned red and smiled.

The judge turned toward her.

"Sorry. I just had no idea you could just find letters like that." She turned off her phone and folded her arms. "I won't interrupt anymore." When the judge looked back at her clipboard, Jennifer flashed Bird a thumbs-up.

The woman finished her interview and then shook Bird's hand and moved on. Jennifer stepped forward and gushed at Bird's display before making him pose for a couple more photos next to his project. Then she turned to stand by his side, looking out at the crowded gym in front of them.

"Where's someone I know that I can go bug?"

"Paul's is in the hallway. His is really good."

Jennifer nodded, not telling Bird that this was where his mother was assigned. Instead, she asked about Bird and Paulie's mutual friends, and then headed off to work her way back toward the hall.

After stopping to talk to a couple of boys she had known for years, Jennifer moved herself within spying distance of Paulie. Elsa was not there; no one was there. Eventually Paulie saw her, and—counter to all of his thirteen-year-old programming, obviously—he beckoned her over.

"I have a sucky location, and no one comes this way," Paulie complained immediately. She started to compliment how his project had come together, but Paulie stopped her. "See if you can find a judge and ask them when someone is going to do this table."

Jennifer stepped back and gave a little salute. "Yes, sir," she said. "Has Elsa been over here, by chance?"

Paulie pointed two tables down. "No, but she's right there."

She saw Elsa, hands gesturing animatedly as she talked and laughed at another student's presentation.

It was Thomas from Izzy's, and he was clearly as delighted as Elsa was with their conversation. Jennifer frowned. She stepped away from Paulie, telling him she'd go find a judge. While most of the gym lay in Elsa's direction, Jennifer headed the opposite way, toward the outer perimeter where she could take another look at Elsa from farther away.

"What the hell, Elsa," she muttered to herself. She leaned against the wall for a moment, processing this odd dose of adrenaline. It wasn't just annoyance at Elsa's failure to support Paulie. Before she could decide what else it was, someone called Jennifer's name.

She turned and saw Craig coming her way. She smiled, taking in his clipboard and his tweed blazer with leather elbow patches. Craig really liked politics, but his greatest love was history. "Look at you, all professorial," she teased. Then she remembered her assignment from Paulie and told Craig that her son was eagerly awaiting his judgment. She pulled Craig to where he could look up the aisle of tables. "He's up there on the right, selling some history of attack helicopters," she said.

Craig nodded. "If it's not war, it's machines, with most of these boys. Paul's in the advanced group, where they manage both at once." He looked out across the gym. "I had visions of political history projects when I volunteered. So far the closest thing was one about cereal companies taking over breakfast." Then his lips tightened as his eyes landed farther down the aisle. "Well shit, Elsa," he muttered.

Jennifer looked back at Elsa as well. "What?" But now she knew what.

"It's that same boy who clearly has a big crush on her, and here she goes again hanging out with him," Craig said quietly, two fingers smoothing beard hairs below his lips.

Together they stared at Elsa, whose conversation with Thomas seemed to glide from serious to humorous and back again. She was shaking her head at Thomas as he grinned wildly and kept talking. They both looked quite happy. It felt conspicuous, like they were generating their own lighting.

Jennifer saw a couple of parents' heads poke around the displays on the other side of the aisle to look at Elsa. Then she noticed two other clusters already watching Thomas and his teacher from tables farther down the row.

"She's getting a bit of an audience," Jennifer said. "Do you think that's just about the Boys Of America . . . ?"

"No. I don't. I mean, it doesn't help, for any parents who knew and cared about that. But I think it's probably getting around that this kid is pretty eager to be this teacher's pet. You know what I'm saying?"

She did.

"Well, we have to do something. I'm going to go get her," Craig announced, and he made a beeline for Elsa.

Jennifer stood watching, unable to decide in time what her role in the matter should be. It wasn't until Craig had gotten Elsa to break away with him that Jennifer unfroze. She and Elsa caught each other's eyes; Elsa smiled. Jennifer raised her eyebrows and tipped her head twice toward Paulie. *Get over there.* Then she ducked away, heading toward the hallway.

There was a table with coffee and cookies just outside the doorway. Jennifer stationed herself there, taking her time in pouring a cup and then rummaging in her bag for a dollar to throw in the fundraising basket. When the principal and his annoying earnestness came by, she shoved a brownie in her mouth, smiled around it apologetically, and stepped away. She stared at the two nearest student projects, rereading all the text large enough to decipher from this distance.

"Hello, Jennifer," she heard as a hand lightly touched her shoulder. It was Katharine Humphrey, from a few years back in her longtime book club. Next to her stood a weathered dishwater-blond man who seemed to have a thing for pockets: cargo pants, a zip-up vest busy with pouches and zips. "Do you remember Michael?" Katharine asked. Jennifer blinked, something snapping into place. The Humphreys had a son: *Thomas* Humphrey.

"Jennifer," she said, extending her hand.

Michael gave a firm handshake and then stepped back. "Good turnout," he finally said.

Katharine bit her lip and then frowned a bit. "I think the kids deserve better, actually." She glanced at her husband, then said to

Jennifer, "I'm glad Michael's here, but I do wish more of the dads would show up to these things."

Jennifer saw the husband's surprise at this statement. But after a moment he took his eyes off Katharine and looked around. "Fair," he nodded. Then he stepped over to the coffee and cookies.

Katharine's shoulders relaxed, and she smiled a smile that seemed just for herself. Then she reengaged with Jennifer. "Sorry. I don't mean to complain. But maybe it's better to just say what you think sometimes?"

"No, you're right, Katharine, hundred percent. I myself came with Elsa Vargas, and neither of our husbands came. You remember Elsa, of course, right?" She sighed and shook her head sadly for a moment with Katharine. This was the action that followed Elsa's name within the veteran members of the book club, because of the way Elsa had phased out of the club after her baby's death and had never come back.

"I saw her recently here at school, and it reminded me of that funeral," Katharine said. "I honestly didn't know her very well, but I suppose you did. Do you remember that funeral?"

Jennifer just nodded.

It was all so long ago. What was it, twenty years ago that Jennifer and Elsa had first met? The two had quickly recognized each other as kindred spirits, then obsessed together by phone about their fears and wishes for motherhood throughout their pregnancies and Jennifer's delivery. But then the day of birth had finally come for Elsa, and it turned out to be a day of death. Jennifer had been kind enough to keep her mothering body out of sight, avoiding the funeral and staying away for years after.

"It really was difficult, wasn't it?" Jennifer said.

"Well, teaching seems to suit her. It seems that she has a lot of ideas, and she really takes an interest."

Jennifer shifted her eyes to the coffee dispenser. "That's Elsa." She nodded. "Well. I should probably find her. She was plowing through lots of kids' presentations. I saw her talking to all the kids on the row where my son Paul is set up." This felt like a useful way to depict things.

"Such a supportive teacher," Katharine said.

A brief hoopla of laughter drew their eyes beyond the end of the cookie table, where a cluster of parents was just breaking up. Coming toward them was Natalie Trowbridge, her eyes lighting up as she saw them seeing her.

"Oh, look, two more awesome mamas!" Natalie scrunched her shoulders up and held her hand against her heart as she moved through the sea of eyes. "Ladies, how are you? This evening is such a smash hit. Almost a hundred kids presenting this year! We're really bumping the trajectory for Lowe Hills, am I right?" Then she looked at Jennifer. "You know, this is so terrible, but I forget. Who is your child again?"

Jennifer told her. Everyone knew Natalie and her beautiful daughter, but Jennifer countered anyway. "And yours is . . . ?"

Natalie continued with her cheery onslaught of words. Jennifer stood patiently for a minute or two. Then she interjected that she saw a friend of Paul's whose presentation she shouldn't miss, and she started to move away.

"So great to connect," Natalie called.

Jennifer scanned a couple of projects, stopping to take in the history of pizza in the Upper Midwest for a few minutes before giving the girl kudos. Then she looked around the wide hallway to see if Elsa was anywhere nearby.

She saw Natalie and Katharine, but not right where she had left them. They stood now close against a corner, farther from the action than moments ago. Katharine was still listening and Natalie was still talking. But Natalie leaned in now, her hand on Katharine's upper arm. The usual bright, selfie-ready expression was missing from Natalie's face, and Katharine looked uncomfortable.

Jennifer frowned and pulled out her phone. Let's make like a tree and get out of here, she texted Elsa.

Chapter 25

Saturday morning, Katharine moved from one task to another with tremendous focus. With the sinks and toilets scrubbed white, the grout between the tub-surround tiles practically demanded to be tackled next. If her mind wandered, she pulled out her phone and flipped to her grocery list, concentrating on the week's dinner planning.

Michael himself had approved their son getting that ride to that ice cream place with Elsa Vargas, she remembered. She didn't need to bother him with this noise.

When the bathroom had no more surfaces to offer, she moved on to the kitchen. The baseboards were painted white, like the window trim, and this highlighted the dinge grown there since her last cleaning. Would she never rid the place of all the damned spots?

She moved on to vacuuming the family room, making piles of abandoned belongings on the back of the sofa: one for Grace and one for Thomas. He was just a charismatic child, Katharine knew, and that was that. Everyone liked talking with Thomas. The camp counselors, the neighbors, the coaches—they all enjoyed him. There was no point in making trouble out of what had always been, just because it was Elsa Vargas this time. Moreover, there was a great deal of dust collected behind the TV stand and only herself to remove it. Finally she put the vacuum away and gathered both Grace's and Thomas's piles, heading up to Grace's room first.

Katharine set the colored pen set and the teen romance onto Grace's desk, surveying the room. She smoothed the bedspread and adjusted the pillows. Then she padded silently down the carpeted hall with Thomas's backpack and his shin guards.

As she opened the door, she saw that Thomas was not out getting hardware with Michael as she'd thought, but was instead lying on top of his bed. He faced a wall, but she could see that he was awake; he was caressing the back of a large pillow he held squished against his chest. As his face pressed into it, tenderly, Katharine realized her son might be imagining romance.

Then she saw the laptop propped open toward him on the bedside stand. On the screen played a phone-shaped video of the school hallway, a woman in a doorway drinking coffee. As the video zoomed in closer to her face, the woman's scanning eyes caught the recording phone and she smiled.

It was Elsa Vargas.

Katharine backed up fast, and in her panic the backpack on her shoulder clunked into the doorframe. Thomas turned immediately, and she dropped the backpack and ran. Behind her, she heard the laptop slap shut and something that might have been the lamp clattering over as Thomas yelped, "Oh my God, Mom!"

Katharine was already halfway down the stairs when the bedroom door slammed.

Chapter 26

On the morning of December 11, Elsa watched from her doorway as the halls filled up. She sipped her coffee and scanned. Still no Thomas. If he was out today, that would make three days absent.

She did see Darnell, who looked right at her as he came toward her area of the hallway. He nodded his head at her. "Hey, Miss, how's it going?" he called out with volume, commanding attention. A couple of clusters of students watched them, looking from Darnell to Elsa and back again.

"Can't complain, Darnell," she answered back. "Coffee, sunshine, a hallway full of eager middle school learners . . ."

Tiana Mosley grabbed Darnell and pulled him against a locker as other kids giggled. She poked a finger into his collarbone and started ranting at him in a whisper, throwing one hard glance over at Elsa as she did so.

"Morning, Shoua," Elsa said as the girl moved by. Shoua gave the briefest nod of acknowledgment, then quickened her pace and crashed into a group of kids, who all collapsed inward, whispering.

The vibe seemed to be spreading. Something was at a low rumble among many of her students.

The fourth-period math class had to squeeze into the room because an extra set of girls huddled at the doorway, peering in at Elsa. Halima in her hoodie-hijab smacked her tongue loudly and spun to storm off, and Charmaine and Emma gave uncomfortable laughs as they followed. Claire called Charmaine back, holding her by the shoulders to deliver some clearly juicy gossip before the two girls separated and Claire made her way into the classroom with an almost haughty bearing.

"Welcome to Wednesday, Claire," Elsa said. "We're doing a little group review today, and you can pick yourself a partner. Then I'll put the pairs into small groups and tell you what to do next."

Claire lowered her eyelids a bit and looked at Elsa from below them, sliding into her seat. "I guess we can't pick Thomas," she said. Elsa could hear that Claire meant something more than just "I notice Thomas is absent."

Darnell gave a small groan. "Get off it, Claire. It's all good. Boy's at home watchin' Netflix."

Claire pointed to Shoua. "Partners?" Shoua agreed.

Darnell turned around to look at the kid behind him. "I'll take Oscar. Right, Oscar?"

Oscar never did his homework and—coincidentally, in his mind—always seemed to bomb his tests. Claire folded her arms and smiled.

Elsa looked at Darnell. "Maybe you can let your Netflix-watching friend know there's a test on Friday."

"Or maybe you can," Faviola snapped at Elsa from the back row, bobbling her head just a bit as she said this. Then she put up her hand to cover the delight overtaking her face and looked over at Claire. Elsa heard a few kids draw in breath.

"He's offline, actually. His phone's been off," Darnell said.

"She knows that," Faviola said to Darnell, her upward palm stabbing toward Elsa for emphasis. Someone made a high and rising hum: the sound of eager spectating on a brewing conflict.

Elsa blinked. "Faviola, find yourself a partner. We're going to do math instead of whatever this is." She moved toward her desk and grabbed the Costco-sized can with numbered tiles in it, giving it a little shake that turned out to be quite loud.

She went around to her chair and sat, taking a moment to say nothing and deflate the momentum. Then she asked the class in a pleasant, unheated tone to send one person from each pair to draw a number and get a group review handout.

After the pairs had formed foursomes by lot, moving desks into little pods, Elsa noticed that Faviola and partner had joined Darnell and Oscar in the back. Darnell and Faviola both leaned forward and whispered assertively, Darnell tapping the group review sheet hard for emphasis. Finally they both sat back. That group sat silently in their chairs for the rest of the time. Eventually, Faviola's partner opened the handout and started reading it silently to herself.

In the front of the room, Claire and Shoua's group huddled close. Whenever Elsa looked at this group, she found at least one pair of eyes quickly darting away from her own.

Elsa slumped into her chair and bounced her pencil eraser off her lips. This was understandable, she told herself. She had managed to frame Thomas as a teacher's pet, and she knew better. She did wish, of course, that she could reassure each of these fragile-aged beings trying to shake off childhood that they were grand, that she liked them, that they, too, mattered to her deeply. But the facts remained: there was no one else in this class who might be Elsa's own flesh and blood, and this she could not yet share. Inside of two weeks, she should have her results. Then things would all shift tectonically. By comparison, the current energy among her students was a mosquito-sized annoyance. She would just let the seven remaining school days until break pass by, buzz or no buzz.

When the bell finally rang, the class streamed into the hall. Elsa was erasing the whiteboard when she heard Darnell's voice in the hallway, loud and firm. "Step off, Claire. You need to check yourself, cuz I'm not hearing none of that." She turned to see that Mr. Anderson from two doors down was moving fast, putting himself between Darnell and Claire. Claire had thrown a hip forward and taken a check-my-nails pose, but her face had turned red. Darnell walked backward a few steps, eyes hard on Claire, before he turned and ambled slowly down the hallway.

The next morning, Elsa watched over the hallway a bit more actively. She made her presence larger, calling out to Mr. Anderson about the week's episode of *The Mandalorian* and asking Aneisha loudly what kind of holiday cookies she'd made. When she tried casually drawing a passing kid into the conversation, though, none even looked her way, instead just turning to talk to a friend or speeding up their gait.

Elsa made light of this each time, but eventually she retreated to leaning against her doorframe and watching her coffee swirl in her cup. That was the danger of middle schoolers: if they wanted to, they still had the power to go all middle school on you. And it still felt the way it was designed to feel, just a little.

But Elsa's real enemy here was time, not thirteen-year-olds. These last two weeks were starting to feel interminable.

During her prep period, Elsa perused the MyTree site all over again, looking for any additional ways to check the status of her submission. Could they have rolled out a new way to expedite results, for a price? Everything else worked that way during the holiday shopping season. She couldn't be the only one in the whole country who really, really needed her results so the mystery of who was actually whose wouldn't ruin the Christmas dinner. Where was the invisible hand of the market when you needed it?

She tried to put her mind onto the current math focus: multiplication of binomials. She went to her cabinet to pull out the algebra tiles she always forgot she had until halfway through the unit. As she was digging past other forgotten items toward the back of the shelf, she heard a little knock on her open door. She turned, expecting Aneisha.

Instead, Katharine Humphrey stood rigidly in her doorway.

"Oh! Katharine, come in! How is Thomas? Is he feeling all right?" Elsa realized how much she wanted relief, how eager she was for his return. And now she felt a surge of real worry for his health.

Katharine said nothing for a moment, her lips still closed. Then she stepped forward into the room and pulled the door shut behind her. "I want you to leave Thomas alone."

Elsa set the algebra tiles down. *Leave him alone?* She dropped herself into the nearest desk, in the back row.

Katharine remained where she stood. "You are a mother. You—you have Bird."

Elsa's skin prickled. *Bird.* Did Katharine know?

Katharine grasped her own hand now, as if she needed the support. "No mothers want their sons to be . . . confused. So you will have to leave Thomas alone."

Elsa stared. She felt her whole body heating up, and she nodded.

"I want Thomas thinking of you as his teacher, and nothing more."

Lies, then. Katharine knew, and she wanted lies. Did that mean she never wanted Bird knowing either? But there was something in Katharine's tone that didn't quite fit. Maybe she didn't know. What was safe to say? Elsa needed to hold herself here—think before she burst out with something.

"Please." Katharine looked less confident now. "We can let this go. That's it. We let this go and move on, all right?"

Elsa gripped the edge of the seat below her, feeling something start to layer on top of her fear. An ache was rising somewhere above her stomach, deepening. She nodded.

Katharine nodded too. Then she turned quickly and left.

Elsa heard the soft tap of Katharine's flats, pattering fast until they were out of earshot. She was gone. Elsa continued to sit in the student desk, unsure whether breathing in or breathing out was what came next.

She seemed to know. Katharine knew she was Bird's mother, and yet somehow she was proposing they all just move on. What did that even mean? Katharine had said nothing about her need to get to know Bird, to have a relationship with her own child. Could she really follow through on that, or would something in her eventually do what it had done to Elsa?

After a few minutes of trying to process, Elsa heard her phone buzz. It was an email from Schusterman, addressed to a list of six teachers.

> Through next week, Thomas Humphrey should be excused from any remaining classwork. Confidentially, his family is beginning the holiday break early because of a family crisis. Please prepare to summarize his progress to this point because after break, Thomas will not be returning to Lowe Hills. Sadly, the family will be moving to Iowa.

Chapter 27

Natalie reached up and ran a finger over Rob Schusterman's eyebrow. How was it that men could still look so damned appealing when they just let their eyebrows do what they pleased, tousled and even growing downward? She was glad he had asked her to sneak in a visit on a Thursday evening. Weekends and school events no longer felt like quite enough.

"So she says this move is all about her mother-in-law's health," Rob said. "There was no mention of Elsa Vargas whatsoever." After a moment he sighed and shook his head. "I don't buy it. I don't buy it at all."

Natalie rolled over and contemplated the ceiling. "Me neither." She arranged the sheet so that her worst stretch mark was covered but her better features were not. "I think Katharine was pretty surprised by it all at the History Day event. She was bothered by the idea that there was talk. You have to understand that Katharine Humphrey is not a person terribly comfortable with attention, let alone this kind of thing." Natalie smoothed her own eyebrows with her fingertips. "Still, moving to Iowa is a pretty big cover, if it's not truly the mother-in-law. I mean, *Iowa.* What was she thinking?"

Rob hit her with the extra pillow. He had grown up in Iowa.

"But really," he continued. "Elsa Vargas clearly has a lack of moral fiber. She can't stand to see schools support a character-building organization, for God's sake. I don't trust her for one second."

Natalie looked at him, and then turned over onto her stomach, propped up on her elbows. "Rob. I think you have to listen to your gut. Maybe she really . . . well, I don't want to even think. But maybe she really crossed a line big-time, one way or another." Natalie paused, watching him stare at the ceiling. "What if she did? I mean, she's still teaching other eighth-grade boys tomorrow."

"And girls. Who knows?" Rob said.

They lay there in silence, Natalie staring at the headboard and Rob at the ceiling. For a minute, each of them watched the terrible little movies coming out of their respective mental projection booths.

"She has to be put on administrative leave," Rob decided. "Lowe Hills needs to be safe, and the guy charged with keeping it that way is not going to sit back and slow-walk this." He turned to look at her. "The district will need to see that something was reported, even if it's not yet provable. You can help me here, babe."

Natalie raised her eyebrows. "Can I, though?" She shifted and put her hand on his stomach. "If people find out about us, that might be awkward. We'd have to back off for a bit, wouldn't we?" She moved her hand just a little, staring into his eyes. She tried for the sad-puppy eyes looking up through long lashes, but this was harder to do from her location above him.

Rob was frowning at the ceiling again, ignoring her pout. "I can't suspend her unless I have something reported," he sighed. Then he got out of the bed. He combed his hair off his forehead, leaving parts of it standing up in a way that Natalie found adorable. He went into the attached bathroom.

Natalie stretched her arms overhead and pointed her toes. Then she pulled up her knees, tipping them all the way to the right and then the left to stretch her lower back. She liked that Rob saw her value as a collaborator, she had to admit. It was never wise to be too hopeful, but they did seem to be a good team.

A memory of her brief foray onto the junior high debate team bubbled up. She and her partner Lewie had been a good team too, killing it until the day Lewie suggested Natalie wear less makeup and put her hair in a bun, for competition. She ended up quitting debate altogether.

She picked up her phone from the bedside stand and scrolled through her contacts for a moment, thinking. Maybe Rob had room for what Natalie was now clear on: it was possible to be a hottie and a master strategist all at once.

"You know what?" she called out over the sound of the faucet. "I think I can help, if you give me a couple days." She saw him pull the hand towel off its ring and stand in the doorway looking at her, hopeful, while he dried his hands. It was endlessly satisfying that no one else got to see him this way, naked and perfectly disheveled.

"It would be a pivot," Natalie said solidly. "We have to recognize that safety is a leading parental issue. And one of our chief pillars in the PTO is communication. If I can help fellow parents to connect a few dots and have a think, then we can target an Additional Item on the next agenda. I'm confident the PTO can run this one in for us." She watched his face, aware that she might be going too far. But he nodded, acknowledging that she was right.

She got out of bed and started toward him. His eyes slid over her body and regained their twinkle. The naked part was easy, Natalie thought; it was the other parts of herself she was still learning to show more of. So far, he didn't seem put off.

"What Schusterman needs"—she winked—"Schusterman gets."

Chapter 28

Elsa felt a lingering churn after Katharine's visit and the news of their sudden move. Her mind bobbed; it was almost vertigo. Still, it changed little about what to do next. She had to wait for the results.

It sure looked like Katharine knew she was raising Elsa's son. But it was possible that she didn't know—even possible, then, that she in fact wasn't. Gradually, a new explanation for Katharine's behavior began to form in Elsa's head, one having to do with the vibe from her students.

Elsa could see now how it might look to her students, that she had given Thomas so much of her attention and her time. In the rain, she had sat so close to him, a fourteen-year-old boy who didn't think of her as a mother. She remembered Katharine's tone: "I want Thomas thinking of you as his teacher, and nothing more." When Katharine mentioned Bird, maybe she meant something else. Maybe it was to remind Elsa of the care one needed to take with a boy filled with a flurry of new hormones.

But then there was the move. It was absurd, doing something as drastic as moving a whole family to Iowa over some attentions from a female teacher. It was an effect that suggested a much larger cause.

"No one wants their children to be . . . confused," Katharine had said. Had she meant *perplexed*? *Misled*? Elsa wondered. More likely she'd meant *mistaken for one another*. Twins could be confused for one another. Babies could be confused for one another. It sure seemed like Katharine knew.

Because the MyTree answer would soon explode into their lives, everything at home this holiday season took on a kind of preemptive nostalgia for Elsa. Their present tense would be the old days, the times before everything changed. Traditions seemed more important. Cookie-making offered Elsa real solace, just as it had for her mother in that first Christmas season without Carlos. When the going got tough, the tough made krumkakes.

It was well after nine o'clock when the batter was mixed and the krumkake iron was hot and ready on the stove. Garvey told the smart speaker to play for the fourth time the Sir Mix-a-Lot song he had just discovered. Ham was slapping Elsa on her big butt, both of them draining the end of their glasses of wine.

Bird had rejected cookie-making in favor of studying. Once the smell of griddling wafted out of the kitchen, though, Bird appeared. Elsa congratulated herself; she knew he wouldn't be able to resist taking a turn at the stove to help make the dainty cone-shaped krumkakes.

Bird took pole position. He ladled batter into one side of the cast-iron mold, closed it, then turned the heavy circle over with its long handles to cook both sides. When he opened it, Elsa used a fork to coax off the imprinted crepe and place it on the cutting board in front of Garvey. Then Garvey rolled the flat circle around the big carrot just so, transforming it into a delicate little megaphone as it cooled.

The carrot had to be carefully selected every year, of course, and Elsa loved the way this kicked off the krumkake project right there in the produce section. She liked echoing the way her grandmother had done it with her and Krista. It made her remember her father too, who'd always pretended to be waiting for the carrot to eat at the end instead of the cookies.

Elsa stepped back and let Ham replace her as the fork wielder. She poured herself some more wine and perched on a stool, watching her family at the stove. Garvey had just taken a particularly perfect one off his carrot. He turned and held it up for her to see, his other hand making a fist and pulling it in sharply alongside his gut. Elsa recognized this little celebratory move as the one he'd picked up at the school board meeting. *Thomas.* She forced herself to smile at Garvey before looking into her wine.

It hurt to think about Thomas, whom Katharine seemed intent on ripping away forever. That wasn't for Katharine to decide alone, though. Once Elsa had the evidence, conversations would replace this standoff of silence.

Elsa watched Bird now as he moved out of the way so Garvey could take a turn at the cookie iron. Bird moved to man the carrot. It was a simple swap, two boys switched in a moment.

When the results came, Elsa and Ham would have to navigate a reality with Bird that scared the bejesus out of her—or surely would have, had there been a bejesus in there. For now, though, there was nothing more to do besides wait.

One method to help time go faster was to make her workday a bit shorter. Why get there so early? Today she'd stopped monitoring students as they arrived in the hallway, first thing in the morning. It was better to remove herself from that drama.

"Hey, Bird, you want a ride to school tomorrow?" she asked. "I'm not going in early."

Bird didn't look up. He was forming his next krumkake, and he suddenly seemed more insistently focused than he had been to that point.

"You want me to take you?" she asked again.

Bird checked that Ham wasn't watching, then pulled his eyes toward Elsa, his face oddly twisted. He seemed to be sending her some kind of a look. When Ham turned back around, Bird dropped the look and shook his head no at the carrot.

"OW! Shit, damn, shit!" Garvey suddenly shouted, his hand waving in the air. He started a loud, panicked crying and shoved two of his fingers in his mouth. Ham turned to give him a calming hug, and Elsa went to the ice dispenser on the refrigerator door. She grabbed a paper towel to wrap around the ice cube and let a drizzle of water from the sink wet the wrapped ice.

Bird was no longer in the kitchen.

Ham helped Garvey live through his finger scorching while Elsa formed the last two cookies from the remaining batter. Then they shooed Garvey to bed. Elsa went to Bird's room to check on him.

"Mom, go away," Bird said coldly.

Elsa stood still. "What's the deal? Do you have something you want to say?"

"No, Mom," he said, full of disdain. "There's no deal, just go away."

"Well, do you want me to check with you in the morning about getting a ride?"

Bird opened his mouth and put his eyebrows high against his hairline. "Seriously? Are you even serious right now, Mom?" Then he smacked his fist down hard on his dresser. Suddenly he was yelling, his face red. "Get out of my room, I don't want to look at you!"

Elsa pulled in her lips and stood there, a mix of guilt and fear running through her. All the drama she'd been trying to avoid was at *his* school—*his* classmates. All of that was in his bloodstream right now, and she'd be stupid to move toward him. Instead, she took a step back.

She took a breath while he glared at her, fists tight and jaw clenched. "It's just me, Bird," she said finally, slowly backing out of his room. She wasn't two steps beyond the doorway before he threw the door closed, making it slam in a way that doors in old houses shouldn't.

A night lasted as long as a school day, Elsa was reminded, when you couldn't fix your kid's anguish. There was just no way to explain things adequately—not yet.

In her minivan the next morning, it was just Elsa. She stopped by the staff lounge to put her lunch in the refrigerator, and then she headed toward her classroom. She peered into Aneisha's room—empty—before entering her own and closing the door. She drank her coffee at her desk, and she felt alone.

After a few minutes of hearing more kids arriving in the hall, she propped the door open halfway and returned to her desk. A student still might come ask for help with an assignment or beg her to grant a test retake. But no one came. No one until Tiana Mosley leaned in to look, then returned to the hallway with her loud announcement: "Oh, she's in there all right."

The corner of her brain that was still thirteen years old said to find a way to retaliate, to tear Tiana and Claire to shreds. But Elsa was an adult. Hell, she was a veteran member of an elite team of professionals: middle school teachers were practically the Navy SEALs. To get through the day, then, Elsa went deep into tactics and maneuvers. To isolate, she leaned in to personal greetings, peeling kids off the herd as they entered. She created a distraction, lobbing the grenade of an unexpected quiz to make them forget their dramas. And she reinforced borders, promising various sanctions if these were not respected.

Weary but not defeated after the battle of her morning classes, Elsa went to get her lunch from the staff fridge.

She opened the door to the lounge and heard an abrupt stop to conversation. A teacher and two aides eating their lunches at the table now seemed exceptionally focused on their food.

"Friday really came," Elsa offered cheerily.

The new special ed aide said, "Right?" but then she opened her sandwich and became oddly intent on squaring up the lettuce with the cheese and meat strata.

Elsa hummed a Cure song to break the silence as she went to the fridge, but when she realized her choice was "Friday I'm in Love," she trailed off. As she reached the door to leave again, she started whistling an Elton John song about Saturday instead. She had never felt so thankful for a spinach salad lunch, which didn't need the microwave.

Back in her classroom eating, Elsa heard a rhythmic knock. It was Aneisha.

"Can I come in, darlin'?" she asked from beyond the threshold. Aneisha wouldn't have even asked, normally. When Elsa waved her in, her own mouth full of salad, Aneisha came and took a seat near Elsa's desk.

"What's up?" Elsa managed.

Aneisha kept her lips together, thinking. Then she tilted forward and extended a few fingers toward Elsa. "You know, that's pretty much my question right there. What's up? I want to know what you know about Thomas Humphrey, because there seems to be some talk."

Elsa sighed. She set down her fork. "I think it's mainly the girls that have this weird vibe going. I think there was a big crush on Thomas, and he didn't seem to be cooperating . . ."

Aneisha interrupted her. "I've seen Thomas come in here to visit you a few times now. And that doesn't bother me, even if it puts the other kids a little on alert. But Elsa. Now the boy's family is moving away."

Elsa nodded. *Exactly,* she wanted to sob. *I think his mother knows he's mine, and she's taking him away all over again.* But she would not cry.

"They are moving away," Elsa said as casually as she could. It was easier to contain herself if she didn't look directly at Aneisha. "And I have to say, I'm going to miss that kid." She stabbed a couple of pieces of her salad and put them in her mouth. When she finally looked at Aneisha, she was pretty sure she had enough of a lid on things to pass as just a little disappointed.

Aneisha kept her eyes on Elsa. After a few moments, she knocked on the desk and stood up. "You might want to consider going to Schusterman with this rumor, hon. Get ahead of this. You've already brewed up some mess a couple of times this year, and you know what they say about third times." She folded her arms and shook her head. She went to leave, turning back in the doorway to offer a brief smile. "You're a magnet for trouble, girl."

Elsa looked at her salad, which now seemed to be looking back at her. Schusterman? What could she say to him now, when she was still waiting for proof? She got up and locked her door, then pulled down the shade on its little window, a shade installed for use during active shooter incidents. Then she lay flat on the carpet behind her desk, focusing on the stress-reduction breathing she had learned from that Charlize Theron movie last summer. *In for four, hold for four, out for four, pause for four. Repeat.*

She would not go to Schusterman. She would simply float, letting time carry her forward until she had her evidence of the truth. Like someone famous had said: the truth will set you free. Probably that someone wasn't thinking of pedophilia, but still.

Once the final class of the day was underway and students were focused silently on their quizzes, Elsa no longer had to think about her breaths. Still, the ring of the phone made her flinch. It was the nurse calling from her office. Bird wasn't feeling well.

"He says he wants to go home immediately, and he wants me to call his dad," the nurse said. "But I thought hey, his mama is here, so maybe I can just keep him and then you can take him at the end of the day."

Bird had never taken himself to the nurse's office before, that Elsa could recall. She thought for a moment. Surely Bird didn't want to ride home with her, not when even looking at her enraged him. Why would he risk it? Then Elsa settled on the likely reason: the bus. The bus ride was far and away the least supervised portion of any schoolkid's day, a daily visit to the *Lord of the Flies* island. Surely someone on his bus—did he ride with Claire? Maybe Tiana or Faviola?—had remembered that this quiet student was actually the son of Elsa Vargas, child seductress.

She told the nurse to have Ham come take his son home, like Bird had asked. "I just can't get out of here soon enough myself," she said, looking out over the current field of enemy combatants.

Shortly after school ended, she called Ham to see how Bird was.

"He says his head really hurts. No fever or anything." This confirmed Elsa's suspicions. Ham continued. "I guess maybe there's something going around. Jennifer said she's sick and their holiday shindig is off tomorrow night."

"Oh, I must have missed that text."

"She left me a voice message, actually," Ham said.

Elsa offered to pick up some food on her way home. "Maybe some lemongrass soup will feel good if Bird's getting congested."

She ordered from the Thai place Bird had always liked. After scanning for any emails from MyTree one last time, she packed up and headed outside. She sent Jennifer a quick text from the warming minivan, to check on her. On the drive toward Selby Avenue, she felt her phone vibrating in her pocket: a message.

Once parked behind Taste of Thailand, she popped open the notification and read the response.

> Elsa. You need to know that things are not looking great. The Lowe Hills PTO is putting an agenda item on their next meeting that's about rumors. I think they mostly want to talk about one involving you and that kid Thomas.

She dropped her forehead to the steering wheel, closing her eyes. The PTO was her burning ring of fire. Finally she opened her eyes and read the message again. During her second reread, a follow-up message arrived.

> I'd advise you to talk to your union rep, Elsa. ASAP.

Then she realized that this hadn't been Jennifer texting back. These texts were from Craig, and he sounded a bit like the lawyer that he was. Elsa stared at her phone, her heart rate climbing.

Whoa. Thanks for telling me. She imagined herself amid licking flames, wearing an orange jumpsuit and handcuffs while Stan "Flat Stanley" Torgeson from the union bumbled to defend her. Her pulse was getting loud in her own ears. She dialed Jennifer; she needed someone to help her absorb this, sick or not sick. But her call went to voicemail immediately.

"Oh my God, please call me," Elsa said, her voice a bit shaky. "I know you're sick, but when you get this, please call. For real. And I'm going to bring you some soup," she decided. She hung up and tried to talk down the rising anxiety. *Right now, breathing. Next, entering the restaurant.*

Twenty minutes later, Elsa pulled up to Jennifer and Ted's. She saw that both cars were there and the lights were on, so she climbed out. She could see Jennifer in the kitchen, talking on her phone. Elsa started to feel better even as she rang the doorbell and moved into the pool of front porch light.

She was just about to ring it again when the door opened: Ted. He motioned her to back up a bit, joining her out on the stoop. "Elsa! What a surprise! I don't think you want to come in here. I don't know if you know that Jennifer is sick?"

Elsa frowned. "Yeah, I brought her some soup," she said. "What does she have, the plague?"

Ted shook his head. "She'll be OK, but she's had a fever, and she's coughing and stuff."

"I really don't mind. I won't touch her or anything. I just really kind of need to talk to her. There's some drama . . ." Elsa waited. But Ted didn't move to let her in. "Maybe I can just talk to her on the phone, though," she said, handing him the lemongrass soup.

"Yeah, maybe eventually," he said. "She's been asleep upstairs for hours now, all afternoon. She's pretty zonked." When Elsa didn't respond, Ted started nodding.

Elsa stood still. *Was she to pretend there were no eyes in her head?* Unsure what else to say, she nodded back at Ted. Finally she wished Jennifer a speedy recovery and said good night.

Tears began to percolate as she climbed back into her car, pulled away from their home, and headed for her own.

Chapter 29

A little smolder set by a few students would have burned out, Elsa knew. This wildfire, though, had moved beyond the underbrush to the serious fuel of grown-ups. Craig and Aneisha were right that it was time to get ahead of it.

More terrifying than the thought of Schusterman or the district was the thought of her whole family. Sooner or later, they would hear about a next Additional Item: *What kind of HOT stuff is Elsa Vargas teaching our children now?*

The real truth would explain it, of course. But that required proof.

Ham stole looks at her all through dinner. Elsa tried to wear a cheerful face as she gave soup to another pretend-sick refugee from the horror she had whipped up. "Feeling any better, Bird?" she asked, playing along for now. First, she would figure out how to talk to Ham; after that, she would move on to Bird.

Bird shrugged into his food. "I guess the headache is better," he said.

"Are we watching a movie tonight?" Garvey asked. "Maybe we could watch something Bird wants, since he's sick."

"Not tonight," Elsa said, overlapping with Bird's "No."

"Then can I play multiplayer in the basement with George and Perry?" Garvey asked.

Elsa looked at Ham, and they said that he could.

After the dishes were in the dishwasher, Ham grabbed Scoopy's leash and looked at Elsa in the kitchen. "Walk?" he asked.

Elsa nodded, beginning her crisis-control breathing.

"Something's up," Ham said as they hit the sidewalk.

"Well, here's one thing that's up," Elsa said after a moment. "Jennifer is avoiding me. She's not sick."

Ham frowned. "She said she was sick."

"She's not sick." Elsa told him about seeing Jennifer in her kitchen, and about Ted.

Ham looked totally perplexed. Then Elsa started to cry. She angled her head away from the streetlamp at the end of the block.

"They're avoiding me," she said, trying for composure. But she was starting to sputter, tears ripping themselves out more violently now. "I'm in a total mess, Ham. And I'm so, so sorry because this is going to suck for all of us."

Ham moved reflexively. He had her wrapped up now, so she let her quiet sobs fill his down jacket until she could steady herself. Then she stepped back just a bit, holding on to his arm. She noticed that Scoopy had chosen this moment to take a dump on the grass next to the street.

"Give me a poop sack," she said. She shoved her hand into the bag like a mitten. Then she grabbed the warm pile without hesitation, flipping the bag inside out around the poop and spinning it shut. She could do this.

"People are saying I have been having an inappropriate relationship with a male student," Elsa announced. Ham stood there as if she'd said nothing, so she continued. "They think I have seduced an eighth-grade boy, and so there's going to be a special PTO meeting to discuss this."

"What in the actual fuck . . . ?" Ham finally said. Elsa waited. He was looking at her, puzzled.

"It's not true. But I can see now that I gave him too much attention." She watched Ham frowning as she breathed in, held for four. "And he has been in my minivan."

"Why?"

"I gave him a ride to Izzy's, remember?"

Ham's face changed, loosening up. "That kid Thomas?"

The boy I heard you call son, Elsa thought. If only she had more to tell him, stamped and certified by MyTree.

His forehead creased again. "Jesus Christ. This is about the school board thing, then. People are accusing you because you came after their BOAs. Is that it? You're godless, so surely you're guilty of anything else they can think up?"

Elsa stood, stunned. Ham wasn't just on her side; he was recasting her as victim.

"Wow," she said. "I guess I didn't want to think that way about—"

"What a bunch of damn hypocrites!" Ham barked, cutting her off. "*Values* my ass. These are the character and values people, Elsa. But trying to ruin someone's reputation out of sheer vindictiveness—no problem." Ham had formed fists, and now he shoved them hard into his pockets.

Elsa frowned and nodded.

Ham shook his head for a minute. Then he spoke again. "Is Bird hearing this shit? And is your principal hearing it?"

Elsa nodded again. "This has to be why Bird didn't want to take the bus home. Or ride with me."

"Goddammit," Ham muttered, turning to look back toward their block.

After a long moment, Ham finally reached out to her and pulled her in for a hug.

"We need to talk to both of them," Elsa said.

Ham agreed. "Let's go around the playground first. I need a little more time."

They walked in silence for another block. Then Ham asked, "Can you ask Thomas to shut this down?"

Elsa explained that he'd been absent. She stopped short of telling Ham about the move, for now.

"His mom told me to leave him alone," she said. "I'm not sure what she thinks happened, but I don't think she's the type to ask the PTO to keep talking about this."

"Maybe you should try to reach out to her and talk to her in person. I mean, this is a big deal. If she could see how this is tied to the Boys Of America thing . . . ?"

Elsa shook her head. "I don't think she'll want to talk to me again, Ham." But she kept thinking. "God, I just wish Jennifer wasn't avoiding me." Tears threatened again.

Ham reached out for Elsa's hand. "Yeah, that totally sucks. I bet Jennifer comes around eventually, Else. But right now, you got me."

Elsa closed her eyes for the next few steps, a drop rolling down her cheek. "It's just that Jennifer knows Katharine Humphrey some, Thomas's mom. She could talk to her, maybe."

Ham slowed. "What, now?"

"They're in that book club together. I was thinking maybe she could, I don't know . . . talk to Thomas's mom," Elsa said. "But Jennifer's probably going to just keep on avoiding me. And Ted too, I guess."

Ham had stopped altogether. He turned away and grabbed his hair. "My God, Elsa." After a moment he turned toward her again. "Fuck."

"Yeah."

Ham held out Scoopy's leash abruptly. "Take him home." Then he shook his head, turned, and started walking down the sidewalk away from them. "I'm new to this whole mess, OK? I'll be home in a bit," he announced without turning toward her. He sounded angry.

She stood with Scoopy and watched him go. Then Elsa looked down, clocking that she was still holding hands with a bag of shit.

With Ham still not back an hour later, Elsa gathered up the boys without him. She asked Garvey to join Bird in his room, and then she got directly to the point, laying out the inappropriateness that people suspected her of.

"None of it is true. I would never have romantic thoughts about a kid, and I would never cheat on your dad even with an adult," Elsa said clearly, looking into each of their faces.

"Why do they think that?" Garvey asked, disgusted.

"Your dad thinks it has something to do with our role in the Boys Of America fight," she said. It felt important for the boys to hear that their dad was on her side. "Maybe some people think I don't hold family values or something."

With these rumors acknowledged, Bird's body looked like someone had finally flipped off the current from a taser. But Garvey stared at Elsa, building up like steam in a kettle. His mouth and his fists started to show the pressure first. Finally he went off, leaping to grab his brother's pillows and whack them against the wall, screaming as he thumped. Elsa and Bird looked at each other, their eyebrows going up at the same time. Bird shrugged.

"I realize now that this was kind of an elephant in the room for you, Bird," Elsa said, moving closer to Bird to be heard over the shrieks. "I'm sorry I didn't say something sooner. I wanted to think it was going away."

Bird frowned and nodded. Then he turned to his brother, holding out an old robot throw pillow. "Use this one instead, Garvey. I don't care if it explodes. But watch out for my plants."

Garvey flopped onto the bed instead and started kicking and pounding the mattress.

"I don't think the elephant has left the building though, Bird," Elsa said. "I think we might have you take some days away from Lowe Hills. It's a tough place for you to have to be right now."

Bird shrugged at the floor. "Yeah. I wasn't planning on going back."

There was just the one week left before winter break now. Elsa agreed that Bird could just stay home for the week, unless and until things came to an early resolution.

Monday did not bring an early end, but instead a more official start to the crisis. At lunchtime, the secretary at the front desk called to ask Elsa to come to Schusterman's office.

"It's about your son," she said.

That was only half true. After inquiring about Bird's health, Schusterman asked Elsa if she wouldn't like to stay home to look after her boy. "This would be your choice," he suggested. Then he sat back in his cheap leather office chair, fingers like a steeple. "The fact is that if it needs to be my choice, we'll want to involve the union representative. I'm sure you are aware that we have some unpleasant rumors."

Elsa thought about Flat Stanley, and her commitment to her collectively bargained rights weakened. "Thank you. I should really take care of Bird, yes."

Back in her room, Elsa sat at her desk and took in the empty seats. In fifteen minutes, her class would file in, discovering that Elsa had been replaced for the afternoon by the assistant principal. The halls would echo with the live update: Ms. Vargas is out!

Her attention settled on where Thomas had sat. She closed her eyes and imagined for just a moment.

He would look over at her and grin. "Can we tell them?" Thomas would ask. Darnell and Claire would lean forward.

"You can tell them," Elsa would say.

"Hang on to your socks, people. Ms. Vargas turns out to be my mom!"

Claire's mouth would drop open, but then she would turn to Elsa. "That's wonderful!" she'd gush, pulling out her phone to send a group text to all the mothers.

But none of this would happen. Instead, the class would simply have no Thomas—and now no Elsa either. She would be on an extended winter break. She rolled that word around in her own mouth: *break*. It was what you did in case of emergency.

Her eyes landed on Phillipe the Philodendron on the back counter near the window. Three weeks was too long. Would three weeks be all?

Minutes later, she made her way to the end of the hallway, loaded down with a full tote bag, her winter coat, and Phillipe. She leaned against the exit door with her butt, but the first side she tried was locked. As she moved to the other, she caught sight of Claire coming down the hall, probably for something in her locker. Claire ducked into the restroom, but not before their eyes had connected.

"A Merry Christmas to you and your mother, Claire," Elsa called out.

If there was one thing a Minnesotan knew how to do, it was how to wield *nice* like a knife.

Chapter 30

That afternoon she tapped on Bird's bedroom door, and he told her to come in. She sat down on the edge of his bed, where he lay on his stomach looking into his tablet.

"They sent me home for the week because of the rumor," she said. Before heading to the house, she had driven to a park along the Mississippi River and walked through now-barren deciduous forest to sit on the cold sand of the riverbank for a bit.

"I know," he said, turning to show her his device. His eyes looked a bit red. The screen showed a meme with an infamous woman teacher and her young student lover. Teachers: changing the world one student at a time.

"Oh, man. Someone sent you Mary Kay LeTourneau." Elsa shook her head. Mary Kay had seduced her young student, gone to jail, and then married him. Her case had been big news in Seattle years and years back. "I am so sorry, Bird."

He turned back over. "I know."

She asked him what he'd been up to today, but he didn't answer.

After a moment he shrugged and gave a bit of a lilting grunt version of "I don't know."

"Well." Elsa slapped her lap and stood up. "I guess while we're in the holiday spirit, I might as well go dig out some decor. This seems like just the time for a string of Santa lights on the front porch."

Bird turned to look at her as she paused in the doorway, and she saw him smirk just a little. For an eighth grader, sarcasm and irony were like candy.

After reheating the leftover coffee in a mug and spiking it with Baileys, Elsa headed for the Christmas storage in the basement. As she dug past the tree ornaments and the stash of wrapping paper and gift bags, she saw the little toy Nativity set that her mother had given the boys when they were small. Today it made her laugh, and she pulled it out. Somehow setting these little plastic pieces out seemed just right: Ham and Garvey would love it.

She was reminded of the Nativity scene outside the church where they held Inga's funeral. Marcy's church, because Marcy had arranged everything. There they sat, two carved wooden parents looking down at their precious baby, still theirs and not yet defined by all that would come.

She dumped the plastic toys out of their box and onto the coffee table in the living room, sheep and shepherd crooks and regal capes and crowns joining the holy family and their exhausted donkey. She picked up the baby. Eventually she realized that his hay and its stand were two separate pieces, and she put him on top of both. Then she set Mary up next to him. "Don't let him out of your sight," Elsa advised.

Garvey arrived home just after four, and he slammed the door as he came in. He threw his backpack on the entryway floor and stormed into the kitchen. Elsa arrived in the doorway in time to see him crash the door to the snack cupboard closed. He plunked himself down on a stool and dropped his face angrily onto his folded-up arms on the counter.

"Another day in paradise?" Elsa asked.

"Justin was telling everybody on the bus about the stupid rumor," Garvey said. "Plus he's a BOA. Of course." He decided against his chosen snack, shoving the unopened granola bar across the counter at her. Then he went to the freezer, coming back with the gallon bucket of ice cream. This was not an approved after-school snack, but he wasn't asking. He opened the silverware drawer and pulled out a spoon.

"Justin needs to get a life," Elsa said. She grabbed herself a spoon and took the stool next to Garvey. "Should we get bowls or anything?"

Garvey smiled and shook his head. They each stabbed a spoon into the potholed vanilla tundra that remained in the bucket and filled their mouths with cold.

"I like Thomas," Garvey said.

Elsa nodded. "I know you do, Sweets." Her eyes felt sour. She got off the stool and moved behind Garvey's line of sight. She put her hands on his shoulders and squeezed. Then she stepped back and pulled out her phone, checking again for any news from MyTree. Nothing—not even from Jennifer.

She stared out the window and relaxed into daydreaming. "Garvey, there's one more Christmas gift for you, one that I couldn't wrap," she let herself imagine saying. "You have another big brother."

Next she imagined a lab-coated scientist dropping some kind of liquid from a little dropper into the saliva samples she had sent, and then watching for the result. How long could it take, for Chrissake? All she needed was a simple yes. She didn't need whatever else was holding things up.

After dinner, Elsa got a text. It was Krista. Elsa. W.T.F. Then she announced that she was on her way over.

Elsa opened the door minutes later, and Krista grabbed her in a hug. "Holy shit, Else." Then she held Elsa at arm's length and looked at her as she reported what she had heard: that Elsa had apparently had sex with a student in a car. Elsa's stomach felt kicked in.

"I don't get why this is happening to you," Krista said. She hugged her again.

Elsa grabbed her own coat and stepped out into the cold enclosed porch, closing the door to the house so that they could have a moment away from the kids' ears. Elsa was halfway into her coat when a whimper escaped, and then her chest gave a quiet heave. Krista wrapped her up and rocked her for a good two minutes.

When she could talk again, Elsa gave her the Ham interpretation: probably related to stirring up the BOA hornet's nest. But this didn't feel very true. Elsa shifted instead to a more confessional tone.

"I gave this boy a *lot* of attention, Krista. I went to his soccer game, and I had him share my umbrella." She reminded Krista of what that would be like for a boy Bird's age.

"Oh my God—Bird." Krista grabbed her arm. "So he's hearing all of this too? Jesus Christ, he's had to picture his mother fucking one of his classmates."

Elsa nodded. "Thank you for that."

Krista turned toward the window now, her mouth open and her hand holding the top of her head, which she was shaking.

"And Mrs. Ballinger," she added now, thinking of their old neighbor and occasional babysitter. "Oh my God, Elsa, Mrs. Ballinger and all the Master Gardeners will be hearing this from their bridge clubs and knitting circles. They're eating their macaroni salad and gossiping about you doing filthy, filthy things."

"Dr. Ramani will imagine my mouth in horrible places while he's checking my fillings," Elsa added. Krista put her hand over her own mouth, but Elsa could see her eyes starting to crinkle.

Krista took her hand away. "I think you can skip hanging your stocking this year, Else. You are *so* on the naughty list."

Elsa opened the door between the porch and the rest of the house. "Glad to be of some entertainment value for you," she said, pointing to Krista's boots in a command that she take them off. Elsa leaned into the house to sleuth out who was where. The boys and Ham were still in the basement, and none had acknowledged the sound of Krista. Elsa pulled her into the kitchen and told her about Jennifer.

"Well, that's not exactly shocking," Krista said. "And you know Mom will try to turn this all pleasant."

"Oh my hell. So I have to tell Mom. And sooner or later I'm going to have to figure out what to actually do. I mean, I guess I have to defend myself." This meantime could stretch out awhile. Maybe just waiting for lab results would not be enough.

"So Ham thinks this is about you playing Super-atheist, then?" Krista said, folding her arms and leaning against the counter. "I wonder if you need a lawyer."

Elsa told her about Joanna, but expressed doubt that the ACLU wanted to spend their resources on slopping around in Elsa's mud.

"What does Ham think?"

Elsa shook her head and shrugged. Ham had hardly been there, and when he was home, he spent time with the boys instead of her. "He's . . . finding some space, taking some time to process." Elsa felt her eyes getting wet.

Krista threw her arms around Elsa again. "Goddammit, Ham." Then Krista detached and got out her phone. She asked for Joanna's number, her old bossy tone back. Elsa wiped her eyes and found the contact information.

"Good," Krista announced. "Oh my God, Elsa, we are totally living in an episode of *L.A. Law*, except for the L.A. part. Is this Joanna anything like that lawyer who was also on *The Partridge Family*?"

Elsa shook her head, managing a single chuckle.

"I bet she is," Krista insisted, dialing. Then she pointed to the stool. "Sit your butt down, Elsa. I got you."

Chapter 31

The Christmas spirit felt a little thin this year to Elsa, knowing what people were saying about her.

Aneisha left her a message when Elsa couldn't bear to pick up. "Are you seeing this, hon?" she asked, telling Elsa to get on the Lowe Hills parents' social media page. Elsa continued to get new notifications from her original Boys Of America posts on the elementary school site, but she hadn't ventured onto the middle school one. Aneisha thought she should defend herself, that her silence was not good. But Elsa refused to look.

Instead, Elsa worked at dousing this Christmas with as much Christmas goodness as she could manage. Candles and Christmas lights could still twinkle, and potatoes could still be transformed into sugared-up lefse. Each day, then, Elsa wrote up a new list and went about her errands, albeit not in the usual places.

The neighborhoods east of downtown St. Paul might as well have been Albania for most living in the Lowe Hills attendance area. But this year they had become Elsa's preferred shopping destination. There were potatoes and twinkle lights for sale there too, and the odds that anyone on the East Side would recognize her as *that math teacher* were slim. Still, the sense of conspicuousness she was trying to shake managed to sneak up on her. It could be just a stoplight, just a stranger glancing over at her, but it made her feel naked. She took to wearing a hat and sunglasses—small protections.

Since the walk when she had told him just days before, Ham had twice had to stay late at work. When he was home, he pulled the boys physically closer than usual: he put his hand on a shoulder, he hugged, he lay down next to them before they went to sleep. In the less frequent times when he was with Elsa, he seemed to swing between two poles. Sometimes he gave her an angry kind of support, railing against the people who would entertain such a horrible accusation against her. Other times he buried his face in her stomach or her shoulder and held on tight. It felt like shame. Maybe Ham felt some responsibility as an accomplice to the anti-BOAs rabble-rousing; maybe he felt ashamed for not protecting his family from this. Or could he actually have doubts about her relationship to Thomas? If he did, he deserved the shame, Elsa thought at first. Then again, he couldn't know what that relationship probably was; she certainly hadn't told him why she might be checking her inbox fifteen times a day.

On Wednesday, Elsa was walking in from the garage with a roll of bubble wrap and the new shipping tape dispenser—today was the last feasible day to send a box of gifts to Ham's family out west—when her phone rang. Because she had just texted Jennifer again, she felt a little lift of hope in her chest. But it was not Jennifer. It was Marcy.

"Mom?" she grimaced. It was past time to tell her.

"Elsa! Are you at home? I've just heard there's something terrible happening to you. Are you at home right now?"

Elsa scrunched up her face more, wishing the rest of her could shrink into a ball as well. "Shit. I'm at home, yes."

Marcy announced that she'd be there in ten minutes.

Elsa released a breath, letting her head drop backward and her shoulders sink. Then she looked at her phone to confirm that the call had ended.

And there was the notification. A new email from MyTree.

She scrolled through the introductory language, opened the attached report, and whipped through everything extraneous. Her shaking finger clicked on the Ancestry heading.

It took a moment to make sense of the evidence, but then clarity rang through her like a bell. Elsa had been right all along.

Chapter 32

Marcy Vargas had had to learn about the traumatic accusation against her daughter from her brother, David, of all people. He had come by to recaulk her tub, something her husband, Carlos, had always done. Her brother had shuffled around looking uncomfortable for a few minutes, then finally told her what he'd overheard in the lobby at the YMCA, after that stationary bicycling class he and his girlfriend did in the mornings before heading over to the medical school.

"These moms were talking about the junior high school. They said the math teacher, a Mrs. Vargas, was suspended without pay." He turned red. "They said there was some kind of hanky-panky with the boys. I don't know how many math teachers are called Mrs. Vargas, so I thought I'd better find out if you know about this misunderstanding." Then he went into the bathroom and started digging away at the old caulk while Marcy followed him, aghast. He had nothing more to say. Marcy called Krista at work to see if she knew what was going on with her sister. Krista confirmed the reality of this situation by groaning and telling Marcy not to get involved, then abruptly hanging up.

And so Marcy had phoned Elsa herself—sure enough, she was at home in the middle of the afternoon—and headed over to offer what support she could. Even as she put on her coat, she shivered to think of Bird and Garvey amid this kind of terribleness.

Walking up to the house, she saw splotches of muck on the front door and on the wall of the house. She smelled it as her eyes found bits of white shell: someone had thrown eggs at this home where her daughter and her grandchildren lived.

Knocking loudly on a clean part of the door, she let herself in. Scoopy was barking from upstairs, so she called out his name to let him know she wasn't an intruder. She heard a bedroom door opening, then the staccato mayhem of the dog's nails as he raced down to greet her.

"Hi, Grammy!" Bird stood at the top of the stairs, behind the dog.

Marcy pasted a smile on her face and gushed another hello to them both. Then she looked at her wristwatch. "Are you home sick?" She realized the likely explanation just as she finished asking.

Bird came toward her for a hug, and he hesitated only a moment. "It's OK, I'm not contagious," he said. "I had a really bad headache earlier."

Marcy put her arms around him and rubbed his back. "I hear your mom is home too." It felt wrong not to acknowledge why, but she couldn't be sure how Elsa and Ham were handling this. If Marcy had learned one thing from dealing with Carlos's mother, it was that grandmothers are most helpful when they follow rather than lead.

"In here, Mom," Elsa called from the kitchen. Her voice sounded different.

Marcy sent Bird back upstairs to get more rest. When she heard his door close, she went into the kitchen to find Elsa at the back of the little pantry room, looking out its small window. She put a hand on her daughter's back. Elsa stayed turned away, but Marcy was patient. After a minute she spoke. "I'm here, Elsa."

Elsa shook her head, then finally turned around. She had tears on her cheeks, but she also had a smile. She grabbed on to Marcy, then a sputter of laughter broke out of her. It brought Carlos to Marcy's mind, somehow.

She tried to laugh with her daughter, but she couldn't. "This *is* ridiculous," she managed.

Elsa stifled another laugh.

"Oh, Elsa. How did this accusation even happen? You poor thing."

Elsa shook her head again.

"This boy Thomas and I just connected, Mom," Elsa explained. Her eyes animated with happiness as she said this. Marcy nodded, inspecting her daughter's face. She must have frowned, because Elsa suddenly turned red and grabbed Marcy's arm. "No, Jesus, nothing like that. It's just more than I can explain right now. I just . . . I have to talk to Ham first, and Bird . . ." Then Elsa trailed off, and her face filled with something dark and anxious. She looked at the ceiling—or at the upstairs beyond it, perhaps—and then at her hands. Tears started to puddle in Elsa's eyes.

Marcy held very still. There was more going on than she could make sense of.

Elsa finally turned her eyes toward her again and started to speak, but then she squeezed her eyebrows down. "No." She moved past Marcy and went into the living room.

She waited a beat before following her daughter, choosing a seat on the other end of the sofa and waiting in silence. Finally Elsa launched herself to the coat rack in the entry and grabbed two coats, holding one out and announcing that they needed to go for a drive.

Two miles later, Elsa directed Marcy into a restaurant parking lot and pointed at a spot on the far edge, one facing the alley fence. Marcy put the car in park as Elsa turned toward her.

"Mom, I just found out, and it . . . it's real, Mom. This boy Thomas. He's my son. I've had his DNA tested, and he is my son."

Marcy's eyes gave a slow blink, then another. She had heard the words, but they didn't make sense. *Son?* Had she missed a part of Elsa's life? How could an extra pregnancy . . . ? There was Inga, but after that Marcy could recall no month, even, that she hadn't seen her daughter live and in person.

"I don't understand."

Elsa reached out and grabbed Marcy's hand. "Bird is not my flesh and blood, Mom. The babies were switched just like I thought."

Marcy stared at Elsa. "There were babies switched? What?"

Elsa nodded. She'd started crying again, and she managed to choke out that Bird was someone else's baby, just like she suspected. "Bird and Thomas were . . . confused."

"Confused?"

"But no one is going to take Bird away, Mom. I mean, if that were a possibility, then I would never say a word about the DNA." Then Elsa covered her face with both hands and broke into sobs. "I don't . . . I just found out, just now . . ."

Marcy reached out to her, put her hand on her daughter's arm. She tried to think through the scenario Elsa had laid out to her. *Babies switched, and now a reunion?* Marcy could feel her own heart rate accelerating.

Finally Elsa regained some control. She started saying something about Thomas's mother—really Bird's mother, she corrected herself.

Marcy let go of Elsa and turned to face forward. *Bird's mother?* Finally she spoke. "How could babies be switched? And what do you mean, just like you thought?"

"Everyone brushed it aside like I was just still crazy. And I knew what would happen if I insisted, so I just . . ." She put her hands to her face and started shaking her head. "I fucked up. But . . . Bird."

"Dear God. You thought you had the wrong baby?" Marcy couldn't imagine. She thought of all the years that Elsa had struggled to let go of poor Inga, how her imagination had infiltrated reality and stuck Elsa in a delusional limbo. "Why on earth didn't they get you a blood test, to be sure?"

Her daughter's expression was sharp. "Because you all were so sure I was being crazy again. Because Ham would have left me if I was like that again. And then after a while, I . . . I couldn't give up Bird."

"Oh, Elsa. I wish I had known all of this."

"You knew! Krista . . . you all said I needed to stop with all this, for Ham's sake."

Marcy shook her head. She imagined how it would feel to have lost her baby Elsa, or Krista for that matter—to have a baby placed in her arms who was not her own. "No, Elsa. I certainly would have gotten you that blood test. You of all people needed to be able to trust reality. I didn't know." She thought briefly of Ham, but she didn't have the capacity to layer anger on top of all this. Instead, she reached out to Elsa. "I wish I'd been there to fix things for you." But events in the past were done. They couldn't go back and redo that now.

"Mom. If you'd been able to fix it, then I wouldn't have Bird at all."

Marcy felt shot. *No Bird?* She threw her hand to her own chest and shuddered.

Elsa leaned over, head landing against Marcy's shoulder. She held her daughter. After a minute passed like that, Elsa straightened, reached over for the key in the ignition, and turned it.

"Ready to go home?" Marcy asked. Her mind felt too overloaded to drive yet.

"No. Let's stay. I just wanted the heater." Elsa punched the button for her seat warmer. Marcy did the same, and they sat next to each other, staring at the chain-link fence in front of them. It was the kind with strips of green woven through, not to offer more strength but to obscure what might lie beyond. Marcy's eyes traced a strip while she tried to process.

Elsa eventually spoke again. "I know this is all crazy. I mean, it's totally complicated and heart wrenching because Bird doesn't know, and it's got this whole teacher seduction thing swirling around it that's eating us alive." She dropped her head against the headrest and closed her eyes. The furrow of her eyebrows released. "But the thing is, I need a chance to feel happy."

Marcy watched Elsa's face gradually fill up with light. Then her daughter smiled at her again. "Mom, I found my son. And you and Krista are going to love him."

Chapter 33

Elsa had not intended to tell her mother first. Having done so, though, she felt grateful for the scrimmage before the big-time events of telling Ham and Bird. It was a mess, it turned out, trying to absorb it and explain it simultaneously. Inside her, waves of different emotions grew and peaked at different times, like sounds not quite falling into rhythm or harmony. Instead of the clear ring of angels finally singing, Elsa's interior was the cacophony of the middle school band room.

As they drove back toward Elsa's, Marcy offered to take Bird and Garvey to her place for the night. They could help their grandma make rosettes, fussy little cookies that both Krista and Elsa had refused to master. Elsa agreed, needing the evening without them. She understood that her mother aimed to give her time to talk to Ham, but all Elsa wanted was some time for feeling the happiness. *Thomas, truly and really her son.* If only she could see him now, find out how he looked when she finally had certainty.

"Do you know that your house has had eggs thrown at it?" her mother asked as they pulled up.

Elsa did not. It barely sunk in; this was nothing, almost, a single wrong note amid her musical mayhem.

"Maybe I should pull into the garage instead, then, so the boys won't have to use the front door."

Elsa pictured her garage, and the minivan parked inside it. It was such a conspicuous vehicle.

"Mom," Elsa said. "I wonder if you could take my car instead. I could get yours washed, to thank you for being so wonderful . . . ?" She knew her mother loved a clean car. More importantly, Marcy did not love bumper stickers or unusual features. Her car did not scream *that Vargas woman*. It was exactly what Elsa needed, just for an hour or two.

Her mother looked at Elsa for a moment, reaching out to fix her collar. Then she fished her keys out of her handbag and held them out to Elsa. "You be careful, Elsa." Elsa nodded and offered her own keys, in trade.

Elsa went up to fetch Bird while Marcy found Garvey. Fear set in first. How many more interactions would they have where Bird could simply see her as his mother—as honest? Next she felt shame. Surely the thought that she wasn't his mother had never occurred to him; it would be a blindside. How had she let herself perpetrate such a massive and ongoing deceit? She hadn't even been comfortable claiming that Santa Claus was real, for Chrissake.

"Bird?" she said, tapping on his door. He was listening to music, so she walked into his room and waved her arms at him like she was flagging down a car in a blizzard. He pulled off his headphones and gave her a bit of a smile.

She sat down next to him on the bed and told him about the invitation to go to Grammy's, reaching out to twirl a coil of his beautiful hair as she spoke. He was happy to go. He got up to look in the mirror, tucking his hair back to how he liked it. Then he turned.

"Mom, I'm really sorry this has blown up on you and stuff. I get that Thomas was just . . . you know, the kind of kid you like being around."

Elsa froze. "I like being around you, Bird. You are exactly the kind—" but he cut her off.

"It's fine, Mom. I'm just saying, you didn't really deserve all this." He moved toward the closet and dug around for his running shoes, then shoved them on and left the room without looking her way again.

Elsa waved at them at the back door as they left for her minivan. She reminded Scoopy that the boys weren't leaving forever. She squatted down beside him and kneaded the fur on his neck and ears.

"We'll be OK, Scoops. You know how it is. I'm not your real mom either, and we still do just fine." Scoopy pivoted his back end toward her, so she scratched above his tail for him. "If it was easy to tell your kid he's not your kid, then everyone would be doing it." After a bit, Scoopy seemed satisfied, so Elsa got up and walked into the kitchen. She opened the refrigerator and stared inside. Her eyes found a container just like the ones Taste of Thailand used, and thoughts of Jennifer tried to rise. Elsa shoved them back down: too many things.

While the fridge glared back at her, Ham phoned to say that he'd be home late from work again. Elsa felt some relief. She wasn't ready.

She went to stare out the pantry window again. She wasn't delusional now; it wasn't a lie. Thinking about Thomas now was just anticipation. She felt for her mother's car keys in her pocket, eagerness running through her gut.

She knew where the Humphrey family lived, if they hadn't yet moved. It was only once that she had driven by, needing to see. Today, there was a good chance that the Humphreys wouldn't be there. After all, Schusterman's email had implied that they were going to Iowa immediately. But that email had also given a reason that had nothing to do with how Thomas and Elsa were connected, so if Katharine had lied about that, then she might have lied about the timing as well. Thomas might be at his home in St. Paul right now.

She went to the entry to grab her coat, fingers passing her usual orange wool one and settling instead on the black down everywoman's jacket. She saw Bird's plain olive-green Carhartt beanie resting on the radiator, and she pulled that on as well. Then she headed out to her mother's little Toyota.

It was only a ten-minute drive to Thomas's neighborhood. Halfway down Snelling Avenue, the autopilot in her almost turned just after the veterinarian's office: a left here would take her to Jennifer and Ted's. She turned on the radio, scanning away from the easy listening station.

She turned right onto the block before the Humphreys', feeling the adrenaline quicken her heart rate as she slowed the car. It was dark now, and a block off the main avenue the streetlamps were more sparse. Elsa glanced at herself in the overhead mirror, pulling her hair forward a bit more across her jaw and drawing the hat down lower on her forehead. She turned down the radio, then at the four-way stop, she killed the music altogether. Checking all her rearview mirrors, she considered turning off her lights and decided that was worse. She turned left toward his street.

Headlights were coming from the left, where Thomas's house sat in the middle of the block. Elsa held her breath, dipping her face toward her lap while the other car went past her. *I'm not even in my own car. It's dark.* She monitored her breathing for a moment. *And I'm not a criminal.* She turned onto his street, her eyes immediately scanning the north side and then resting on the two-story house that sat just a slight bit higher than the two before it.

Some lights were on in the front windows of the first floor. It reminded her of seeing Jennifer in her lit-up kitchen, and a moment of shame shocked through Elsa. She gave her head a quick shake. *I'm not a gross molester. I'm his mother.*

There was a car parked on the street on the Humphreys' side, but not directly in front of their house. Elsa rolled by, too cautious to stop, but as she approached the end of the block, she knew she couldn't yet go home. Instead, she turned twice to enter the alley running behind the garages on his block. His would be the fourth house in, maybe the fifth. She slowed to a trawling pace, looking at each garage for a house number.

Just as she thought she might be at Thomas's garage, the one next to it began opening. She braked in horror. Then she backed her mother's car up a bit, moving farther to the side in the alley the way one did to make room. She slumped behind the steering wheel. What if she had miscalculated, and the Humphreys were about to back out and point their headlights this direction?

Instead of a car, she saw a man walk out of the garage with a full kitchen bag. He was Black: not Thomas's dad. He lifted the lid on his dark poly cart next to the garage and tossed in his trash. Then he went back into the garage, and a moment later the automatic garage door started its trip back down.

Elsa's eyes went to the garage she had figured was Thomas's, and to the second-story windows on the back of the house. No lights—or was that a glow, blocked by a shade? She moved her head forward to the windshield, and the glow seemed to move with her: just a reflection, then. She let go of the brake and rolled through the rest of the alley.

She turned back onto Thomas's street and pulled over two houses west of his house. From here, she could see if anyone came in or out of the front. Elsa stared at the door, waiting.

Time passed easily. It was overdue, this space of nothing in which to absorb her new reality. It had angles, this new truth, and you had to walk around in it the way you might take in an art installation. This tall house, for instance—this was where Bird would have grown up. He would have been called Thomas, and he would have had family in Iowa. He might have had a math teacher named Ms. Vargas one year, and never met Garvey or Ham in his life.

And Thomas Humphrey? He was Thomas now, but he wasn't *really* Thomas. He was Baird, her tiny boy who had started off with blue eyes, amazing her with his very aliveness as she held him in her arms. He was the baby she had let float away to an unknown life, to events inside this house that she had done nothing about. There were always scars; even parents who didn't inflict abuse couldn't protect their children from moments of terror, tangles with shame, and the way wills got bent to those in power. A family, Elsa knew, had a secret internal logic that set the dials on its children, adjusting the amplitudes and magnitudes until they grew into something genes alone couldn't explain. She wondered if Thomas would resent her for the way he had been sculpted inside this house.

What if Thomas walked out that front door into the evening all by himself? She imagined stepping out of the car and calling to him. She tried out words in her head that might come next, imagining both her own and his.

But then a person did appear. It was a woman on the sidewalk ahead of Elsa, entering and then leaving the direct light of a streetlamp with her wiggly little mop of a dog. It looked like that mom of a herd of high schoolers, somebody Windell. Elsa condensed into something smaller, moving slowly like prey.

The jittery little dog gave a yip just ten feet ahead of where Elsa sat, and the woman turned alert, scanning. Her eyes seemed to catch on the Toyota, and Elsa felt a rush of terror. She turned her face away from the woman, toward the street. *Fuck. Why does a person just sit in a car?* Panicked, she reached for her phone and held it to her ear. She nodded, as if in conversation, and the traitorous phone brightened and shone on her cheek.

When the Windell woman had disappeared around the next corner, Elsa sat up and reached for the key in the ignition. Her eyes clung to Thomas's house as she drove past, out to the main thoroughfare. She tapped the seat heater on and remembered her mother. Marcy knew about this new grandson, Elsa thought. He was *real.* Elsa might be skulking around like some kind of sketchy stalker, but the truth was on her side.

She thought of her mother's insistence that she would have gotten Elsa the blood test. It was overwhelming, how much would have been different. But she couldn't have a past with Thomas without having no Bird at all. There was nothing to do but let it go.

Her brain went to the Disney song. She hummed "Let It Go" to herself, trying.

A left onto Snelling pointed her back toward home—toward telling Ham. Once he knew, they would be together in this. And they were a team that could take on anything.

Chapter 34

After Elsa had forced herself to eat a late dinner of Cheerios, Ham finally texted that he was on his way home. She warned him about the eggs on their front door, right where a wreath should have hung, and he updated her on the latest social media topic: even if she hadn't had sex with that boy, it was only because pedophiles groomed kids first.

Once she had trudged her weary body upstairs, she felt drawn to Bird's room. Maybe it was a need for penance, for this eagerness for Thomas. She lay down on Bird's bed and wrapped her arms around herself.

She'd been there for twenty minutes when Ham poked his head in the open door. "There you are," he said, coming into the room. Elsa sat up, and he sat beside her, both of them backing up to lean against the wall behind Bird's twin bed. She could let Ham decompress for a moment, she thought, while she prepared for how she would begin.

They looked around the tidy room. Shelves neatly displayed Bird's collection of brachiopod fossils and Petoskey stones and his rows of sci-fi and fantasy books, including four full series. He had one poster showing the galaxy with a *YOU ARE HERE* arrow and another showing the evolution of man, beginning with an ape and ending with a man playing the French horn.

Ham reached out and put a hand on Elsa's thigh. "How's Bird dealing with it all today?"

She almost snorted. If Ham thought having a mother accused of molestation was hard, wait until he contemplated Bird finding out he wasn't theirs.

Elsa moved herself to face Ham, and she picked up his hand and held it in her lap. "I have to talk to you about something else."

Ham looked frightened, but she forged ahead. Fear had no power to change things.

"Do you remember at the hospital when we had Baird, how I was so afraid our baby was switched? Well, it turns out I was right. We'll still love and parent our Bird. But he's not biologically ours. And now I've found our true son."

Ham registered only confusion.

"Our babies were switched, and I found him. I had his DNA tested, Ham. It's Thomas." Ham stared at her. She pushed onward. "I've been suspecting he was ours, so I submitted his DNA without him knowing about it." She told him how she had tricked Thomas into spitting into a vial, and how she had finally gotten results just today.

Ham shook his head. He looked at the Milky Way poster for another minute, processing. Then he looked back at Elsa, frowning. "What do you mean, you had his DNA tested? What does that mean?"

"I used MyTree," Elsa said. "I sent in his saliva. And I . . . well, I sent in yours too." She cringed exaggeratedly. "I might have, like, kind of soaked up your drool one night with this little sponge thingy . . ." Admittedly, it had been skeevy of her, Ham sleeping blissfully through her covert maneuvers in the dark with the sponge on a stick. But sometimes you had to stoop pretty low and ask forgiveness later. After all, sending in Ham's instead of her own had been a stroke of strategic genius: he didn't have that inconvenient blood relationship. Lois was not his aunt.

Ham's face tightened up. "You took my drool to test my DNA against this kid's."

"I'm sorry, but yes. I would have used mine. But, well, I had to avoid popping up on my Aunt Lois's chart, so it was better if it was yours . . ."

"And you didn't think I had a right to know anything about this."

Her volume increased. "Ham, please hear me. There is a big giant piece of news here, and it is not that I stole your drool with a sponge on a stick. It is that we have found our actual flesh-and-blood son. Bird and Thomas were switched. You know I couldn't tell you what I believed, right? I couldn't tell you how that sense just didn't go away, that this child was not really Baird . . ." She couldn't think of more words that would help now. She needed him to get to the part where he understood: Thomas was their son.

Ham kept his eyes and his hands closed tight. He sat that way for half a minute. "Fuck," he said.

"But, Ham . . . it's not all fuck," Elsa tried. "It's also not fuck. We won't lose Bird; there's no way that could ever happen. We're his parents now. We just . . . we also have Thomas, even if we don't *have him* have him." Ham did not open his eyes or release his hands.

After another minute, Elsa tried again. "Ham, we have a new son. And he's a great kid."

Ham got up and walked past her, into the hallway. He went downstairs, and Elsa waited only a moment before following him. She, too, could use a shot of whatever he was probably about to pour.

After the whiskey, Ham began crisscrossing the house: it was not so much pacing as it was erratic bursts of walking. Finally he took a position in the doorframe between the entry and the kitchen. Then he spoke.

"Elsa, this is insane. This is about Inga. I know that her death made something go very wrong with you. But I can't believe you let that come back and mess with your head about Bird. Your son Bird, Elsa. He wasn't switched, he was just, I don't know—not Inga. I can't let you fuck with Bird's life like this."

Elsa's mouth fell open. "What? Ham, you aren't understanding. We can decide what we tell Bird, or what we don't, but he isn't our biological son."

Ham slammed the side of his fist against the wall. "Elsa! They put an ID bracelet on Baird right in front of me, when they got him out of you! He had a red splotch on the back of his neck I *know* I saw immediately, and you know that didn't go away for like a year! Of course he is ours! You were just nuts!"

"I have the genetic results, Ham. Thomas is our son."

Ham gave his head a couple of violent shakes. His face turned red and his voice sounded off, ready to cry. "Goddammit, Elsa. Thomas's DNA matches mine because I'm his father. I'm his father"—he dragged in breath, his voice now shaking—"because apparently Katharine gets pregnant pretty damn easily. I slept with her one time. One time, and it was—I just, I broke, right after that time I left you in Duluth."

Ham's eyes were overbrimming. "Thomas isn't your son, Elsa. He's mine."

Elsa stood frozen in place.

Ham moved toward her tentatively, but Elsa stepped back. Then he launched forward and veered around her, heading toward the back door. "I have to get out of here," he said, now high pitched. At the back door, he fumbled to undo the deadbolt. "I'm sorry," he yelled at the door. Finally he threw it open, stormed through, and slammed it closed behind him.

And then it was quiet.

Elsa's head was pulsing, a jumble. Ham had cheated? She looked around the empty kitchen, silent and hollow. She went to touch the doorframe where he had been; it was solid and steady. But Ham had cheated.

Ham had made another baby. Katharine's baby.

Elsa felt the emptiness starting to pull. Thomas wasn't their Baird, lost for so long and finally found. He wasn't Elsa's baby at all.

First Elsa slid to the kitchen floor, then her body crawled her toward the radiator. It remembered this hole. She pulled herself into a ball, fetal, and hugged her knees desperately against her cheek.

If Thomas wasn't her baby, then who was? She had nothing to go on to find him now. The son she had let go of was just gone.

Chapter 35

When Marcy picked up the phone and heard Elsa's wailing, she immediately went around to Krista's door, carrying the phone with her. While she listened to Elsa, she covered the phone and told her other daughter to get the boys from her side and turn off the stove, which was heating oil for rosettes. The boys would have to stay with Krista tonight while she went to help Elsa.

Eventually through the sobbing into her neck, Marcy understood where things stood now. Ham had a son, but the boy was not Elsa's. And somehow—most heart wrenching of all—Elsa still could not understand this as meaning Bird was truly her own. She brought her daughter back to her duplex and put her to bed, holding her until she finally cried herself to sleep.

At five in the morning, she called her brother, David, knowing he arrived at that indoor bicycling class by six and at the medical school by eight. "It's Marcy. I need you to arrange a blood test, and I need it to happen today," she decreed.

By nine, they had an appointment for noon. She told the boys she was concerned about their nutrition in this time of crisis and all she wanted for Christmas was for them to get a full nutrient panel. This required a blood draw. Elsa, she announced, would get one alongside them.

After the appointment in Minneapolis, she took them out for lunch at a vegetarian restaurant farther still from St. Paul and made a show of pointing out healthy proteins. She did her best to cover for Elsa's dazed silence and her total failure to eat, and then she returned the boys to their home.

The following morning at eleven, David called to confirm exactly what Marcy had expected.

"What took you so long?" she asked him.

She went directly to her bedroom, where Elsa had reburied herself beneath the covers with the old green teddy bear that Marcy had clearly not hidden well enough.

She sat next to the mound that was her daughter and pulled blankets away from her face. "Elsa, honey. He's yours."

Her daughter blinked twice, then sat upright. "Bird?"

"Everything is OK. The blood test came back. Bird is definitely your baby."

Elsa tore off the covers and ran out of the room, leaving Marcy still perched on the bed. In half a minute, Elsa reappeared, her feet in their shoes and her coat all but zipped. She threw her arms around Marcy, tipping her over onto the puffiness.

"I'm real! He's real!" Elsa started to laugh, and Marcy started to cry.

Then her daughter wriggled back to standing, holding out a hand toward Marcy. "What are you waiting for, Mom? You have to take me home to my two sons."

Chapter 36

Katharine was unpacking the box of Thomas's books and sports magazines in her mother-in-law's spacious house when she heard a notification on her phone.

It was the text she had hoped never to receive.

> I know now that Thomas is my son.

Ham asked her next to confirm that this number was right, that this was Katharine, but she didn't reply. Maybe if she said nothing, she could ride this out too. She wanted to have left it all behind her in Minnesota. Even without confirmation, though, he continued to send her messages.

> Please understand that I had no idea until recently. Now that I know, I want to support him in any way I can.

Katharine sat down right on the wood floor and closed her eyes. It seemed impossible that he had only now figured it out. Perhaps it was Elsa, meeting the Other Woman's child and seeing her own husband; Elsa the math teacher, doing the math.

Somehow, those fourteen years back, Katharine had indeed become the Other Woman. She had never seen the misstep coming. From the first day on the project she'd been assigned to at Morton & Dunworth, she had recognized Ham. He was that poor father from the funeral three years before, the man who had apologized for his wife's disturbing demeanor. While he didn't remember Katharine, he talked openly about that funeral when he learned she had been there.

Across the weeks that they worked with each other, Katharine had rarely filled the silences. They weren't uncomfortable for her the way they seemed to be for Ham. Maybe that was unfair; maybe he just needed words to help him sort out complex emotions. Whatever the reason, his confessions about grief made their conversations begin to feel intimate, and this was new. With Michael, the silences were simply respected, particularly at a point when they had the noise of two tiny daughters filling the house.

Looking back, it made a terrible kind of sense, what happened that one evening. She hadn't known the power that this kind of intimacy with words could have on her body's desire for touch. The way Ham laid bare what he thought and felt seemed so real—brave—and it pulled her in. He had a need, and she felt a kind of pulsing attraction to her own ability to meet it, one only made more compelling by her awareness that she, Katharine, was stepping into recklessness.

She wasn't proud. She wanted to honor her commitments to a husband she loved, then and still.

These days she could see that her marriage was many wonderful things, but it relied on leaving much unsaid, perhaps particularly by Katharine. She was trying; she was showing more of herself, watching Michael to see whether more of her could ever be better. Still, showing more was quite different from telling all.

From the time she'd realized she was pregnant, she had known that the baby was Ham's. She chose to keep this quiet. She gave her notice at work soon after the tryst—they agreed never to repeat their guilty mistake, but she wanted to be sure—and she did not stay in touch with anyone at Morton & Dunworth. It had only been a part-time job, and she was already busy with mothering. When Michael suspected nothing, not even after the dark hair and brown eyes, she'd followed the path she felt he was offering: silence.

When Ham's wife transferred to Lowe Hills from the high school at the start of Thomas's seventh grade, keeping him enrolled there had seemed just fine. Later, of course, it had not. When Elsa started showing interest in Thomas, Katharine realized they must know about this son, that Ham's confessional ways must have led him to tell Elsa about his infidelity. But Katharine couldn't be sure. She'd stuck to her path of silence on the matter for as long as she could. Then, of course, it became clear. It was time to get her family out of there.

Ham's next texts came when she was wrapping the new mittens she had crocheted for her eldest daughter.

Elsa is in a lot of trouble, it said. I can understand you wanting us to stay out of your life. But I have to ask. The situation is desperate.

Katharine read that last text several times. Was not responding a way to ride this out, or would it only push Ham and Elsa to act?

Next he sent her screenshots of what some people were posting about Elsa. Katharine and Michael didn't participate in social media, but she knew that these posts were disturbing. My daughter's friend says there were naked photos taken of this boy, probably to pass to other pedophiles, one said. If the district won't do something about her, there are plenty out there who will, said another.

Katharine could see that they had a compelling need. But she couldn't just go along, defer. She thought of Thomas's frustration with her. What she really thought—what she really needed to just say, then—was that she needed to keep her family safely intact. For that, she needed both Ham's and Elsa's cooperation: their silence. It meant that meeting their needs was relevant to meeting her own.

That night after watching her children help her mother-in-law up the stairs, Katharine went into the guest bathroom, the only room in the house with a lock. She needed to establish a clear pact.

I will speak to whomever I must, at the district, to have these allegations dropped, Katharine texted. In return, I need your word. Never tell my husband the truth.

She saw the phone indicating that Ham was typing something in return. So she made an addendum.

And never contact me or my family again.

Chapter 37

For real. When Elsa woke up in the morning and when she went to sleep at night, that was the refrain. The way her body felt when she repeated the words told her just how overdue they were. Still, it was a lot of real to process.

After he'd dropped the news about Katharine and stormed out, Ham had gone to a motel. His texts began in the middle of the first night and continued through the next day, piling up while she was with her mother.

> I am so sorry, Elsa. I hate myself for what I did.

> I understand if you can't forgive me. But please. You are everything.

Elsa had barely read them at first; there was no room left in her for this. Her whole world, that first night and day, had been about her lost baby, gone. It was only when he had been found—Bird, himself!—that she had the capacity to absorb the revelations about her marriage.

Ham. He had left her in Duluth; he had decided to throw it all away. Just like that, he had gone to his consolation woman, somehow waiting and ready.

She pictured Ham's naked body tangled up with Katharine's, his hands grasping her not-so-fleshy ass. Elsa's own body, one she had long ago come to accept, now taunted her: it was bulgy, loose, dimpled. Like a crappy fairy tale, her prince had magically turned it back to ugly.

His messages continued on the second day.

I can't think of how to tell you how sorry I am. It's so much, Elsa.

Right then, I thought you were never getting better. I should have gotten you more help, and instead I just gave up. I failed you.

She remembered the little ruffled swimsuit from the water park gift shop, how Ham thought Elsa bought it for a little girl she might abduct instead of for Jennifer's daughter. She had chosen to be patient, to let him take his own time in trusting that she was done conjuring up an Inga. But after three years of her cycle of promises and failures, his trust had been gone.

And then she'd gotten pregnant, and he had wept his apologies like a big drama queen. Elsa had granted him forgiveness so easily. It was OK that he had left her all alone in Duluth; she had let him go. Now, though, she understood what was really behind his tearful sorrys.

Did he think it counted back then, saying sorry without clarifying what for? That took the cake, if so. It was up there with thinking that "I'm sorry you got mad" qualified as an apology. But at least he'd been racked with guilt then as well.

Bird is ours, she had managed to text. It was something more than silence, enough that Ham said he would come by that evening.

Elsa looked at the words she had typed. *Bird is ours.* Of course this wasn't news to him. It answered a question no one had been asking but Elsa.

She was working to make new sense of the baby switch she had invented. Of course her infant son had felt different, off; he was warm and alive, and Elsa was used to a tiny corpse or a bag of sand. She and Ham had expected Baird's arrival to heal past traumas—maybe even erase them. But Bird was not Inga. And if you tried to force a Bird-shaped piece into an Inga-shaped hole, it didn't really work. It was like with a jigsaw puzzle: if you pushed it in there anyway, then all you felt at the end was like a cheater trying to sell yourself on completeness. It had felt like the truth: *This is not my baby.*

Still, there he had been, this little living wonder who became Bird. *Are you my mother?* If only she had known the truth all along. But seeking the truth hadn't been worth the risk of losing him.

Then Thomas happened, so suddenly and seemingly so right. Her gut turned it from theory to knowledge, fast; she'd never really imagined being wrong. That he was Ham's flesh and blood explained so much.

Unfortunately, it was an explanation that couldn't be shared. Worse, Elsa had already counted as chickens all the eggs in that basket. She realized now how much she had been relying on the news that Thomas was their son to clear up all this Mary Kay LeTourneau business. And while she waited, Elsa had been doing not a damned thing to fight back and protect her own children.

Things were getting pretty real on that front too.

Within two days of her night-stalking drive by Thomas's house, Elsa understood that she'd been spotted. It was secondhand information, and the spotter could not be sure, the post said. Even so, it was enough to trigger a new flurry of activity. The rumor was passed on the sledding hills and in the yoga studios, attracting new attention to both the middle school and elementary parent sites. Most piled on in a heap of agreement, sure that no one should let their children roam the streets alone in a town where Elsa Vargas might be on the prowl. There were occasional voices of reason and calm: let due process happen. None of the voices were Jennifer or Ted.

When Ham finally returned home after her brief text, the boys were in their rooms. They didn't know their father had slept elsewhere; as far as they knew, he'd just been out late. Elsa heard him enter, but she stayed put at the stove, unable to go greet him. Her eyes focused on the frying pan; finally, her fingers turned off the burner. She moved to lean against the sink.

He came into the kitchen, hesitant. His face contorted. "Elsa." Then his eyes filled.

"Ham." She moved her eyes to the window. It was impossible, returning his gaze. They stood still for a full minute, and then Ham took a step toward her. Her body leaned away before she'd decided how to react, and he stopped.

"I know you're sorry," she managed, speaking to the refrigerator. "And I'm trying. It's not like I don't see what I put you through. I'm sorry too."

"No," he objected. "You have nothing to . . . I love you, Elsa."

Elsa shook her head. *Love?* She turned her eyes to his face, and her teeth clenched. "You have a fucking lame-ass way of showing it, Ham. You're a lying, cheating piece of shit, you know that?" Somehow her voice remained at the same volume.

Ham nodded. "Truth."

She wanted to read his body as wilting, but part of her knew it was relief setting in. He was still Ham, who knew her better than anyone.

"You can sleep in the car out on the street," Elsa announced. "Keep a watch. Protect us. Your boys do not deserve more violence against this house." Too late, she heard what she knew Ham heard: *your boys.* Now he had another. Bird and Garvey were a subset of Ham's children.

"I'll keep watch. And I'll bring the baseball bat," he said.

Elsa couldn't say if he was trying to be funny; she knew he'd seen the way the online energy was only rising. She kept her arms folded across her chest. "Maybe you could use some time to think," she said, less venom in her voice.

"Thank you," Ham nodded. "And maybe you could use some space."

They stood there another minute. Then Elsa let her arms unfold, pushed herself away from the sink. She turned the stove back on under the meat she'd been browning, her back to Ham. *If you can't stand the heat . . .* she thought. But maybe they could. They were both here in the kitchen.

Their dinner performance seemed to pass as normal, each parent interrupting Garvey's perpetual freestyle here and there to draw out Bird. Afterward, she sent the boys to the basement. She cleared the table while Ham rinsed the plates and loaded the dishwasher. Eventually, she broke the silence, trying out what could be said next.

She told him about their rapidly maturing child. When Bird had learned about the egging, he had set his jaw and researched how to best clean it all off. He had enlisted Garvey in a massive LEGO project the day before, the bricks strewn across Bird's ordinarily tidy bedroom rug, and he had brought in Garvey's book of riddles. He kept his shades down, and he handed his phone and his tablet to Elsa. "Keep them turned off," he had told her.

Ham wiped his hands and watched Elsa talk. She could see his gratitude. When he finally spoke, his voice sounded a bit huskier. "What do you think about that, the social media? I think I'm with Bird. I'm thinking you and I should stay out of the shit online too."

Elsa nodded in agreement. There was plenty to wade through right here in their house, she thought.

She filled a glass of water and nodded at Ham one more time. Then she reminded him where the best sleeping bag was, and headed for the stairs. She was ready to shower and head to bed; it was enough for one day.

The next evening, the two of them again felt pulled to the kitchen. When Elsa said yes, she was ready, Ham offered his own updates: he had reached out to Katharine, who refused him any involvement in his son's life. After shoving aside the images that came back into her head at Katharine's name, Elsa heard him. *Thomas.* For all the loss Elsa herself felt for him, still she was not his actual parent. Ham was. And Ham had gained a son and then lost an actual father-son relationship, all in extremely short order.

Never tell my husband the truth, the text Ham showed her said. Elsa recognized this—maybe good mothers sometimes lied. But now Ham had to as well. He would have to learn the skill Elsa had long ago mastered: how to live in a state of possibly interminable deception and separation. It was a pain she wouldn't wish on anyone.

Or at least mostly.

"So . . . Katharine?" she asked, ten minutes later. "Of all the women in the world, she's who you picked?"

Ham hid his bowed head. "Oh, Else. I can't justify any of it. She was just there. And listening. And . . . uncomplicated."

Elsa squeezed the sponge tighter over the sink drain. "I guess I can't compete on that one."

"You have no competition, Elsa." He turned his sorry face toward her. "You're Usain Bolt. Michael Jordan."

"I'm Serena Williams," she corrected.

"You're Abby Wambach marries Simone Biles and has a baby," Ham said.

"And then thinks that baby isn't theirs," Elsa added.

Ham stifled a smile. "Nobody's perfect."

Nobody's perfect? How rich—her cheating husband had jokes.

"Too soon, Ham," she snapped. She fished in her leather bag for the car keys and then slapped them on the counter. She left the kitchen and started up the stairs. "Don't forget your damn bat."

Chapter 38

Christmas Day arrived like an uninvited dinner party guest, awkward and puzzling. Still, whatever lumps of coal Santa might have strewn about this year, the rest of the adults committed themselves to giving the boys some needed joy.

They gathered at Marcy's, and Elsa found herself feeling genuinely happy. All day long, she could not take her eyes off her new son.

Watching Bird was different not just because *he* was different, but because she was looking through a new lens. It wasn't as if he were bigger or really even clearer; she still found Bird to be a bit of an enigma, as always. This was less like a new prescription than like someone had finally wiped a strange tint off the glass. Now, there was no interference. When she looked at Bird, she saw her son.

When she looked at Ham, she still saw a husband, but of course that was different too. Maybe it always would be from here on out. More and more, though, Elsa found that the emotions she was wrapping herself up in didn't feel quite right on her skin. The fuzzy ache of his betrayal was interwoven with wiry fibers of her own guilt. Elsa had hidden important things from him too. She *had* been off her rocker, not just for three years but then for fourteen more. Forgiveness would have to go both ways.

At four o'clock, Marcy drew them all to her Christmas dinner table. When they were all seated, she asked for a moment. She reached for Garvey's hand. "Not a prayer, just a moment."

Bird closed his eyes, and Ham focused hard on his glass of water. Elsa's eyes toured all of their faces, these people she loved.

"To Jesus," Krista finally cracked, holding her wineglass up toward Marcy.

"And to this strong family," Marcy smiled, raising her glass as well. She put her other hand on Ham's shoulder. He closed his eyes and swallowed hard.

The adults gathered all knew the truth: about Bird, about Thomas, about Ham and Katharine. To Elsa, this honesty felt fresh and clean—almost minty. One day she would have this with her sons too. For now, she'd have to fall back onto her well-trodden path, this time with a companion. Now Ham was a liar too.

"Thank you for the dinner, Grammy," Bird said. "You always make Christmas really special."

Elsa melted.

"And scrump-dilly-icious!" Garvey added, holding up his forkful of buttery mashed potatoes.

"Also, thank you again for the telescope, everybody," Bird added. "I'm going to set it up at home tonight. I want to be ready for the semicolon on the twenty-eighth." He drew one in the air as he explained. "Venus is going to be the dot, and the moon is going to be the comma part." He smiled.

"Wow, I want to see that," Elsa said. "Do we even need the telescope for it?"

"In the city you can see Venus better with a telescope," Bird said. He launched into an explanation, and Elsa was entranced.

"Aren't you keeping the shades closed, though?" Garvey frowned.

Elsa saw everyone remember what she had stirred up outside their home.

Ham reached over to mess up Garvey's hair just as Marcy suggested Garvey challenge his dad to a round of his new strategy game. Ham gave a big grin and pointed at Garvey. "Game on!" Then Ham insisted that, first, he and the boys would clear the table and clean up in the kitchen.

"Me too," Marcy said, touching Ham again. "It's my kitchen, and I want to be one of the boys today. After that, I want Bird's help with my new tablet on the porch." She was all smiles, but the one for Krista included a pointed look toward the wall shared with her side of the duplex.

"I guess the daughters are supposed to get out of here," Krista announced. She told Elsa to grab the open bottle of wine, since all the holiday-fancy stuff was here on their mom's side.

They entered Krista's apartment through the back door off the shared patio. Elsa kicked off her shoes as Krista flipped on the lights. "I've made such a huge mess, Krista. Mom's right to get me out of there. Maybe they can forget about the whole damn thing."

"Get your mess out of Mom's Christmas, would ya?"

"But for real, Mom is kind of great that way sometimes," Elsa said, following her sister into the living room. She could see the tenderness Marcy was offering to Ham and to her children.

"Not sometimes," Krista corrected. "Remember: she's always there for you, Elsa." She sang the last part in her best Marcy parody.

Elsa frowned. "I don't know, Krista. I feel like maybe she is always there for me."

Krista rolled her eyes and dropped into the sofa, her feet quickly kicking up to land on the stupidly furry ottoman.

Elsa sat on the edge of the armchair, watching her sister as she continued. "You know, Mom told me she would have insisted on a blood test way back then, when I thought Bird was switched."

"Oh, yeah? But she didn't do anything way back then, did she?"

Elsa looked at her sister in silence for another moment. Then she pulled open the cork on the bottle and topped off what remained in the glasses they had brought along from the other side.

"Mom didn't even know I thought my baby was the wrong one."

Krista shrugged. "Whatever, Elsa. Happily, it turns out you were wrong about him being the wrong one."

"You know what I think? I think you never even told Mom what I was saying, Krista. I think you just talked me out of insisting this wasn't my baby, and acted like Mom was with you on that."

Krista stared at her. "What the fuck. Merry Christmas to you too." The sisters glared at each other, each waiting for something.

Finally Krista spoke again. "You were about to lose Ham, Elsa, when you got pregnant. I know you were. Because—because I knew. I didn't know who she was or anything, but Ham isn't all that good at hiding guilt. And to tell you the truth, it made a gross kind of sense to me. You were just so damn stubborn, staying in your pretend world and not moving on." She closed her eyes in a moment of pain, remembering. "You put a fucking toddler toilet in your bathroom, Elsa."

"But this wasn't that. This was later, when they brought Bird back to me and I was just totally convinced he was—"

"This *was* that, Elsa!" Krista barked. "This was *all* still that! And if you were going to still do the 'where's my Inga' thing, then you were going to burn it down and lose your husband! Jesus." Krista shook her head. "Mom would have been with me on that, Elsa. She just didn't see what was happening in Ham. She didn't know he could break."

"So you just pretended that you told her?" Elsa demanded. Now she leaned forward and put her finger in Krista's face. "When you did that, you robbed me of that blood test. *You.* Mom would have nipped it in the bud!" Elsa got up and moved behind the chair, trying to calm herself. Then she turned back toward her sister. "I mean, what the hell, Krista? You thought I should just shove that feeling under some sleep deprivation, see if it went away? Well, it didn't." She slashed the air with her hand. "It never did. But I took Bird home and loved him anyway. And then before long, it was just too late." The anger was giving way to what was underneath, and she turned to leave the room.

Elsa put her elbows on the island in Krista's kitchen. After about a full minute, Krista followed her and took a position leaning against the refrigerator.

"I didn't know you would hang on to that suspicion, Else," she said. They stood in silence. "I guess, in retrospect, I should have remembered just how good you are at hanging on to things."

Elsa thought of that iceberg trip down the Mississippi River at the dog park. Krista was so adamant that Marcy had failed by not doing something sooner. But then when Elsa had suspected Bird wasn't hers, it had been Krista who had made sure no one could save Elsa.

"You were like the Santa man who jumped on my iceberg," Elsa said, turning. She faced her sister. "You tried to help, but all you did was shove me out into the river." Elsa thought of the fast-moving current she had hit, raising Bird and doubting he was hers. She had gone so far down that river.

"That's lovely. Now I'm that creep," Krista snapped. But as she looked at Elsa, her eyes grew pink and shiny. Krista scrunched up her mouth and shook her head no. Then she closed her eyes and nodded it yes. "Fuck you, Elsa," she said, her voice thick.

Elsa reached out an arm toward her sister. "No, fuck you, Krista." And then they were in a hug, where they decided to stay awhile.

Chapter 39

Three days after Christmas, Elsa found an email from Schusterman in her inbox. It wasn't addressed to the whole staff, and it certainly wasn't to all the parents. Only Stanley from the union and Natalie Trowbridge from the PTO were copied.

> Happy holidays, to those who celebrate! It truly is the "most wonderful time of the year," isn't it? Time flies when we're heading into the New Year! :)
>
> It is with great relief that I convey some news. Thomas Humphrey's mother has made it clear to me that rumors of any kind of impropriety by Ms. Vargas were completely unwarranted. No official complaint will be filed on this matter.
>
> PTO Chair Natalie Trowbridge has shared with me, via an email, that the PTO will host a special meeting on Tuesday, January 7th. What a wonderful opportunity to come together and clear the air! I have ordered a substitute math teacher for the first few school days so that we adults can sort things out before the kids are with Ms. Vargas.

I look forward to seeing you all on the 7th! I'm confident that Ms. Vargas can put these rumors and resentments to rest, as she has with previous concerns. Happy parents make a Happy New Year! 😉

Good Tidings,
Robert Schusterman, Principal

Elsa felt the relief: no formal action.

But that was tempered by the rest of the news, that now she had apparently graduated from *Additional Item* to *Only Item*. Elsa would be the whole damn "special" meeting. She would have no slides or civil libertarians, and the facts that would have been most enlightening had been deemed inadmissible by Katharine's request for secrecy.

She forwarded the email to Ham, changing the subject line to *special* and pasting Dana Carvey in his wig and horn-rimmed glasses above Schusterman's message.

In another life, one without lemongrass soup, she would have sent the email to her concerned best friend as well. But Jennifer was still offering total radio silence. Fifteen days of zilch had ticked by, including Christmas itself, which Elsa felt should count at least double.

It was hard to face just how low she'd set the bar for that friendship, across time. Where had Jennifer been after Inga died? Where had she been when Elsa had almost drowned in denial for more than two years, when she had almost lost Ham? And in the modern era, where had Jennifer been when Elsa was the Additional Item? Where was Jennifer, fellow nonbeliever and Garvey fan, in the online Boys Of America battle? What about at the school board meetings, where everyone's eyes had been on Garvey and Elsa as the root of the whole fiasco? But clearest of all was now, when Elsa was accused of being an actual pedophile. What Would Jennifer Do? Not a damn thing, it turned out.

"Heard from Jennifer yet?" Ham had asked the day before.

"You mean Casper?" Elsa had corrected.

It wasn't just the ghosting, though. It was the outright lie, delivered with Ted's complicity. Maybe Elsa should have seen it coming. How many times had Jennifer invented a fake scheduling conflict when she didn't want to deal with Ted's combative brother at his parents' dinners? And hadn't Elsa been right there when Jennifer told her daughter's friend that no, Sarah couldn't come to the slumber party because she was babysitting? That was a lie too, one that only served to teach Sarah that you didn't have to tell a friend when you didn't like them anymore.

Elsa imagined leaving Jennifer a voicemail: "Goodbye. It turns out I don't like you anymore."

But it wasn't as easy as that. They were like string art, the two families, with tight connections across different pairs of points. There was a Bird and Paulie friendship; there was the Ham and Ted one. More, there was Ted letting Bird have a try when he showed his own son how to recaulk a tub, all three of them stunned to see Elsa moved to tears when she came across this scene. Maybe these other strings connecting their families could survive, if Elsa snipped the one between her and Jennifer. But what about the one between Garvey and Jennifer? That one had first been woven in taut years ago, when Jennifer had peeled five-year-old Garvey's bloody lips off the pavement, collected his tooth, and regaled him with stories about pirates and dinosaurs in the ER waiting room for three hours. When Elsa and Ham got out of their movie and finally turned on their phones, the last voicemail was from Garvey, giggling and telling them about a T-Rex with an eye patch and a tiny hook at the end of his itty-bitty arm. He had loved Jennifer ever since. Was there a way to not throw Garvey out with the bathwater?

Maybe the coming PTO meeting would help. Elsa would bet a year's salary that Jennifer would avoid it, but still—its very purpose was to clear the air. Surely it would move them in the right direction.

Ham thought so. He kept repeating bits of the email to Elsa to stoke their optimism. "Completely unwarranted," he would remind her, reaching past her at the sink. "No official complaint." She knew that this part of their mess—the community versus Elsa—was by far the clearest for Ham. Here, he could just support her, fight righteously for the truth. The rest of it was not easy, Elsa knew: the newfound son, the betrayal that produced him, the promise to not father his son to save his wife. What did you do when grief and shame and honor and joy were all tossing around together inside of you? If you were most men, Ham included, you waited until a woman helped you put words to it.

"Maybe stay inside awhile tonight? You could sleep on the sofa," Elsa suggested. She needed words too.

When Ham went out to grab the paper late the next morning, he saw a few neighbors huddled across the street looking his way. Just as he held up a hand to them and turned to go back inside, Emmet Clarkson's dad called out.

"Uh, Ham, you'd better come out and see this. You got tagged, looks like."

Once the neighbors had dispersed, Elsa went out with the boys to see the two-foot-high retaining wall in front of their yard for themselves. Someone had spray-painted across it in all caps, red, some letters having dripped like the title on a slasher movie.

I RAPE CHILDREN.

Elsa sucked in a breath. *Rape?* She had doubted the accuracy of Ham's description, but here it was. Who would do such a thing? She looked up and down the street, now emptier than it had ever been, and her skin felt grazed by a hundred eyes behind curtains. She shuddered and turned her focus toward her boys.

Bird touched Elsa's fingers. Garvey's hands balled tight.

"Call the cops!" Garvey spat out. "I hope they were caught on camera. They can rot in jail. Forever!"

Bird reached out for Garvey's shoulder. "I think they probably need help. They're pretty messed up."

Elsa felt disoriented; it sounded like something her mother would say. But Bird was not her parent.

"The cops will get it removed today," she reassured her sons. What did you say to your children when the world was using you to spew shame? Marcy would remain calm, Elsa thought, closing her eyes for a moment. And somehow she would remain forgiving. But when she opened her eyes again at the terrible redness, Elsa thought only of Carlos, the way he pointed at horror and revealed that it was ridiculous. That was his legacy; that was the Vargas she wanted to pass on.

"In the meantime, I guess free holiday decor," she cracked. "It's certainly a merry tone of red, really adds a certain *je ne sais quoi*. Maybe a little *joie de vivre*. We'd better enjoy it while it lasts, boys, am I right?" She did her best to douse it with jazz hands and wobbling eyebrows. Laughter would sell it best, she knew. But that was more than any of them could muster.

Chapter 40

Bird and Garvey stayed out of school in the first days after break, alongside Elsa. When Tuesday the seventh arrived, Bird helped Garvey iron a button-down shirt and get ready for the PTO meeting at Lowe Hills.

"They shouldn't come," Elsa objected. But Ham and Marcy both insisted: the boys wanted to do this, and it could only be helpful to remind these parents that she, too, was a mother.

It was dark out when they loaded into the minivan, Ham driving. Snow was still falling over the fresh inch that lay on the ground, and the city had fallen quiet.

"Maybe more people will stay home," Ham said. The car ahead of them slid a few feet at the red light.

"Be careful," Elsa said. Dying just now didn't sound half bad, but she didn't want her family brought down with her.

The middle school parking lot was not empty. It was not even half empty. Ham found a space and turned off the car. No one reached for their door handles.

Elsa turned around. "You don't have to go in," she reminded the boys.

Bird unlatched his seat belt and pulled open the sliding side door. "Let's go." Garvey scrambled after him.

A sign on the front door to the school said the meeting was in the gym. The library couldn't hold this many people, Elsa understood. Reflexively, she took Ham's hand; then she remembered, and dropped it. She forced herself to move forward.

"I wish I could do this for you," he said. "I'm the reason this all happened."

"Just tell me I can do this, Ham."

"You're a badass and you got this, Else," he complied.

The gym was humming with the sounds of voices and metal folding chairs. They entered from near the back, moving up the center aisle. Faces turned to look at them, then look away. There were the scientist parents; there was the Windell woman; there was Shoua, a lone non-adult ready to translate the meeting into Hmong for her mother and father. Elsa found herself scanning for Jennifer or Ted; she was just picking at a scab. A man wearing his BOA shirt and his Anaconda bandana glowered hard at Elsa, refusing to look away.

Her mind flashed to another aisle, years ago: a sea of smiles surrounding them as she held her father's arm and processed toward Ham, happy and certain. Today's aisle was clearly its evil twin.

Marcy and Krista sat in the front row, and Krista stood up and waved her arm. "Ham, Elsa," she called out brazenly, pointing now to empty seats next to her. Marcy stood up too, as they arrived, holding out her arms and giving each of them a quick hug as they shuffled past her. Krista and Marcy sat down again on either side of the four of them.

Schusterman and Natalie Trowbridge hovered near a lectern, leaning in and talking in quiet voices. Their eyes occasionally moved in tandem to land briefly on Elsa. Finally Schusterman approached her and lowered himself to a squat in front of her.

"How we doing?" he said. "I'm going to speak to the group very briefly, and then I can turn it to you for anything you would like to clarify. Stanley couldn't make it tonight, but since we have no action being filed, I'm not concerned about that."

Elsa nodded.

"Wonderful," Schusterman said, extending his hand toward Ham even before he shifted his eyes off Elsa. "Rob Schusterman. Thank you for coming out. You must be Mr. Vargas."

Ham finally shook his hand. "Hamilton, actually," he said.

Schusterman blinked, clearly not following.

"I'm Elsa's husband. Father of . . ." Ham trailed off for a moment. "You know Bird Hamilton, and this is my son Garvey. We're eager to see this cleared up. Obviously this is very painful for my family."

Schusterman gave his best pained expression, looking toward Elsa and then back at Ham. "I can only imagine." Then he got up and moved to rejoin Natalie.

"Fucker," Ham said quietly.

"I hate him," Bird said. Elsa and Ham exchanged looks, eyebrows up.

Elsa reached over to touch Bird's leg. "Let that shit go, Bird. If anyone can stay out of the hater club, it's you."

Schusterman called for the gym's attention. He welcomed everyone and then ran through a list of upcoming student and family events. "So many wonderful opportunities in the next couple of months, people. And that is all because of your incredible support of our young learners." He held his hands up to clap, motioning for everyone to join him. A brief ripple of half-hearted applause followed his lead.

Next he held his arm out toward Natalie. "I want to thank our PTO chair, who has called this meeting. Natalie Trowbridge, thank you. Would you like to say a few words?"

Natalie stepped to the microphone in her pantsuit, oozing authority. She nodded and made her face serious. "This has been a difficult few weeks. Principal Schusterman and I have seen the social media page, as many of you have, and both of us have heard directly from people expressing a very, very serious concern. That concern was about inappropriate behavior—alleged inappropriate behavior—between a teacher here and a student. I synergized the full set of data points and questions for Mr. Schusterman, and he has done a wonderful job of handling this incident. We all hope to see our schools err on the side of protecting our children. That is just what he did, in providing a substitute mathematics teacher, and I think we can all be proud of that."

She held out her hand toward Schusterman, letting the heartier applause roll for a long moment. He gave a little bow with his head.

Natalie continued. "I have no role in what comes next from a district process standpoint. But I felt strongly that we, the parental stakeholders of this community, needed a huddle on this issue. Let's get some altitude to fully understand where we are, get locked in on those coordinates." Here she paused and looked into faces with seriousness. "As your leaders, we are committed to open communication. I thank you all for showing up tonight, showing that you, too, feel that full transparency is what we deserve."

The Boys Of America father stood up now, clapping loudly. Several parents joined him in applauding.

Natalie nodded and asked Schusterman to please take it from there.

"What the hell is this?" Ham asked in a low voice. "They haven't even said yet that you have been cleared." Elsa had noticed.

Schusterman situated himself in front of the microphone. "Parents, teachers, we want to offer you complete transparency. When the issue arose, the next step was to consider a formal complaint, which would trigger a full investigation. Here's where we are: there will be no action taken. While I realize that there are questions you all have—should a teacher be giving a ride to a student, for example?—the allegations have been . . . quelled. I have heard from the family of the student in question, and they do not, I repeat, *not*, believe that any of these rumors of impropriety are in fact truth."

The noise level in the room rose a bit, people all seeming to turn to whoever sat next to them.

Schusterman continued. "As Natalie has shared on the social media site, there will be no formal complaint filed whatsoever. That means no investigation, and this is now over from the district viewpoint. This is because the family simply has no complaint with Ms. Vargas."

The room got louder. "No investigation?" someone yelled, sounding indignant.

"Does the family know she had him in her van?" someone else called out.

Schusterman tapped the microphone and held up his hand. "Ladies and gentlemen, we are a civil and transparent community. We can have discussion, but it will remain orderly. I have assumed that Ms. Vargas may have an interest in speaking to us, and if she would like to field your questions, then I would ask that you put your hands up."

People quieted. A few hands went up immediately.

"Ms. Vargas is not currently the subject of any investigation. No complaint has been filed, nor will it be filed, against her. She has every right to our courtesy as we give her the opportunity to speak." Schusterman looked over at Elsa. "Would you like to take this opportunity, Ms. Vargas?"

Elsa had changed her mind: even Bird should hate this man. "I would," she said, trying to keep her voice strong. She got up. She could feel the heat on her face, but she stretched her head higher. She smoothed her blouse, noticing that her hands were not as steady as she had hoped.

She went to the podium and turned to face the masses, looking first into the helpful eyes in the front row: her mother, her sister, her husband. Her two brave sons. Finally she moved her gaze upward to take in more of the crowd, much of it glowering. She cleared her throat, and then she looked again at Ham, for strength. Immediately he got up and closed the gap between them, taking a position next to her. He squeezed her hand once and then let it go.

Elsa adjusted the microphone on the lectern. "My name is Elsa Vargas, and I teach math here," she began, her voice only slightly trembling. "I have never done any touching or said anything inappropriate to a student. I gave one student a ride to an ice cream gathering after a school board meeting, in my minivan. I imagine that what those in the parking lot could not see was that my younger son was with us, already in the minivan. This student got his parent's permission to get a ride before joining my son and me," Elsa said slowly and clearly. Elsa turned to Natalie now. "As happens with our children, I'm certainly aware that sometimes people see something and start to gossip about it. But sometimes they don't have all the information."

A man shouted out now. "The kids saw you giving this boy a *lot* of your time. What the hell is that? If the kids think something is going on, why is that?"

A woman's voice: "We need an investigation."

Elsa took a breath. What could she tell them? She couldn't think how to reframe the umbrella on the bleachers, how to take back her attentions at History Day. "I thought he was my son" was not an option. She nodded at the shouting man and raked her lip with her teeth, desperately searching for what she could say instead. So many stern faces were lobbing disgust and righteous anger at her head. Speed pumped through her veins; her animal brain yelled "FLIGHT!" telling her to actually run. Her eyes darted to the propped-open double doors at the back.

There, her eyes met Katharine's.

Katharine Humphrey. Elsa moved her forearm to touch Ham's.

They watched Katharine move into the gym, followed by both her husband and Thomas. She led them up the aisle, the two behind her walking tall. "I would like to speak," she said shakily, her eyes on Ham briefly before moving to Elsa. "Could I speak, please?" Her face was pink, deepening toward red.

Ham pulled Elsa away from the microphone. Then he leaned into her ear. "I—he's right there. I have to sit down." Elsa nodded at him, and he returned to his seat.

Katharine went to the microphone. She bent it down farther and it squawked, making her jump back. Then she stepped cautiously back up to the mic and began, her voice trembling. "My name is Katharine Humphrey, and my son is Thomas Humphrey." She looked at her son and took a big breath. "And I have something to say."

Elsa could see that Thomas and Michael Humphrey were both transfixed, nodding, while the room waited. Katharine looked out at the masses. "There have been a lot of terrible insinuations about my son and Elsa Vargas. Let me tell you what I think about that. I think that is disgusting and irresponsible and flat-out wrong. Many of you should feel ashamed about spreading these horrible rumors. And the rest of you should stop listening to them, because they are lies."

Elsa felt something break loose inside. Tears sprouted, and a little hic barked from her throat. Katharine stepped back from the lectern and turned to look at her. For the tiniest moment, she started to reach her hand toward Elsa. Then she quickly pulled back and locked her arms across her body, her pained face going crimson all over again.

Now Thomas stepped up to the microphone. He looked over at Michael Humphrey, who gave him a silent nod. Thomas began to speak.

"Listen, you all have gone crazy," he announced, looking toward the back wall. "I'm the one who you all are saying Ms. Vargas did something to, which is just, like, a total lie. She didn't do anything wrong or inappropriate. And oh my God, she's not molesting kids. You can't just say something like that about someone when it's a hundred percent not true." Elsa looked at her sons reflexively. Bird was pink with embarrassment, but Garvey was gazing at Thomas with unabashed admiration.

Thomas took a big breath, then frowned. "It's true I got a ride from her and her son one time. But people get rides, right? I mean"—here he turned to address Natalie Trowbridge directly—"when I saw you leaning into the window of Coach Schusterman's Camaro, I just figured you were getting something you had left in his car. I mean, people can carpool, right?"

Natalie's face whitened, and she glanced over at Schusterman, whose eyes had lost their usual luster. The room fell briefly silent, enough so that Elsa heard the delayed gasp. It came from Shoua, sitting up straighter in her third-row seat, her eyes widened. As Thomas cleared his throat to continue, Elsa watched the girl's thumbs fly into action on her phone.

"So anyway, Ms. Vargas is an awesome teacher. She's funny and she actually likes middle schoolers, which I guess is, like, not that common. She stands up for what she believes in. Or what she doesn't believe in, I guess you could say. I guess that made some of you mad at that whole school board thing." Thomas looked directly at the dad in the Anaconda getup.

Next Thomas looked at his hand, which Elsa could see had words written on it, and gave a nervous half chuckle before pausing to compose himself. "OK. So. What I'm telling you is that the only thing Ms. Vargas did was be a person who cares, which, I guess, maybe some of you think is not what teachers should be like."

The room was dead quiet.

Thomas looked over at Michael. "My parents taught me that lying is wrong. So I'm telling you the truth. Also, maybe it would be good if more people would stop and think before you spread lies next time." He looked now at Elsa before they both shifted their eyes to Katharine. Katharine nodded at him.

"I guess that's it," Thomas said, stepping away toward Michael.

Michael put his hand on Thomas's shoulder and looked at Katharine, tipping his head toward the aisle. He and Thomas moved to leave, heads held high. Jerrod and Craig stood up and clapped. Aneisha popped up near the back as well. As a small wave of applause gradually gathered, Garvey jumped up to join the people standing. Just as quickly, he sat down again.

Katharine had gone back to the microphone instead of the aisle. She spoke louder now. "Please leave my family alone." She looked out at the crowd, and then she looked right at Ham, pausing for what Elsa understood as a pointed reiteration. Then she turned to Elsa. "And please leave Elsa Vargas and her family alone." Elsa heard something different in Katharine's voice, a new fullness to its timbre.

Katharine moved to follow her family out. Elsa touched a hand to her chest, but Katharine did not look back.

Unsure of what came next up front, Elsa felt heat return to her cheeks; she looked at Schusterman and moved tentatively toward her seat next to Krista. Just as she turned around to sit, though, their mother stood up. She turned to address the whole family. "Shall we go?" Marcy smiled firmly. Then she gathered her coat and her purse and she led them up the aisle, through the hallway beyond the gym doors, and out into the cold white stillness.

Chapter 41

As the four of them drove home, everyone but Garvey was quiet.

"I thought it went really good. I didn't see Ted or Jennifer, were they there?" Garvey asked, trying to spin on his fingertip a little Nerf basketball he had found under the seat.

"She's still sick," Elsa said.

"Thomas totally did good. And his mom." Elsa looked out the window while Garvey continued to monologue. "I'm sad they moved away. He's nice. I mean, I guess maybe it's better because of this whole stupid thing? I don't know. Still, he's cool."

Elsa didn't have to look at Ham to know this was hard. She turned on the radio, found some classic grunge that could pass as a favorite, and turned the volume up loud enough to make conversation untenable.

Once inside the house, they each found their own comfort. Bird went to the solace of his bedroom; Ham and Garvey went to play a video game in the basement. Elsa filled the bathtub, threw in a bath bomb the boys had given her for Mother's Day probably six years before, and eased herself into the now-clingy water to steep in her thoughts.

Thomas. By now he was gone again, headed back down the freeway to Iowa with the family that didn't include them. Elsa wouldn't get to watch him grow into those qualities she so loved about Ham: itching to fight injustice, but readier still to do it with humor. Iowa couldn't possibly stay boring with Thomas now in it.

His family was all right, Elsa had to admit. Katharine had some mama bear behind all that mouse. And how about that husband? "My parents taught me that lying is wrong," Thomas had said tonight. That credit went to Michael; he was the only one of the four parents whom Elsa didn't know to be a liar.

It didn't feel wonderful, playing along with Katharine's lie and letting Thomas go. But Katharine had more than fulfilled her end of the bargain; they had to honor her demands. She was his mother, and that seemed like it deserved some deference.

Not for forever, though. Maybe it would be when he moved out of his parents' house or maybe it would be sooner, but sometime downriver they would let Thomas know. Ham was his father too, and they would always be there for him. Even in this case, family meant never quitting the long game.

Elsa got out of her bath, wrapping one towel around her torso and another around her hair. She wiped the steam off the mirror, and her head reminded her of Jennifer's last-minute stabs at a Halloween costume this year. "Is this offensive?" she had asked, her head in some kind of sweater-turban. The wine had made this hilarious; right now, it made Elsa's throat ache.

You couldn't choose your family, people liked to say, as if you could really always choose your friends. No one in their right mind would choose friends who weren't there for you, friends who ran and hid from conflict, who did exactly nothing when nothing was all it took for the yuck to grow. But then, Elsa herself had done adamantly nothing about her own lie for Bird's entire life.

Maybe Bird was right: maybe when people acted like assholes, they were just doing the best they could. Maybe quitting the long game just because someone *wasn't* family kind of sucked as an approach to life.

Elsa sat down on the toilet lid and grabbed her phone from the shelf.

She tried to imagine airing her injuries, how she'd been hurt by the soup lie and the ghosting. But Jennifer wasn't going to face this level of conflict and stick around—it just wasn't in her makeup. All the strings between their families could end up going slack and unlacing.

Sure, real honesty was a better policy than most. But only some relationships could bear its weight. In others, you had to respect the load limits.

Elsa composed her email:

> Jennifer! I hope you get better soon, my friend. What a lame-o Christmas for you. I'm sure your grateful children waited on you hand and foot.
>
> So you missed a whole drama that has been super cray-cray, but it's better now. You'll probably hear about it once you're back among the living. Maybe we can grab a beverage later this month and I'll tell you all about it.
>
> Hugs.

It felt a little sad, hitting send. What used to be was gone, to be replaced by something else. But there was something more than Jennifer in that sadness.

It wasn't always so easy, figuring out what it meant to be there for someone. Was sticking around enough? Was love still worth something if you were holding something back? Elsa thought about how much she and Ham had each hidden of themselves, fearful. And now? Now they were showing it all. Strangely, the world had not ended. In fact, it was beginning to feel like maybe showing more of themselves could be the way.

Chapter 42

Elsa tapped on Bird's door that night.

"Come in," he called out. Elsa found him stretched out on his bed, his clothes still on. He smiled at her as she entered, but then his face fell back into a frown. He pointed to his reclaimed phone, which now lay on the floor below him.

"Apparently everyone's talking about Claire's mom and the principal now," he said. "That's probably really embarrassing for Claire."

Elsa's own reaction to this new drama had been heavier on the happy: it was about someone else. But maybe she could learn to be like Bird when she grew up.

"I'll make sure the teachers remember to look out for Claire."

Elsa went to the chair by the spider plants. She said nothing for a few moments, just looking into space the way Bird was now doing. Then she turned to him. "I know this has been confusing for you, Bird."

He grabbed his old robot pillow and tossed it up in the air, catching it again.

"You know I didn't do anything gross," she said. "But I feel like it was probably hard for you that I gave Thomas a lot of my attention."

Bird shoved the robot behind his head. "I think he's your style of person," he said.

Elsa got out of the chair and went to lie down beside him on his narrow bed. He scootched over to give her room, and they both looked at the ceiling, shoulders touching.

"Bird, you are always going to be my style of person. Just in a different way. You're not just like me, and I don't always recognize myself in how you see things. But that's how real love works, you know?" She tapped a knuckle against his arm. "Finding the real them."

Bird gave her hand a squeeze. After a while, he turned on his side to look at her as she stared at the ceiling.

"Mom, I know you have something empty, where Inga was. Grammy and I talked about you, and we can both understand it. Inga was inside you that whole time when you were pregnant. I guess that kind of empty sort of just lasts."

Elsa's eyes filled up. She closed them, and a tear was pushed out, rolling toward her ear. She turned her head and looked into his face.

He touched her tear. "I know you love me and Garvey. But you're like an atom with three protons, and we're only two electrons."

Elsa loved this boy. "Does that mean I could start a nuclear meltdown?" she asked.

"No, you're just maybe a little bit unstable. But not in a bad way."

She looked around his room. It was here, the walls then painted violet, where she had rocked the little stuffed bear who wasn't Inga. Later these walls were baby blue when she had renamed this boy Bird, after the character on a journey to find his mother. But now the walls were full of his scientific mind, his love of fantasy, his focus on the good.

She grabbed Bird's pillow from under his head and batted his stomach once. "You're not just an electron in my atom, you know."

"Well, OK," he said.

"You get to be your own atom."

"Then we're a molecule," Bird offered.

Her eyes fell on his poster of the Milky Way. *YOU ARE HERE*, it announced. Why had she always understood that *YOU* as singular, lonely? It wasn't about the bleakness of the universe. It was about being exactly here, together—here for each other.

"We are," Elsa agreed.

Acknowledgments

So many people deserve acknowledgment for their role in helping this novel to be its best self. Some lived parts of the story, including the hardest parts; others helped me find what to revise or leave out; still others pulled off the stunning creation of the actual published book you have here. It takes a lot of time to go from first draft to debut, I learned, and much of it is grueling. The massive upside, though, is that it brings into an author's life the active support and work of many wonderful people.

Heartfelt thanks go to Jodi Warshaw at Jodi Warshaw Edits and to Jenna Land Free and Margaret Sutherland Brown at Folio Literary Management. How did I get so lucky to have women whose amazing literary skills and savvy are accompanied by such top-tier human care and warmth? I nominate all of you for Best Ever.

To Nancy Holmes and the many teams who make the magic happen at Lake Union Publishing: you are all incredible. Your insights, your meticulous work, and your enthusiasm along the way have been so encouraging.

I am so grateful for the support of the Loft Literary Center in Minneapolis, including that of everyone involved in the mentorship program. It has been such a joy to build lasting community.

Joel Haskard, your contributions are too essential and encompassing to capture in words. I might try interpretive dance.

Many people I love have read drafts, given space to retreat, and offered amazing cheerleading and commiseration. Thank you to so many others, but particularly to Andrea, Ann, Anne, Alexis, Cokie, Dad, Dorcy, Elizabeth, Ezra, Farley, Joel (again), Kristin, LaTreena, Lori, Matt and Megan, Mindy, Mom, Sahnya, Sara, Stacey, Sua Sponte, Susan, and Swati.

At the time of my writing this, no strangers have yet bought this book with money and then read the entire thing. But maybe you are one, reading this now. It's hard to convey how wild that is, from my side: wow. Thank *you*.

About the Author

Cindy Jiban holds a PhD in educational psychology, and like the novel's protagonist, she was a member of an elite team of professionals: middle school teachers, or the Navy SEALs of the education world. She was awarded a Mentor Series Fellowship funded by the Jerome Foundation and the National Endowment for the Arts through the Loft Literary Center in Minnesota. She grew up in the Seattle area and now lives in Saint Paul with her family. *The Probable Son* is her debut novel.